The end days are upon us
Who will triumph?
Who will die?

•

HELMAN

His blue, hunted eyes have seen too much horror. Now, what those eyes are about to see, his mind won't be able to explain.

ADRIENNE

Her kiss had the power to transform a man. Her will held the last chance to save a world.

THE FATHER

He's the oldest and most awesome of the vampires. But no amount of good he'll perform in the future can atone for all the evil he has done in the past.

DIEGO

He's survived many centuries and absorbed much wisdom. The global havoc he's poised to set loose will be his greatest victory—and one beyond the realms of God or the Devil.

*

"*Bloodshift* contains the best elements of Robert Ludlum and Anne Rice. It is a fast-moving international adventure with a rational horror element served up with corkscrew plot twists and an unexpected ending. If you want something different and exciting in revisionist horror, *Bloodshift* is your book."

—Chelsea Quinn Yarbro,
author of *Beastnights*

Garfield Reeves-Stevens

POPULAR LIBRARY

An Imprint of Warner Books, Inc.

A Warner Communications Company

POPULAR LIBRARY EDITION

This Popular Library Edition has been published by arrangement with the Author.

Cover design by Joe Curcio
Cover illustration by Mark and Stefanie Gerber

Popular Library books are published by
Warner Books, Inc.
666 Fifth Avenue
New York, N.Y. 10103

A Warner Communications Company

Printed in the United States of America

First Popular Library Printing: May, 1990
10 9 8 7 6 5 4 3 2 1

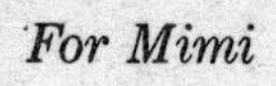

For Mimi

Prologue

For the first time in centuries, he had awakened from a dream.

The dream had spoken to him.

For a long time before they came for him, he stared up into the darkness of his resting place and thought about what he had seen. It had been so long since the last time he had dreamt, that he despaired of ever knowing what the images had meant.

At first he had been moving through his house, among his familiars, yet they had not noticed him. He had watched them at their work. He knew that the things he watched them do were the things they actually did that day, as if he had left his resting place while his body slept.

And then he had been . . . elsewhere.

Those images were a blur of fog-shrouded billows. Nothing was in the proper order or place. Except for the feeling: release. After all these years, the salvation he thought would be forever denied him, shone from some distant horizon like the first light of dawn.

Things would happen. Salvation.

"Dear God," he said as he stared into the darkness, "let it begin *now*."

And it did.

PART ONE

THE CONTRACT

One

The assassins were at the airport twenty minutes after the sun had set.

Three of them carried weapons of wood and plastic. They passed through the detectors of the inspection points quickly and calmly, as they had rehearsed.

The fourth, clothed in black and having no need for weapons, moved in the shadows of the tarmac, invisible in the darting headlight beams of the aircraft service vehicles.

He was older than the others, and his knowledge of the Ways far deeper: as he moved to his position in the darkness, he left no footprints in the light snow that covered the ground beneath him.

The director of Heathrow was in the control tower preparing to close down his airport.

The snow had come as forecast and the reports from the Ministry confirmed its growing intensity. In an hour at most, Heathrow would be unserviceable. Already, inbound flights had been diverted so his snow removal equipment could concentrate on the outbound flights. The director detested stranded hordes camping in his lobbies. He wanted everyone out.

Twenty-seven flights had been rescheduled to take off in

the next forty-five minutes, most trans-Atlantic or Europe-bound. He gave those flights priority. Buses and trains could handle the local traffic.

But still, he thought as he watched the snowfall speed and thicken in the shafts of airport signal lights, there were some passengers who wouldn't be going where they had planned that night.

The assassins were at his airport to ensure exactly that. For them, one passenger could not leave Heathrow. One passenger must be stopped. The threat must be neutralized.

In washrooms and storage rooms, weapons were assembled; special weapons capable of delivering the Final Death. The threat *would* be neutralized. The order *would* continue. Alternatives were unthinkable.

The assassins began their sweep of Heathrow.

There was a new clerk at the Travellers' Aid booth. The regular clerk had phoned in ill but had arranged for a friend from the London office to fill in for her. The harried senior clerk had agreed to the arrangement, relieved. He did not remember seeing the new clerk at the London office, but knew that the staff there turned over rapidly.

The replacement clerk knew what to look for. She identified the first assassin by an improper line beneath a large, open trench-coat, a set to his mouth which she had been trained to recognize.

She excused herself to the couple she was serving, an older couple from Bonn whose children had not met them as planned, and lifted her phone.

A call was made to another phone in Heathrow. The diversion was begun.

Two men wearing blue British Airways stewards' blazers accompanied a woman in black along the wide corridors leading to the departure gates. One steward wheeled a hospital gurney, the coffin upon it draped in a tan, quilted movers' blanket.

It was quite irregular, but the woman was to accompany her husband's body back to New York in the lounge of a 747.

The man had been wealthy. His devoted widow had purchased every lounge seat for the flight. It was the only way the airline officials would allow the coffin in the passenger section. Money had smoothed the irregularities, even to the borrowing of two blazers for the widow's companions.

The second assassin was impressed with the obviousness of it. They had been searching for a face, a nervous figure sneaking out of England; instead they had found an object leaving in plain sight.

The coffin was an appropriate attempt appreciated by the second assassin. He made the proper signals. The two others joined him. They moved toward the stewards, the widow, and their target hiding in the coffin.

The gurney rolled by the Travellers' Aid booth.

The first assassin saw the slight nod pass between the clerk and the widow and knew he had been identified. If the assassins continued they would have the stewards in front of them, the clerk behind. Pincered.

The first assassin slowed his pace. The clerk opened a drawer and reached inside. Her eyes locked with his.

He spun to face her, lifting the crossbow from under his coat. The clerk raised her gun.

The assassin felt relief at the sight of the gun. It meant their true nature hadn't been revealed. He tightened his finger on the release.

The clerk dived behind her desk.

The crossbow's bolt ripped through the air above the desk. The man from Bonn was impaled on the wall beside it. His twitching feet just brushing the floor.

The silence of the diversion and the attack was finally broken by the old woman's scream. Then by the hiss of silenced gunshots.

The widow had fired her weapon through her coat pocket. The first and third assassins were both hit and spun off balance. The third assassin's crossbow fired blindly into the ceiling.

The second assassin released his bolt. The widow's throat

was pierced. She gurgled softly as she collapsed, clutching at the coffin's blanket, dragging it with her to the floor.

The two assassins who had been shot by the widow were standing, hurriedly recocking their weapons. One steward advanced on them.

The second assassin saw the Travellers' Aid clerk rise from behind her desk. Blood from the old man had splashed over her, plastering her hair to the side of her face. She raised her weapon toward the second assassin.

He attacked.

Two bullets tore through him before he was upon her, ripping at her unprotected throat with his hands.

The old woman screamed louder as the clerk's body was thrown to the ground, neck arteries broken and spurting.

For one brief moment, the assassin realized that more people should be screaming, but the long corridor leading to the departure gates was deserted. He didn't have time to consider the implications. He saw what the attacking steward held in his hands and knew that their nature *had* been revealed. Totally.

While the second steward wheeled the coffin away, the other approached the reloading assassins with a billy club, its end sharpened to a deadly point.

The third assassin, his reloading not completed, threw his crossbow at the attacking steward and leapt.

The steward ducked below the crossbow and thrust forward. The club sank into his attacker's chest, the momentum of the impaled body wrenching it from the steward's hands.

Weaponless, the steward turned to face the first assassin.

The stock of the crossbow swung faster than the steward could sense, lifting him off his feet as the impact shattered his temple.

The steward's body crumpled. The impaled assassin slowly crawled to the entrance of a washroom. A white, thick fluid smeared the floor behind him.

The two other assassins took aim on the second steward racing away with the coffin.

Then the reason for the empty corridors became obvious.

Six British soldiers appeared at the end of the corridor. Four carried Sterling submachine guns. Two carried crossbows.

The steward halted. He hadn't known of the soldiers' presence. He looked nervously behind at the two assassins, then again at the soldiers.

For a moment, there was silence in the corridor.

The moment ended when a metal outside door burst off its hinges and the fourth assassin, clothed in black, hurtled through the air at the steward.

His black-gloved hands twisted the steward's head one hundred and eighty degrees. The crack echoed down the corridor.

The fourth assassin turned to the coffin.

The soldiers with crossbows released their bolts.

One flew wild. The other struck its target at the waist, sinking to its vanes.

The fourth assassin ripped the bolt from his flesh and held it like a dagger above his head. He tore open the coffin lid and brought the bolt down in a blur of awesome speed.

The bolt splintered.

The coffin was empty.

The assassin in black screamed in deafening rage and flung the coffin and gurney fifteen feet to smash on the far corridor wall.

The Sterlings erupted in a murderous volley.

As if molten, the assassin in black rushed through the doorway he had burst open. The two other assassins followed, running wildly, countless bullets tearing through them in explosions of cloth and flesh.

Unable to believe that they had seen two men withstand such bombardment, the soldiers ran to the door and shone a flashlight down the metal staircase that led to the tarmac.

There were no bodies heaped upon it.

Through the mist of the soldiers' breath in the winter's night air, smears of white liquid glinted in the light on the stairs, but the snow before them was smooth and unbroken, and stretched undisturbed into the darkness.

Two

In a small office in the British Ministry of Defense, an officer listened intently to a soldier's phone report from Heathrow. The officer's eyes were fixed on the small patch of white over the throat of the man who sat across from his desk. In the half-light of his office, the patch of white seemed to glow.

The officer's hand tightened on the receiver as he heard the details of the horror the man with the patch had involved him in. People were dead at that man's orders, and that man said he was a priest.

The officer was Colonel Noel Tremworthy. He was sixty-three and had served the Crown well for forty-five of those years. As he listened to the sergeant's report from the other end of the secured line, he realized his years of service were coming to an end. The only word he could think of to describe what had happened at Heathrow was awful. Awful.

There had been too many witnesses, too many casualties. Nothing had gone the way any of them had anticipated. He dreaded telling the priest, but there was nothing else to be done. Tremworthy felt engulfed. If he ever saw his wife again, he wondered, would he be able to explain? Would anybody ever know why he had done what he had done? After forty-five years of military service, Tremworthy knew what the only answer could be.

Finally the Colonel spoke. "All right, Sergeant. Please stay on this line." He pressed the intercept button on the phone's scrambler unit.

Father Clement waited expectantly.

"There was a diversion," Tremworthy said.

"Whose?"

"I don't know. The Sergeant said there appeared to be another group after her. Four men. With crossbows. The Sergeant's team and the other group ran into each other. In the confusion, she got by us. Did *you* send in a back-up team without informing me?"

The priest hissed. "I had your assurance, Colonel. There was no need for another team. Close the airport. Now!"

The Colonel shook his head. "It's too late. The snow was unexpected. Schedules changed. Local flights were canceled and the trans-Atlantics were pushed through. They've all left. She appears to have made it after all."

Father Clement jerked to his feet; his face reddening, his eyes darting.

Tremworthy felt himself flinch as though the priest were going to strike him.

Clement paced furiously.

Again the Colonel spoke. "Five people are dead. Perhaps six."

"What do you mean 'perhaps six'?" The priest still paced.

"One of the four men was stabbed in the chest by one of the people who were helping her escape. It was a knife or spear of some sort. The attacker crawled into a lavatory. By the time the men had checked him out, he had managed to escape. Probably in disguise. They found the clothes he was wearing but . . ." The Colonel slowed, as if realizing what he was saying, what he had heard, for the first time. "When he crawled away, the Sergeant said, it was sticking right through him. They're looking for the body. He can't . . ."

The priest looked at Tremworthy with contempt.

"After all you have learned, you can believe that story? That body will *never* be found, Colonel Tremworthy. 'Stabbed in the chest' is impaled through the heart. That body is dust on a lavatory floor. Gone. Dissolved. When will you accept what we have told you as being the truth?"

Panic edged in on the Colonel's voice.

"Five people were *killed.*"

The priest mocked him, goading him.

"You are sure they've counted all five bodies are you? There are no more of them lying about waiting to be found with spears through them, are there?"

"Five," said the Colonel, trying to restrain himself, unsuccessfully. "The four who were helping her and a *civilian.* An old man from Germany."

Tremworthy looked pleadingly at the priest.

"For the love of God, Father Clement."

The priest exploded.

"Don't you dare, Colonel. Don't you dare presume to judge us. To judge me." He leaned over the desk, loomed over the Colonel. His voice became a whisper.

"These are the closing days of a conflict you can't begin to understand, Colonel Tremworthy. Never. I am just one small part of it. *She* is just one small part of it. You and your men, the people at Heathrow, they don't begin to matter to what we face. These are extraordinary times, Colonel. They require extraordinary measures. Don't ever dare question them."

Clement straightened. The Colonel trembled, tears filling his eyes. The interrupt button flashed silently.

Finally, the priest spoke.

"Five deaths. Were guns used?"

Tremworthy nodded.

"On just the five who died or on some who, shall we say, from a witness's viewpoint, 'miraculously' escaped unharmed by bullets?"

"Who . . . escaped." Tremworthy fought with his tears.

"And if some of those who escaped were the targets of your men's machine gun fire, I imagine your men have some questions for you."

"Yes . . . the Sergeant asked . . . and the crossbows . . . it's insane . . ."

"Not insanity, Colonel. A mistake. You will have to deal with it. The mistake mustn't spread."

Tremworthy stared vacantly. "How? It happened."

"You will deal with it in the way certain elements of your Majesty's government have always dealt with it. We both knew there would be a cost to failure, Colonel. Or do you need another incident? Another example to convince you of my authority?"

The Colonel thought of his wife and her accident. The doctors had said she would be fine. That she was lucky. The priest had said something else. Something sickening. It had not been an accident.

"No. I know. A posting for them."

The priest nodded. "That's right, Colonel. A posting. To Belfast. A transport truck. A terrorist mine, or attack. A minor tragedy. But no more questions. The mistake doesn't spread."

The Colonel stared at the flashing button. There were thirty-four of his soldiers at Heathrow. Thirty-four.

The priest went to the coatrack by the door, slipped on his overcoat, and bent over.

Tremworthy stared uncomprehendingly as the priest who had killed five people and sentenced thirty-four others to death, struggled with his galoshes.

No, said a voice within him, *you are sentencing the thirty-four to death. That man has ordered it. You are carrying it out. After forty-five years. A traitor and murderer.* For my wife, he thought. Lila, for Lila. *Murderer, murderer.* The years were coming to an end.

"Perhaps," said the Colonel, "perhaps Washington will have more success with her now that you'll be operating in America."

Clement's face hardened. His hand tightened on the doorknob. The look of contempt returned.

"You poor fool. You understand nothing of this. You think that I . . . Washington? Washington is an *obscenity.* They work together, Colonel. Washington and she, together. Why else do you think we must stop her at all costs?"

Tremworthy felt sick. Too many things. Too much to think of. "But your organization? The way you operate. Where does the power come from? What's your control?"

The priest paused, letting the look of utter confusion and loss grow on Tremworthy's face. He considered his answer carefully.

"Colonel Tremworthy, despite all we have revealed to you, do you actually think that I am other than this?" He gestured to his cleric's collar. "Do you consider us an insane group of terrorists? Or government spies or agents or whatever you will? This collar is no disguise, Colonel. Many years ago I even served in a parish, a terrible parish with mines and poverty, ignorance and disease. I came to know my parishioners well. I came to know how they reacted to the pressures and forces of a world far too complex for them. I could look at a man, Colonel Tremworthy, and from the tone of his voice and from an understanding of what he had recently experienced, tell just what that man was going to do. How he was going to deal with his situation. If he could find the strength." The priest paused again, staring at the Colonel, then at the Colonel's desk. The right side. Where the drawer was. Where the gun was kept.

"I've never thought to ask you, Colonel. Are you still a Catholic?"

The Colonel nodded once, almost imperceptibly.

"I shouldn't worry about it." The priest looked toward the right side of the desk. "Extraordinary times. I can make the proper arrangements afterward. It will be all right for you."

Colonel Tremworthy was motionless, recognition slowly growing in him. Recognition of action he knew he had already decided upon.

"To answer your question, Colonel. *Ad majoreum Dei gloriam*. I take my orders from Rome."

The priest closed the door behind him as he left.

Rome. For the greater glory of God. The enormity, the hideousness of the words echoed in the silence. It was the Jesuits' creed. All of what had happened had happened for them. For *Rome*. Old men caught up in costumes and rituals most people no longer took seriously had come to this? Is this madness what became of them when the world had turned away? Jesuits who killed? On orders from Rome?

After a long time, Colonel Tremworthy depressed the interrupt button and talked to his sergeant. When he was finished, he telephoned an aide to release the prepared story of an aborted IRA attack on Heathrow, then began the paperwork which his staff would complete, sending his men to their silence in Belfast. *Murderer, Murderer.*

He did it all for his wife.

For himself, he knew as well as the priest that the gun was there, in the drawer. The priest had said he would make it all right. Like an invitation to escape from the insanity which surrounded him.

The priest—no, not just a priest, the Jesuit—had said it. The world had grown too complex for the Colonel's understanding. Rome, his deeply held base, had risen like some monstrous worm, twisting and writhing in impossible, unbelievable directions. And those monsters from the shadows, they had somehow become real. Colonel Tremworthy was too tired to struggle with them any longer. He was too tired.

He left it to the Jesuit and to whomever it was who was so important, so inexplicably dangerous, now hurtling across the Atlantic to America.

He left it all to them.

Sometime later, he opened the drawer.

Ad majoreum Dei gloriam.

Rome.

Three

The darkness that enveloped her was her comfort, for in that darkness was her strength. Just as her hope lay within the drone and soft vibration of the engines pushing her through the night, high over the Atlantic.

The brutality of Heathrow was behind her now. The risks, for her, had been worthwhile.

She had survived.

But after the switch she had heard the gunfire as the decoy coffin was rolled through the waiting area. Her familiars could not withstand such weapons. She knew the last of them had been killed as the price of her escape.

Now she was safe in the container marked *Medical Isotopes*. Its radiation warning labels granted her protection far greater than any lock against the prying of customs officials.

Cramped and confined in the container in the baggage compartment of the 747, she thought of her freedom. Freedom from the container would come first. Then from the darkness, and from the danger. Most of all from the hunger. With that would come her final freedom: from the Conclave.

Lost in her thoughts of the future, images of sunrises shone in her darkened eyes. She smiled because she was travelling at 600 miles an hour away from those who would destroy her. She thought she was safe.

But eight miles below her and over twenty thousand miles above, it had already begun. The voices, deep and sibilant, whispered their way through the web of trans-Atlantic cables, flew through the tenuous net of satellite relays.

For the first time, a conflict was to reach overseas. But the voices often considered the impossible and contingencies had always been available.

Someone new would be drawn in; someone whose usefulness had long ago been calculated, noted, and filed. Now he would be found and activated. It had worked with others in the past. It would work again.

Inquiries were made. Dormant networks came alive. A location was established.

Hours later, as the aircraft began its descent, all was in readiness. The voices were silent.

Within a day it would be known where she had landed, and the conflict would reach its final, inevitable conclusion.

Then Rome and Washington would be as dust in sunlight, swirling to oblivion, and the Conclave would rule.

Forever.

Four

The man in the blue parka stopped to study the tracks he had followed in the snow. They had not yet filled in with new snowfall. They were minutes old.

He took a deep breath of the winter air, enjoying its bite as it chilled his throat and lungs. The cold had flushed his cheeks, bringing back color and taking off years. He was nearing forty but his face did not show it. The skin was tight; his nose sharp. It was the face of an athlete long used to taking care of his body. His age showed only in his eyes; large, blue and hunted. There were too many lines around those eyes. They had seen too many things he would have preferred not to witness.

The man stood up slowly, staring ahead at the thicket a hundred yards away. The large, soft snowflakes had formed a mantle of white across his shoulders and salted his black toque to a shade of gray.

He brushed at the snow caught in his eyebrows and remained still. He knew the deer would be in the thicket, rooting through the light snow under the trees for winter forage, but he could not summon the will to go in after it.

He carried only his Olympus with its motordrive and

telephoto lens, but he couldn't move. The thrill of the chase, if he could call it that, had left him. Even in this harmless situation.

The man hooted and yelled at the deer he couldn't see, slapping his mittened hands together. For a moment he thought the noise hadn't carried in the snow-muffled stillness. Then a doe burst from a seemingly solid section of the thicket, its legs drawn up in a perfect, gravity-defying bound, and was gone.

That moment of its disappearance triggered the memory. The snowbound landscape fell away from his eyes, replaced by that fine mist of blood, sprayed out in tiny droplets, beaded upon the filthy floorboards and slowly sinking into the grooves and cracks. The memory staggered him. He gasped for breath in its ferocity. He saw the startled face, eyes open, still moist, staring lifelessly at the delicate tongue tip, inches away, lying useless in the dust.

He shook his head to lose the image. Behind him was an old fallen tree trunk. He walked toward it, needing to sit down.

When he had calmed himself, his breathing steady, and his hands without tremors, the man prepared to examine the memory in detail. He had long ago learned that his subconscious was an important element of his success, and if something could affect him this strongly, he must review. It would not be the first time he had noted a mistake after the fact. But this time, it was far enough after the fact that he might not be able to do anything about it. He could only wait for them to come and get him.

With that, Granger Helman gazed out over the snow-covered hills of New Hampshire and reflected on the Delvecchio closing, the twenty-third and last time he had killed for money.

One year ago, Joe Delvecchio had vanished on his way to a luncheon appointment with business associates. Delvecchio was the president of the Interstate Handlers Brotherhood and had been implicated in a number of quasi-legal actions involving pension fund misappropriation, election rigging and, it was rumored, the murder of union officials and non-union protesters who had opposed him. The Handlers were approaching a level of power equal to or surpassing that of other major transportation unions when Delvecchio disappeared. No one seemed too surprised; it was known with whom he was dealing. Certain organizations which had made considerable investments in the shipment of goods across state lines, without the intervention or taxation of government, did not tolerate interference.

Most people believed Delvecchio had interfered. It was generally assumed he was dead, even though no body had been recovered, and no charges had been laid.

Helman had sources different from those of most people. He *knew* Delvecchio was dead, and for the reasons most people suspected, even though those reasons were wrong. Helman also knew why no body had been found or would ever be found.

The organizations Delvecchio appeared to be moving against routinely invested in legitimate businesses as a method of disguising their cash income from other sources. There was not a single similar organization operating in the United States which did not own or control at least one funeral parlor as one of its legitimate businesses.

Business was carried out as usual at these places, except when, occasionally and late at night, a delivery was made of an unidentified and unclaimed body.

After the next scheduled cremation, the body did not exist. True professionals left no traces.

Joe Delvecchio had been invited into the car of an associate who had urgent news. Delvecchio's knuckles were scratched with a needle held in the barrel of a ballpoint pen. Three seconds later his striated muscles were useless. The drug was a curare derivative developed for certain types of brain surgery during which the probing of brain tissue might trigger sudden body movements. Delvecchio could see, hear, and breathe, but he couldn't move.

He was taken to an underground garage and transferred to a private ambulance.

The ambulance delivered him to an independent funeral parlor. A cremation was already scheduled for that evening.

His captors told Delvecchio exactly what they were doing. They also told him that the drug prevented the development of the shock syndrome. Despite his panic and terror, Delvecchio would not pass out or faint. He could count on being conscious for the rest of his life.

He was placed on a corpse in a coffin and slid into the crematorium. His last sensations were of the thud of the fire door being sealed behind him, the rush and bump of the gas jets igniting, and the air searing his lungs as the first flames crackled through the lid of the coffin.

They told Delvecchio to expect all of this, but they didn't tell him why. If they had, he wouldn't have understood. They had killed the wrong person.

Six months later, when the political bickering and maneuvering among the Handlers Brotherhood subsided and the transfer of power had taken place, the people who had arranged for Delvecchio's removal realized the connections they had tried to sever were still operative. They were hidden, convoluted, but untouched by Delvecchio's elimination.

Delvecchio had been a puppet. New puppets were already in place.

The real power had lain, and still remained, with Delvecchio's wife, Roselynne. Wife, mother, killer of the innocent.

At this time, negotiations were begun with a specialized broker operating out of Miami. Granger Helman was brought in to correct the situation. As he thought of it, to close the deal.

The fee was exorbitant for a non-political, domestic closing: $250,000 American, in cash.

Helman's broker took a third from the top. Helman's share was delivered in cash, some of which would appear in his bank account after his return from a Las Vegas vacation, duly reported as gambling winnings. The rest was left with one of three 'soft' casinos in Las Vegas. For another percentage off the top, the management would invest Helman's cash in a number of prominent corporations where it would be turned around into consulting fees paid out to bank accounts owned by individuals who would carefully report the income to the IRS and pay full taxes. All the individuals were Helman. They were his "drops."

When in doubt, the government audited those whom it suspected of illegal activities. Helman's cautious use of a broker, which gave him the opportunity of refusing a closing—something which would lead to his own death if he attempted it as an independent—and the careful, complex manner by which the broker hid the source of his income had contributed to his survival. Helman had seen too many top professionals lose everything because of a simple tax audit in which they were unable to explain the presence of twenty thousand dollars in small bills.

The excessive fee was justified. Other people had developed an interest in the activities of Roselynne Delvecchio. Helman would have to complete the closing while the deal—his target—was under the surveillance of the FBI.

Other conditions were also established. In this case, the body must be found. A lesson would be taught to the people dealing with Roselynne Delvecchio on both sides. There must be no doubt that she was deliberately executed.

The last condition was the most difficult. The Justice Department was expected to call a grand jury investigation into the operations of the Interstate Handlers Brotherhood within three weeks. At that time, Roselynne Delvecchio would disappear into the impenetrable security of protective detention.

Helman reviewed the conditions again, and analyzed the methods he chose to meet them.

One. He knew the deal could not be closed while the FBI was involved because he could not guarantee his safe withdrawal. For the same reason, he could not kidnap her and remove her from the FBI's presence. He must arrange for Roselynne to remove herself from surveillance.

A threat had to be made. One obvious to her but invisible to the watchers. Roselynne was a mother. The threat would be made against her children.

Helman paused in his review, uncomfortable as he recalled the ease with which he had made that decision to involve the innocent. The change which he felt struggling deep within him pushed that much closer to the surface. He gathered his thoughts again and continued, uneasy.

Two. The location of the closing could be made as secure as possible. The body could always be found as a result of a short phone call to an interested party. For the lesson to be evident, the call must not go to police or newspapers. Instead it must be made to members of the groups working with Roselynne; high-ranking members who believed they were unimplicated, untouchable. Panic would ensue and the lesson would be learned.

Three. For an execution to be obvious, many methods were immediately unsuitable. The undetectable drugs which Helman favored, disguising themselves as heart attacks and insulin shock, were too subtle. Mechanical methods like bullets and cutting instruments left too many possibilities for forensic detection. A drop of blood, a single filing of metal, and a chain of events could be followed back to Helman. He would use his hands. If records were checked to assemble a list of all those who had the training to inflict such injuries, Helman's name would probably be on it. But unless a list could be assembled naming all those who had the will to use their training, he would be invisible in a list of thousands.

Helman could see no flaws in his reasoning. The plan had taken him a day to develop, two weeks to prepare. He was ready to close the deal a week before the grand jury was convened. He moved immediately.

Breaking into Delvecchio's house was the riskiest phase of the operation. But Helman knew how the FBI worked, how they thought, and acted accordingly.

He penetrated the FBI's surveillance at night. He took three hours to carefully move through the unlit back garden and conceal himself in the well of a basement window. If he had entered the house then, the first perimeter of the house's commercial alarm system would have been activated and he would have been caught. Instead, he waited.

In the morning, as Roselynne's three children left for school and she for union headquarters, the alarm system was deactivated to allow them to move out of the house. Helman, at that time, moved in.

Ultrasonic motion detectors were not in use because the children's cats were allowed to roam the house. The alarm system's second perimeter was a system of pressure-sensitive mats concealed under carpeting by windows and on stairways and set to react to intruders heavier than the cats. Helman avoided windows and climbed up bannisters.

When the house was empty, Helman moved into the kitchen. The FBI listening post had shifted its attention to the union headquarters' telephones. Helman was able to attach two devices to the kitchen telephone without alerting them.

In the refrigerator, he found the unopened carton of milk he had observed Roselynne purchase after work the evening before. His hypodermic slid easily into the top seal of the carton without leaving a visible puncture.

Helman returned to the basement. He had fasted for the two days previous to prevent the need for elimination, enabling him to stay hidden in one area for many hours.

When the children returned home and deactivated the alarm system again, Helman moved back to the window well. Later that night he withdrew through the garden past the unsuspecting FBI agents.

Again and again Helman reviewed his penetration of the house. He was convinced it was flawless. He did not know there had been other watchers in the garden that night, equally invisible to the FBI.

At three o'clock that morning, Helman placed his first call to the Delvecchio house. Roselynne answered, her voice sleep-blurred and annoyed. The FBI agents listened intently.

Drunkenly, Helman demanded to speak with Mr. Till. Roselynne was confused, she did not know anyone by that name. Helman read off a phone number. It was Delvecchio's number with the final two digits transposed. Roselynne slammed down the phone.

The FBI judged the possibilities. The phone call could have been a coded message, an attempt to determine if Roselynne was home, or a call which activated a listening device concealed within a phone in the house. As Helman had anticipated, the FBI immediately investigated the number he had given to Roselynne. It belonged to a Paul Till. The FBI called him and yes he had received a phone call moments after the call to Roselynne from a drunk who demanded to talk to *Peter* Till. The FBI left the investigation there. The phone call, as far as they were concerned, had been a legitimate wrong number. Meanwhile, Helman's listening device in the kitchen phone had been fully activated and was working perfectly.

The next morning Helman listened as the Delvecchios awoke and prepared themselves for another day of work and school. After he heard the sounds of the children in the kitchen eating their cereal, Helman placed his second call.

What Roselynne Delvecchio heard terrified her. What the FBI heard was unintelligible. The second device Helman had attached to the phone was a scrambling unit compatible to the one he spoke through. The garbled transmission was decoded when it reached the device in the kitchen phone. Where the FBI had placed their intercept on the outside cable however, all they heard was interference. Eventually, they would get around to reacting, but Helman knew it would not be soon enough.

Roselynne threw the receiver onto the kitchen counter. She ran towards the breakfast table and with a wild sweep of her arm sent breakfast cereal bowls and glasses to shatter on the floor. As she had been instructed she took the now almost empty milk carton into the living room and poured a few drops into the aquarium tank. From behind her, she could hear the confused crying of her youngest child as the others tried to clean up the mess. The sounds were masked by the rushing of her blood as she saw the fish in the tank begin to violently twitch and shudder and sickeningly float to the surface.

The man on the phone had told the truth. There was a

nerve toxin in the children's milk. The fish, being so small, reacted immediately. Her children had, at most, an hour.

She went back to the phone, shaking, and agreed to everything Helman told her.

The children would remain at home. If Roselynne did everything as she was told, a man would come to her house with a fruit drink. The children were to drink it. In it was the antidote.

But for the man to come at all, Roselynne must be at a certain location within five minutes. The phone went dead.

Seconds later Roselynne screeched out of her garage in a late-model Cadillac. She was leaving an hour before her regular routine. The FBI was caught without a pursuit vehicle. By the time instructions were issued to local police, Roselynne had arrived at the designated parking lot and transferred to another car. Helman was the driver. He had two conditions left to meet.

There was a storage yard ten miles away. A construction rental company kept job shacks there; offices built like mobile homes to be driven wherever they were required. They contained nothing of value and the one guard at the gate was old and slow. He was unconscious before he had a chance to think that Helman might be any threat.

Helman drove to a job shack he had already prepared. A wire stretched from it to the telephone pole outside the guard's shack. Roselynne went first, directed by the gun Helman held.

The woman seemed oblivious to the danger she might be in. She demanded Helman order the antidote sent to her children. Helman said they had been watched in the parking lot; her children had already been treated. She had nothing to worry about.

In reality, the children had never been in danger. The substance he had injected into the milk carton was a naturally occurring poison derived from a species of sole found in the Red Sea. The Navy used it to allow divers to work in shark-infested water. It was deadly to fish yet had no effect on humans. There was no need for a second party to be involved in any of Helman's closings. His security, he thought, was impenetrable.

He placed the phone call which would inform his clients that the deal was to be closed. They would make their calls to alert the people behind Roselynne's actions. The phone call was brief. The clients hung up after Helman spoke the coded message. But Helman held the receiver to his ear and pretended confusion. He held a one-sided conversation with the dead line for a few seconds before hanging up.

Roselynne looked at him questioningly.

He explained that a mistake had been made. Certain people had suspected Roselynne of directing the misappropriation of pension funds. She was to be killed because of it. But new evidence had come to light. The real thieves had been detected. Roselynne was to go free.

The dark terror left Roselynne's face as exultation took over. She spun, still dressed in her nightgown and housecoat, to stare out the one dingy window in the shack. She had given up everything in the last hour, and now it was being miraculously restored. Freedom was her last thought, her last experience, as Helman's knuckles drove into the base of her skull, severing her spinal cord and crushing her medulla oblongata.

Roselynne Delvecchio was dead before she fell to the floor.

In her last second, she must have been licking her tension-dried lips. The violent snap of her head had brought her teeth together, tearing her tongue tip away from her in a fine mist of blood.

It was the blood that startled Helman. It was to have been a clean closing, a simple closing. He had given her her last freedom as an act of compassion, an apology that for the successful completion of this business deal, she, unfortunately, must die.

Helman shifted on his New England tree trunk. He knew why the blood had startled him. He knew why it returned to him again and again.

It was the one element he hadn't planned.

Everything had been meticulously organized. He had run through each step so often before undertaking the actual closing that it was mechanical. A business deal, nothing more.

But for Roselynne licking her lips, the mist of blood sprayed out in tiny droplets, beaded upon the filthy floorboards and slowly sinking into the grooves, something new had been added. Something that did not fit into his precise plan.

Roselynne's startled face, eyes open, still moist, staring lifelessly at the delicate tongue tip lying useless in the dust, framed by that dark halo of blood, made her elimination more than a closing.

It was murder.

At that moment in the job shack, Helman knew it had been his final closing. He stared transfixed by the thin trickle of life which slid from between those lips that had talked and eaten and kissed, and saw in its moist glimmer the sparkle of the snow which awaited him in his New England. His refuge, his comfort. The hundred thousand he would realize was the final amount he needed to buy his own farm, a few miles from his sister Miriam's farm. He would be rid of his profession. His freedom would be real, not the ephemeral promise made to Roselynne.

The blood focused him and his thoughts. He looked into it and saw the twenty-two others he had murdered, always calmly, sometimes proudly, telling himself he was punishing those whom the law could never touch, doing his duty for justice as he had that first time, for his sister. And Helman knew in his thoughts that it was a lie and that he was finished with it.

But it was only now, alone in the hills, enwrapped in the gentle snow with the warmth of Miriam's farmhouse less than a mile away, that he, for the first time, *felt* it: that all that he had done *was* finished. The change burst free and his struggle stopped.

Whitened by the falling flakes, ears heavy with the

snow's silence, Granger Helman wept for the life that now was behind him.

Later, the tensions and realizations released, Helman stood up from the tree trunk and stared out at the blue-white hills, slowly darkening in the late afternoon sun. The old life had left him. It would be years perhaps, before the final wounds were healed, safely forgotten in the depths of unwanted memory, but for now, there were new things to consider.

The day before, he had given his deposit to the real estate agent in Goffstown. In the spring, the farm he had wanted for so long would be his. The things he had put off for so many years, telling himself that some day he would get to them, were going to fill his life.

It would be a good feeling to be able to have Miriam and Steven and Campbell, her two boys, visit him to repay them for all the love they had shown him over the years he was constantly traveling and out of touch. Helman's life was changing today. He was happy. And for no other particular reason he shouted.

He listened carefully to see if some faint echo might come back to him. Instead he heard the rumble of a van as it drove away from the front of his sister's house.

He stared after it as it flickered between the bare trees at the side of the road. It was too late for the Sears truck to be delivering from Concord, too light in color to be a UPS van. Like the FBI agents who had immediately moved to check out a seemingly innocent phone call to a wrong number, Helman knew that the unusual was always something of which to be wary. A small tingle fluttered through his stomach. The van was gone. He wondered if he should return to the house.

Then the back door of the house opened and a figure came out, looked around, and, spotting Helman on the rise, began to wave at him. Helman held up his Olympus and sighted through the telephoto lens. It was his nephew

Steven, not waving to him, but waving *at* him to come back.

The tingle grew into tautness that spread through his abdomen.

For a sickening instant, Helman knew the van had a connection to him. His lightness of only a few moments ago sped away from him as an all too familiar feeling took over: the adrenalin-honed concentration that engulfed him as it had before each closing. That awful, purposeful concentration which he had decided never to feel again, owned him.

All was as it had been. With a clear mind and unfeeling body he trudged through the snow toward the shadow-darkened house and the message from the van.

The package, slightly larger than a shoebox and carefully wrapped and sealed in heavy kraft paper and adhesive paper strips, sat on an upright firelog against a tree in the back garden.

Helman stood in the back porch, out of sight of any neighbors who might have puzzled over his walk to place the package so far away from the house, and carefully wrapped a heavy blanket around the barrel of his old Remington 722.

He was as ice.

Behind him stood Miriam. She had sent the boys inside, warning them to stay away from the windows which, if his suspicions were correct, Helman thought might shatter. Miriam, however, would not leave her brother's side.

She was older than Helman, though he jokingly called her his younger sister. Yet she shared with him the legacy of their parents with an unwrinkled face and sharp, clear features.

But now her face was darkened with worry; her eyebrows drawn together, building shadows over her eyes. She had always carried the guilt of believing she had started her brother in his career, and now that feeling had grown to impossible tension because she had accepted the package which sat waiting for its first bullet.

It had a typewritten label. There was no postage, no return address. The courier who had delivered it had offered no bill of lading to be signed.

It was addressed to Helman, even though no one knew he was at his sister's farm. His life was too controlled. No one knew him.

But Miriam had betrayed him in her confusion, and accepted the package, acknowledging his presence.

Helman drew careful aim, letting his years of experience with weapons compensate for the blanket's awkwardness. He held his breath, braced himself for the explosion to follow, and squeezed off the first shot.

The package flew off the log, and fell lightly in the snow.

He fired four more times. Scattering half the package in sprays of tattered paper. Nothing.

Helman exhaled. At least it was not a bomb.

He walked back out to the package and inspected the snow around it. There was no evidence of chemical venting. No aerosol device had been triggered by the violence of the bullets.

He knelt beside the package and in the deep shadows of the sunset carefully unwrapped what was left.

The contents were quite simple, quite direct, quite terrifying.

The first was a newspaper clipping. Half of it, with a headline, had been shredded by a bullet's impact, but enough of it was left for him to see what it was about: Roselynne Delvecchio's murder.

The second was a small piece of electronic circuitry. It was the scrambling device he had placed in the kitchen phone.

The third was a panel cut from a carton of milk. The brand and size were the same as the carton he had injected.

All thought left him. His insides rippled like water. His dreams were threatened with collapse.

Granger Helman, the professional who had covered himself and his actions with a genius and perfection no one had ever seen through, had been completely and totally uncovered.

His world stood on the edge of destruction. He would do anything to ensure his life would not be next.

He stared at the package's contents until the sun had set and there was no light left to see them.

He heard Miriam call him, a dark silhouette against the warm glow of the open back door.

There was a phone call. For him. The person no one knew was there.

Thoughts and emotions tumbling and warring within him, Helman entered the house, took the receiver, and heard the voice.

It was deep, sibilant, and had a suggestion for him.

Five

Dr. Robert Massoud misjudged the distance in the darkness of his bedroom. The phone receiver crashed into the bedside table and slid off, taking the rest of the phone with it to clatter on the uncarpeted floor.

Beside him on the bed, his wife was finally awakened. She had stirred from time to time, trying to ignore her husband's early morning conversation—a common enough event since their move to Stockholm—but the crash of the phone had finally done it. She reached out for him and asked what had happened.

"The fucking rats died."

It was four o'clock in the morning. As far as she knew, her husband's rats were always dying of one thing or another. She was confused.

"Which rats, dear?"

"My fucking rats back in Berkeley. The fucking computer fried them."

Erica Massoud pulled herself up so she was sitting against the bed's headboard, and reached out one hand to rub her husband's shoulder.

"Could you try that one more time? I don't know what you're talking about."

Robert sighed and stretched for the phone. A recorded Swedish voice was telling him to hang up and try his call again.

"That was Frank," he explained, "at Berkeley. He went into the isolation lab this morning and all the rats, the inoculated group, the infected group, *and* the two control groups were dead. Every single fucking one. Two years down the tube."

Erica was still confused. She didn't understand her husband's work. Sometimes he was happy when his rats died.

"I always thought that if they died it meant that you had isolated something; proved it was dangerous."

Robert lay back on the bed.

"Usually it does. But this time the rats didn't die of cancer. The computer made an error in regulating the temperature of the isolation cages. It boosted it to over a hundred and twenty. The rats fucking cooked."

"How does a computer make a mistake like that?"

"I don't know. Frank doesn't know. I didn't even know the temperature control was hooked into the lab's computer. I thought it was just a thermostat control."

Erica thought her husband might be in danger of crying. She had to talk him out of it. The other doctors at the Institute might mistake red eyes as a sign of too much drinking the night before. That could be a setback in her husband's incredibly fast-rising career.

"Won't Major Weston look after it? Get it all straightened out? He did promise you he'd see that the experiment was finished so you could take the appointment at Haaberling."

Robert threw his hands up. "Oh, Christ, I don't know. He said a lot of things that haven't come through."

Erica stroked her husband's chest, trying to distract him. "The appointment at the Haaberling Institute came through, didn't it?"

Robert thought back on it: the first meeting with Major Weston; the incredible honor of being offered a position at the renowned Haaberling Institute while in one's twenties was unheard of. Still he was reluctant to leave his experiments at Berkeley. He felt that after two years he was finally close to the breakthrough he needed to isolate the mechanism by which certain cancers appear to simultaneously invade the body at several sites rather than developing within it at one location, then spreading. But Weston was insistent. It was good for the country to have an American at Haaberling, and when his appointment was finished at Stockholm Robert could expect an immediate offer from the Centers for Disease Control in Atlanta and work on anything he wanted.

Besides, Weston had promised that he would look after the experiment being left behind, personally.

With a little misgiving, but enormous excitement, Robert had accepted. And now the rats were fried by a computer that shouldn't even have had control over the temperature.

"I suppose so," he sighed finally. "But Weston seemed to be spending a lot of time in Washington. He's a pretty busy guy to be looking after my rats."

Erica giggled. "I know how to look after your rats," she said, and began whispering into her husband's ear.

He laughed and rolled on top of her, kissing her. But afterward, as she slept again, he stared at the ceiling trying to figure it all out.

"Dammit," he said to the darkness. "I was so close. I know I was."

When the bedside alarm went off two hours later, he was still thinking. But he never once thought that it was anything other than an accident.

Six

The flickering darkness Granger Helman stared up at disappeared in a wash of light as the Greyhound bus he rode drove into the tunnel.

The discontinuity gave him that vague sense of having forgotten what it was he had just been thinking. He settled back into his seat, trying to regain his body position of a few moments before to see if that would, by association, recapture his thoughts. It didn't. All he could think of now was that for the first time since he was a child, he was frightened. Not as in his closings, apprehensive or nervous about possibilities which he had anticipated and must avoid, but truly frightened.

He remembered as a child, alone in the house, a ball he had been playing with rolled through the basement door and down the wooden stairs. He had to get the ball, yet he was too small to reach the basement light switch. He had made it halfway down the stairs before his child's mind penetrated the darkness and saw what waited for him there. They were grinning their idiotic grins, dim light from the kitchen behind him glinted off their spittle-flecked teeth, the oily fur and the eyes that always watched him through the floors. They had been waiting for him to come, just once, into the basement when he was alone and it was dark. He could feel the kitchen door slowly shutting behind him as the light faded and the darkness grew and the long grabbing things stretched silently through the wooden stairs for his feet. He had flown up those stairs in two jumps and slammed the door shut behind him. In the basement, he knew he had heard them exhale and settle back to begin their wait again.

A few days later his father found the ball wedged in behind the furnace. Granger knew it couldn't have rolled there on its own and never played with it again.

That's what it was to be frightened, and that's what Helman felt as the wash of light vanished and the bus rolled out of the Lincoln Tunnel onto the night streets of Manhattan.

The Port Authority Bus Terminal was fluorescent bright, crowded, and still under construction or renovation or just falling apart. Half the walls were covered with thick plastic sheeting or grafitti-covered plywood. The other half were covered with people, leaning and sitting, bus travelers, or pretending they were, waiting away from the snow and cold outside. Helman studied each face, peered through each wall of plastic. Somewhere, he knew, the caller was watching him. He had tried every switch and dodge he could think of in the past twenty hours, but he was certain they hadn't worked. Helman had lost control.

The voice on Miriam's phone had suggested Helman attend a meeting in Manhattan.

"When?" Helman had asked.

"Twenty-eight hours, Mr. Helman. Eleven. Tomorrow evening." Helman had never heard a voice like it. He assumed a masking device was distorting the speaker's normal voice. He couldn't be sure if it were a man or a woman.

"Where?" Helman knew he had no choice. He must agree with whatever the caller set forth. The threat of the evidence in the package ensured his compliance.

"Manhattan," said the voice.

"Where in Manhattan?" Helman protested. "A bar, hotel, address?"

"We know where you have been, we know where you are. We will meet you in Manhattan, by whichever routes you choose, at eleven, tomorrow evening. Yes?" The word was drawn out, like a hiss.

"Yes," said Helman, and the line went dead. The next

morning, Helman drove his sister's Rabbit to the Budget lot in Concord. There he rented a Citation to be dropped off at LaGuardia that evening.

He drove south on 93, varying his speed, searching for following cars which matched his variations. None did.

He exited at Manchester and parked at the airport. At the American Airlines desk he bought a ticket for a LaGuardia flight in two hours and went into the Skyline bar to wait.

Thirty minutes later, he went into the men's room. When he came out, his brown hair was black, he had a moustache, and his cheeks were swollen with cotton batting, giving him the look of a man twenty pounds heavier. His L.L. Bean boots had been replaced with black broughams with two-inch thick metal inserts that wedged uncomfortably against his heels and arches, altering the way he walked. His jeans had become black pinstriped suit pants, and his blue parka, now folded and belted across his stomach to add to the illusion of his extra twenty pounds, had been switched with a black leather topcoat. Instead of the casual duffle bag he had started with, he carried a small, thin attaché case. In his left hand he carried a brown paper bag, obviously holding a bottle of liquor which he grasped around its neck.

The liquor bag was the element of misdirection necessary to a successful disguise. Packages were always examined by people on surveillance duty. Packages were how weapons and cameras and stolen items were smuggled. They could not be ignored unless their content could be identified after a few seconds inspection, as Helman's liquor would be. Anyone who watched him could see the bottle top where Helman had carefully peeled back the bag. However, those few seconds of inspection diverted attention from the build and face of a subject. Those few seconds established the subject as existing background to the scene. The examination that followed was usually less critical, especially if a number of people requiring attention were also entering and exiting the surveillance area. It had worked for Helman before. He didn't know if it would work now, if indeed he was being watched, but he had to try.

As a commuting businessman, walking with slumped shoulders and a tired gait, seemingly eager to find the nearest Holiday Inn and settle down with his bottle, Helman walked over to the Eastern counter and bought a ticket for Newark. The flight left in twenty minutes.

There were only twelve people on board. He recognized them from the airport corridors or the bar. Either none of them was following him, or someone was better at disguise than Helman.

In Newark, Helman took the cotton out of his cheeks and sat in a bar. The Port Authority bus left the airport every twenty minutes. He waited until what he thought would be the last moment, and took the ten P.M. bus.

He was walking up the exit stairs to Eighth Avenue at twenty minutes to eleven. He was prepared to attend the meeting as scheduled. In his circles, few made threats they could not back up.

For no reason other than to keep himself moving, he began to walk toward Times Square. The shows were letting out and the side streets were jammed with taxis and limousines. Horns sounded in a continual undulation of impatience. Clumps of people walked briskly on the sidewalks and into the choked streets, eager to make as much headway as possible before the show crowds had dispersed, leaving the area to the street people who made the visitors nervous.

Another time, Helman might have been caught up in the lights, the activity, and the excitement of so much life surrounding him, but that night he was caught up in other things.

It was ten minutes to eleven.

If contact wasn't made by twelve, he had made up his mind to go into hiding. His sister and her two boys would unfortunately have to go with him. Somebody wanted him. He could not afford to leave anything behind by which they might snare him. He loved them too much. They were his only family. His only refuge. Miriam was waiting for his call. He searched the Times Square crowd.

It was five minutes to eleven.

He decided to cross over to Nathan's for some coffee. He could sit near the window and continue to watch.

Two hands grabbed his upper arms. Two men flanked him.

"Look straight ahead, Mr. Helman. Keep walking. Your ride is on its way."

A hand took away his attaché case. He was made to walk faster, along 42nd to Sixth.

A silver Fleetwood limousine, almost as common in Manhattan as a yellow cab, waited at the corner, exhaust forming an ominous ground mist around it.

The two men guided Helman toward it. The windows were darkly tinted. He could not see who waited for him. At least, he thought, they won't kill me in this car; it's too expensive. But somehow their surveillance had picked him up, despite all his efforts, within minutes of his arrival in a darkened city of millions. Perhaps expense was of no concern to them.

Steps from the limousine, the door swung slowly open. No hand appeared to be on it. Helman was guided inside. The two men did not follow.

Another figure sat in the far corner of the car.

"Thank you for being punctual, Mr. Helman. I am Mr. King. I will accompany you to your meeting."

Helman felt a tightness constrict his chest. It was the voice from the phone call. Exactly. There had been no masking device. Mr. King actually spoke like that.

"Your surveillance is very good, Mr. King." Helman controlled himself, resisting his temptation to lash out. The situation belonged to the man across from him. Helman must wait; carefully choose the proper moment to react.

Mr. King leaned forward and Helman saw his face, deeply shadowed from the overhead light. It was completely unremarkable. Except for the eyes. For one moment they seemed to shine with a tiny highlight of their own. Yet they were so dark in shadow.

Helman did not have time to consider it further.

Mr. King reached out, peeled off Helman's moustache and removed his wig.

"Our surveillance has to be good, Mr. Helman. As do all

our procedures." He put the hairpieces in a plastic bag and placed them on the back window ledge. He spoke again.

"And now, Mr. Helman, your reputation does precede you. Please lie face down on the floor."

Helman didn't move.

"There is a chance, Mr. Helman, that you will walk away from your meeting. In that case, it will be a distinct advantage for you not to have any more information than you actually require. Do you understand?"

Helman stretched out on the floor, his face near the man's feet. They didn't want him to know where they were taking him. It was a good sign, a reason for hope. Just as he had granted Roselynne Delvecchio her freedom, seconds before her death.

Helman felt the man's hand on his neck. He felt the strong thumb and forefinger lightly position themselves on the proper spots, and felt nothing else.

Only then did Mr. King press the button on the console to signal the driver that it was safe to drive on.

Helman woke in stages.

First he became conscious that he was thinking and tried to place himself. He remembered lying on the car floor. He was puzzled because now he could feel himself in a sitting position. The seat was soft and comfortable on the parts of his body which did not feel numb. He couldn't feel any of the car's vibrations.

Then he remembered his eyes and he opened them.

Eleven pairs of eyes stared back.

He jerked his body upright from the chair, twisting to see his position, to see if he were trapped. His neck and head caught fire with pain and he collapsed back into the chair, sweat bristling on his face. He fought back the urge to moan.

"There are aspirin, water, and cognac, if you wish any, on the table beside you." The voice came from Helman's right. It was the voice from the phone, from the car.

He turned his head slowly and saw Mr. King sitting a few

feet away in a similar chair. For a moment, Helman thought he was in some sort of club.

The walls were dark and fabric covered, the ceiling high and crossed with gleaming dark wood beams, catching innumerable highlights from a brilliant crystal chandelier.

Then he saw the eyes again. All other thoughts ended.

Eleven people sat behind a massive, intricately carved table. They stared at him and their faces were just eyes. He stared back, willing his eyes to focus, to show him the truth of what he saw.

Each face *was* just eyes. The rest was covered with a black cloth which hung from a cord tied behind the head and crossing just over the bridge of the nose. Their bodies were draped in formless black jackets—perhaps robes? Even their hands were swathed in black cloth, like improbable mittens.

"Who are you?" he said, quite softly. The movement of his jaw ripped into the back of his neck like scalding blades.

A voice began. It took Helman some moments to tell from the movement of a black cloth that the speaker was the figure seated third from the left.

"You are Robert Granger Helman. You are also David Michael Franklin, William Terrence Rosner, Stephen Phillip Osgood." The figure paused. He seemed to smile through his mask, then continued. "*et al.*"

They were the names of Helman's "drops." The dummy identities he and his broker used to funnel payments, and which Helman used as operating identities when closing deals. He had more than the three the figure had named, all backed by passports, credit cards, social security payments, and mailing addresses, but the ones named were his active ones. The rest were dormant until he had a need for them. Helman was not concerned with the revelation. He had expected it.

The figure continued.

"All of them born about 1975 it would seem. About the time you came in contact with a 'broker'—Helman noted with interest that his broker was not named—and became involved in the closing of certain 'deals.' "

A third person at the table began speaking.

"Mr. Helman, you are what is commonly referred to as a contract killer, a hit man. We have knowledge of twelve of what you call your deals. We have direct evidence linking you to seven of them. We suspect your total number of assassinations at between twenty and twenty-five. However, we feel seven is more than enough to interest the FBI. And any indictments filed against you would be certain to more than interest your past 'clients.' Panic, we are sure, would be much more likely considering the names you might be persuaded to reveal to save yourself.

"If you live through to your trial date, you can be certain your sister and her children won't. We shall see to that personally."

In the silence that followed, Helman felt the trap inexorably closing. He looked around at the room he was in: the paintings, the sculptures by the double doorway, and the rich oriental carpet beneath him. All spoke of wealth, old and considerable. The people who faced him, their voices all curiously similar to the man's beside him—a regional accent from a language other than English would fit in with his suspicions—were talking of murder.

Murder, wealth, and a group based in a common foreign location meant only one thing to him. A war was to begin. One of New York's families had linked him with some closings which might have been arranged by another family. They had somehow set him up in the Delvecchio deal, and now wanted him to give evidence about who hired him and why. That evidence could be taken to a war council as justification, in the end, for taking control of New York City. Helman had always tried to stay away from organized crime. Now he felt he hadn't tried hard enough.

It was time for him to react.

"You probably have more information about the closings you're talking about than I do," he began. "All of them are arranged through the broker you mentioned. Except when a name or a face has been in the papers, I often don't know who the deal is, and I *never* know who my client is.'' His first approach would be to make them think he was a pawn.

The group at the table reacted oddly, as though of all the things Helman might have said, his last statement wasn't one of the expected ones. The masked figures looked at each other in silence for a few moments. The figure in the middle, who hadn't spoken before, turned to Mr. King and asked, ''Does he wish to be commended for his ignorance? Surely that is the only way he can operate?''

The man in the chair addressed the group.

''No, my Lo-,'' he stopped abruptly and began again. But Helman had caught it. Was he actually going to call the man at the table ''my Lord?''

''No, sir. He believes you are one of the organizations his assassinations have been directed against. He will no doubt assume that his latest assassination, evidence of which we have presented to him, was arranged by you to furnish a hold over him. He believes you will now request him to furnish information about his previous employers so you may use that information against them. He is trying to establish himself as blameless in the planning of the assassinations so you will not kill him.''

Another figure at the table seemed impressed with the explanation of Helman's statement.

''Is this true, Mr. Helman?''

Helman was confused. Nothing here was making sense. He felt as if he were on display, not about to be subjected to interrogation on the eve of a gangland war. And why was one of the men at the table called ''Lord?''

''Who are you people?'' Helman had run out of theories. He had no idea what he was doing there.

The figure third from the left spoke again.

''We wish to offer you a contract. We wish you to assassinate for us.''

A cold, detached part of Helman accepted that as a legitimate request. That was the reason they had approached him: they wanted to buy his services. He examined them closely. Eleven indistinguishable figures. All with black cloths obscuring their faces and hands. All with the same whisper-hiss way of speaking. Their request seemed legitimate, even if they did not. But the request made no sense. What were they hiding?

They had the resources to completely uncover one of his closings. They had the ability to locate him within minutes of his arrival in New York. They were surrounded by the trappings of wealth. Helman had no doubt that they also had the sources and ability to hire anyone in the world to kill anyone else. Why did they come to him?

"I've retired," was all he said.

Instantly Mr. King was behind him, his steely fingers pressed deeply into the soft muscles just below Helman's skull.

The room turned red. Blood roared through his ears. Helman's head was twisted slowly and painfully up to meet the incredible eyes of the man who held him motionless. The eyes *did* glow. Or was it the blood being forced from his head? As if at a great distance, Helman heard Mr. King's single word. "Respect."

And then the man steadied and the warm light of the chandelier returned. Mr. King was no longer behind him. He was sitting in his chair. Helman had not been aware of any movement. The group at the table came into focus once more. The figure third from the left spoke again.

"You are an assassin. You will not speak to us otherwise. Your fee shall be the destruction of the evidence we hold against you."

Another voice spoke. From which figure it came, Helman could not be sure.

"Remember your sister and her children. You have no choice."

Helman rubbed gently at his inflamed neck. He knew what the penalty was for saying something to these people which they did not want to hear, but he had to risk it.

"With all respect, why have you chosen me for this? I'm an independent. I don't compare to the capabilities your organization has shown in bringing me here. Surely there are others who would be more suitable?''

Mr. King spoke.

''Mr. Helman. They have chosen *you*. That makes you suitable. I strongly advise against questioning their judgment.'' A lesser man might have punctuated that threat with an ominous clenching of a fist or some other reminder of the pain which had been inflicted, but Mr. King simply sat still. Everything about these people was understated and brutal. They had no need to threaten, they simply got their way. They were in complete control.

The confusion was leaving Helman. The resolve and, from the shadows, fear were growing.

Again a masked figure spoke.

''It is precisely for those reasons about which you have expressed concern, that we have chosen you.

''There are spheres of influence operating in the world which are far removed, in goals and power, from the areas in which you find yourself. You are involved in the petty circles of criminal endeavor, of corporate enterprise, political machinations. None of them concerns us. Just as we, at present, are of no concern to them. We all of us go our own ways, and only time will tell who is the master.''

Helman listened in fascination. Were they mad? After crime, business, and politics, what was left?

The figure continued.

''These spheres are quite rarified and open only to a few. Much power is exercised among them but a drawback is that all within are known to each other.''

Helman saw what they were driving at.

''You have never operated in such concerns and therefore are useful as an unknown quantity.

''Simply, we wish to punish one who has fallen away from us and our ways. This person is to be your target. Our usual operatives, and our usual methods, are known to the target, and certain defences are possible. We wish you to carry out this contract because you will be able to move freely without being identified, without causing alarm, until it is too late."

Helman asked the question his training demanded.

"There have been other attempts against the target?"

The figure nodded. "There have been other attempts."

And there it was. Nothing more had to be said. Like the Delvecchio closing, Helman was being brought in to correct a mistake. Only this time he had no idea whose mistake it was. His retirement, it seemed, was over. He had to kill one more time or risk the lives of the only people who mattered to him. His dreams and his life were secondary. They did not have to mention their evidence against him again. They had said it once. He doubted that these people would ever bother to repeat themselves.

"What guarantees do I have that after I complete your contract, the evidence will be destroyed? My family will be safe?"

Mr. King spoke. He seemed to be taking the role of interpreter, as though Helman represented a completely different world to the group at the table; a world which needed constant explanation.

"You have no such guarantees, Mr. Helman. Frankly, you're not in a position to demand them. You also have no guarantee that upon completing the contract we simply won't kill you ourselves."

Helman had known that.

"All I can offer," Mr. King continued, "is an appeal to your professional instincts. Each death is another opportunity for unpredictability. A careful plan can unravel with unanticipated inquiries from those who investigate bodies and death. You represent no threat to us. You don't know who we are, where we are, our motives, or the victim. Why risk a murder investigation when there is no need?"

Helman had no doubt that his body could disappear, just as easily as Joe Delvecchio's.

"Besides, Mr. Helman, at the very least, cooperating with us will buy you time." For the first time, the man's expression changed from one of deadly earnestness. He smiled at Helman.

For no particular reason he could think of, Helman noted that the man's teeth were perfect. White and even and regular, contrasting vividly with dark, brooding eyes.

Surrounded then, by a man with deadly fingers and a movie star's smile, and a mysterious group of people who wore bizarre masks in a peculiar room which, he noted for the first time, had no windows, Helman realized he must make his choice. And he realized that, in actuality, there was no choice to be made. There was only one course of action open to him.

He asked, "Who do you want me to kill?" and the briefing began. An envelope was produced containing pictures of the target, lists of recommended strategies and conditions which must be met.

The first thing he learned was that his target was Adrienne St. Clair, a woman who had just arrived in North America from England. The second thing he learned was that she was deadly. And after he had learned all that they would tell him, Mr. King, again without movement which Helman could sense, was behind him, fingers of steel pushing into his neck.

Helman collapsed, unknowing, without a shudder.

And now that the human would be removed from their presence, the masks could come off.

Seven

Lord Eduardo Diego y Rey rose from his position at the middle of the meeting table. His fingers worked delicately through the covering layers of loose black cloth wrapped around his hands, until he was free of its disguise.

His hands were gaunt and white. Each bone and tendon marked out in high relief. Not even the blue of arteries showed through the whiteness of his skin, as though something other than blood coursed through him.

His nails were inch-long wicked talons of brilliant white. They seemed to glow in the warm light of the meeting room's chandelier. He moved his hands behind his head to the fastening clip of the mask cord, and it too came free.

King felt envy as he gazed upon the face of Diego. It *was* the face of a Lord, unmarred by the necessities of the camouflage needed for dealing with the humans. Diego's rank was such that he never had to deal directly with them. Or else the humans he did deal with were of such rank that he did not have to disguise his true nature.

Diego's skin was paler than any albino's. The white was not just an absence of color, it *was* a color of itself. And his fangs, pushing delicately against his lower lip, had the appearance of marble: a true Lord of the Conclave, ruler of all *yber.* It was the name they called themselves. Humans called them by one far more foul.

"Mr. King," Diego said, his pale lips drawing back from the exquisite, needle-sharp incisors. His own kind would consider it a smile, as if it amused Diego to call King by the name he took while working among humans. "The situation seems controlled. When it is settled, consider traveling back with me to Spain. There is work there for you which would not require masks, of any kind."

"Of course, Lord Diego," King replied calmly. But in his thoughts he was thrilled. Lord Diego had just offered to be his mentor, an escape from the cruel mutilation of his own fangs so that he might pass among the humans. And such offers led to others; a century or two from now, he might even be allowed a seat on the Conclave itself.

"When this matter is completed," Diego said.

"When the heretic St. Clair has been given the Final Death," King agreed.

"And the human, Mr. King. It would be best if his body could be easily recovered and tied to whatever actions he might commit. When the human authorities have the dead suspect, they will not look further into it."

King nodded. Implicit in all his plans was the fact that Granger Helman could not be allowed to live. If the foolish human had believed what King had told him about going free after the heretic had been dealt with, so much the better. If Helman did not expect any treachery, the treachery would be that much easier.

"What shall be done about his sister, my Lord? And the children?"

"That depends on what his actions are likely to be. You were correct when you said he would react favorably when we threatened them. In truth he reacted more strongly to the threat against *them* than the threat against himself. Do you think he will attempt to contact them?"

"As soon as he can, my Lord."

"Then we will have to establish our presence. He cannot be allowed to think that we have no actual power over them. What do you suggest?"

"Methods he would understand, my Lord. An audible phone tap to begin with, so he will know all his communication with them is monitored. I also suggest some familiars place themselves in a position of watching. he must often communicate over unsecured lines. He works extensively with subtle codes. Quite likely he might have some way of alerting her."

"And afterward?"

"If she does not try to elude us and we do not have to contact her directly, she is nothing to us."

"Still, from what you have told us of him, he is unusual for a human. Are the children related to him by blood?"

"They are, my Lord."

"And what are their ages?"

"Steven is twelve. Campbell is ten," said King. His research had been extensive.

"Very good. When both Adrienne and the assassin have

been given their respective deaths, kill the sister and bring the children to me. A decade or two as familiars and if they share any of their uncle's attributes, they will make worthy additions. Yes?"

"As you wish, Lord Diego."

"Delightful." Diego waved his hand at the unconscious form of Helman, his claws flickering through the air like scythes. "Take him away. Start him on his journey."

King picked up Helman as if the unconscious form were only the weight of its empty clothes and carried him through the doors at the end of the meeting room. The doors were closed behind him by two young men, their eyes dark and sunken, with black cloth wrapped around their necks: Diego's familiars.

"And now we shall deal with the Jesuit who dared come too close and spy on our place of meeting," Diego announced.

The ten others at the table agreed. They had removed their own masks and hand cloths as Diego and King had decided Helman's fate. All, like Diego, bore delicate, needle-sharp fangs and white, polished claws. It was a full gathering of the Eastern Meeting. The last had been fourteen years ago to plan a foray into the politics of humans which had ended disastrously five years after it had begun in an unprecedented scandal at the highest levels. The reasons for this gathering were even more urgent.

The first reason was Adrienne St. Clair, but Diego was satisfied with King's arrangements, and felt the matter was settled. The threat had been neutralized and the Conclave was safe from within. But from without, danger grew stronger each passing night. Something had happened within the Jesuits of the Seventh Grade. The equilibrium of centuries was being threatened and, ironically, it had taken the heretic woman to bring it to the Conclave's attention.

The fiasco at Heathrow was, without question, the work of the Jesuits. By itself, it was meaningless. Such attacks occurred from time to time, from both sides. But what was chilling in its implication was that for the first time in over four hundred years of conflict, the Jesuits had involved outsiders, and those outsiders had been told what to expect. The British soldiers had carried crossbows: weapons of the Final Death.

For the past two hundred years, the conflict had been contained. Both the Jesuits and the Conclave had skirmished incessantly, but each had kept their battles secret, for each held awesome weapons against the other. The Jesuits of the Seventh Grade knew the true nature of the Conclave and through the world-wide missions of their brothers of the first six grades, that truth could be told to the world of humans. Some of these humans would believe and the Conclave would be crushed, not by the strength or intellect of humans, but by their numbers.

But before the Conclave would let that happen, the catacombs of Rome would also be exposed to the world: the sordid truths of actions taken by the hypocrites who for two thousand years had existed in the Jesuits' Holy Church, were cataloged and ready. The *yber* had also moved within that same church for generations. Documents existed concerning certain saints, certain phenomena, and, more damning in these times, certain political expediencies. One of those expediencies was known to the world by a special name. And if the Conclave were threatened by any revelations by the Jesuits of the Seventh Grade, than those documents would find their way into the hands of those who would not hide them.

Madmen, removed from the seat of the Church's power, but acting for it nonetheless, had drafted those documents so they might survive the storm that threatened Europe. Those documents engineered the insanity that followed. The insanity that the world called the Holocaust.

The Conclave might not survive, but the Jesuits' beloved Church would be swept into oblivion with it.

Thus each had battled, constrained from using their ultimate secrets against each other. Until Heathrow. Until Adrienne St. Clair. Lord Diego would learn why the enemy had involved humans in their conflict or the bound and captive Jesuit his familiars now brought before him would pray for eternal damnation for release from what Diego would do to him.

The Jesuit's arms were tied behind his back and he was firmly held on each side by the familiars. He was old. The hair that was left to him was sparse and white. Though he appeared frail, he stood proudly before the massive table. But his eyes were closed and his mouth moved silently in the words of prayer.

Diego walked around the table and stood in front of the Jesuit. He held his claws lightly against the face of the praying man. Slowly he pressed into the flesh, depressing it, deeper, until tiny wellings of red formed at each claw's tip.

"Open your eyes, Father Benedict," he hissed. "Look into the eyes of *Hell*." The last word was screamed. The startled Jesuit jerked backward, eyes opened on the hideous fanged monster before him. His face was shredded by the knife-sharp talons.

Father Benedict wailed in agony, blood streaming from ten deep slashes down his face. Diego lifted one blood spattered claw and slowly guided it to the Jesuit's left eye.

"Don't you like my face, Priest? Does thine eye offend thee?"

The Jesuit strained backward against the solid grip of the familiars, his eyes transfixed by the closing tip of Diego's outstretched claw.

"What is it your bible says about thine eye offending thee? What is it, Priest?"

Father Benedict mumbled prayers feverishly, not moving his eyes from the evil point inches from his face.

Diego's other hand shot out and slapped the Jesuit with a crack like lightning. Blood sprayed from the wounds of his face.

"What is it? What is it? What does your bible say?"

Father Benedict looked into the eyes of Hell, looked into the face of Diego. "Pluck it out," he whispered.

Diego's claw thrust out before the Jesuit could blink. It sliced through his eye, gouging savagely. The eyeball burst from its socket, collapsing as its inner fluid ran down the

Jesuit's face, mixing with the still-dripping blood. Diego pulled back with a sudden twist. The upper eyelid hung grotesquely over the gaping socket like peeling paint. The Jesuit's screams were deafening at first, but changed quickly to deep sobs, obscured by the constant mouthing of prayers which still he continued.

"Perhaps if you thought of something to say to us other than your cursed pleas for help from your insipid god, I might do something about the pain. And you would still have at least one eye left by sunrise."

Father Benedict said nothing. He squinted through his right eye. It was impossible for him to open it wider because of the massive damage to the other.

"What are you to your god that he would let this happen to you, Priest? What can this be worth?"

The Jesuit, finally, spoke. "Salvation." The word was garbled. Blood and other liquids gathered in his mouth.

"I can give you that," said Diego, stepping away slightly, decreasing the threat.

"There is no salvation from the devil."

"No, Father Benedict. I am serious. If you wish 'salvation,' as you call it, let me make a proposal."

"Never."

"Where is the famed logic of your order? Listen first, then answer. To begin, you must understand that tonight you will die. Your uncivilized behavior before our Meeting makes your death a necessity. Do you understand?"

The Jesuit had no reaction.

"What we have left to deal with then, is the manner of your death. It could be easy and clean, and delayed long enough for you to complete whatever rites of contrition you think necessary. No doubt your god will greet you at the gates of heaven. Or else, I could give you to them." Diego gestured to the others seated behind the table. "And you would die in a manner that I'm sure you'd find repugnant. And then, Father Benedict, *after* you had died, I would chain you in a small cell below us. And each night I would stand by the door and listen to you rage and bellow against the thirst. And Priest, believe me, *it is a terrible thirst*. Then, when you could stand it no more, I would send in children. Do you understand, Father Benedict? The blessed innocents would walk in to give themselves up to you, and you will rend them and consume them until you are sated and full of shame. Then I shall chain you again in the midst of the ruin of their bodies, and we shall all wait until the thirst returns and we do it again and again and again. Throughout eternity, Father Benedict. Eternity. Do you understand?''

The Jesuit's face was pale. ''No,'' he whispered. ''Please, no.'' The mumbled prayers had stopped.

''It's very simple to avoid. Tell us why you staged the attack at the English airport. Tell us why you involved the British soldiers. A few questions. A few simple answers. And the pain will stop. We'll give you a small injection. You'll last long enough for us to deliver you to another who can give you your last rites, if that's what concerns you. You can confess everything. Your god will understand. The flesh is weak. He knows. He forgives.'' Diego's voice was almost calm, almost reassuring, then he dropped it to a dry hissing whisper. ''But he'll never forgive the children, Priest. *Never.*''

The Jesuit was silent, unmoving. He stood only because the familiars held him so tightly.

Diego held up a talon. ''Madeline. My patience is gone. He is yours.''

A woman rose from behind the table and came toward Father Benedict. Her mouth was wide. Her lips were moist and her mouth was gaping. The fangs within glistened.

''You already know why we're after St. Clair,'' the Jesuit said, looking at Diego in desperation.

''Of course we know already,'' Diego lied easily, convincingly. He motioned Madeline to stay back. ''You won't be telling us anything new. You won't be betraying anyone. Confirm it for us, and you shall have peace.''

''The final war is coming.'' The Jesuit's voice was weak.

''Armageddon?'' Diego seemed amused. ''Again?''

"The signs are there. It has been foretold."

"Forgive me, Priest, but you're babbling. Has there been a rapture? Has the Antichrist announced himself? Have there been more stars over Bethlehem?"

"You are all of you the Antichrist. The forces of darkness are combining. The threat grows. The End Days are here."

For an instant, Diego was chilled. *Could* the Jesuits have heard about the *yber's* Final Plan? Is that what drove them? The Jesuits were superstitious fools. The Bible spoke of such a conflict and in each generation the wise among them decided theirs was the time in which it would come to pass. But still it worried him. Perhaps St. Clair knew. Perhaps she had already contacted the Jesuits.

"What forces of darkness do you see combining, Priest? Tell us who our allies are against you."

"This country rises from the Pit to join you. The beast rises from the west."

"What do you mean, 'this country'?"

"The United States. We know that Adrienne St. Clair is your contact with Washington. It can only mean you are to combine and the power of this nation will be subverted to destruction. To damnation."

Diego sputtered on the word. "Washington? We are 'combining' with the Americans? What nonsense are you speaking?" He grabbed Father Benedict by his neck. The talons dug deep. "Who told you this? How?" Diego glanced frantically back over his shoulder to assess the others. All looked as confused as he.

"Contact has been observed. You cannot convince me otherwise. These are the End Days."

Diego squeezed harder. "They *are* the end days, Priest. For you. Now tell me how you know this or you shall be sucking the innocent blood of children before the moon changes."

The Jesuit was gasping, his face turning purple from the unrelenting pressure. "Word comes from Rome. St. Clair must be stopped. At all costs. Must be . . ."

Diego released his grip.

"From Rome? Rome wants St. Clair stopped at all costs? Because she is representing the Conclave to Washington?"

"Yes."

"*Es increible.*" Diego turned away from him. "Madeline, take the poor fool from his misery."

Madeline moved in front of the Jesuit. Her slender, taloned fingers stroked gently across his blood-drenched face. She brought the coated fingers to her mouth and slowly, deeply sucked on them. Her eyes held him. Father Benedict shouted, "The injection. You said I would be spared this. The Last Rites. You promised me."

Diego resumed his seat in the middle of the table. He bared his fangs in a smile. "Look into the eyes of Hell, Father Benedict. Look deeply, and you will see yourself."

Madeline pulled on the simple white shift she wore. It floated down around her feet. She stood naked before the Jesuit. Her body was the perfect form of just awakening womanhood, and had been for more than eighty years.

"*Nous connaissons ce que vous revez*," she whispered to him, and reached out her moistened hand to his groin. And the Jesuit, his body old and torn, facing the demons he had fought from afar for the fifty years he served the Holy Father, God have mercy, he responded to her touch. The power of the *yber* reached into him, shaming him. She squeezed at his hardness, pressed her body tightly against him, and forced his bloody mouth to her own. Her fangs cut deeply into his lips and he felt her suck upon him, felt the constrictions as she hungrily swallowed, the constrictions of her hand as she pulled upon him. Her lips trailed blood from his mouth as she moved across him.

"We know what you dream," she whispered into his ear, her breath hot, exciting him more. Her fangs sliced into the soft flesh of his ear lobe. She moved further down.

The Jesuit, his voice a feeble murmur, said, "Oh God, oh yes." And then she had entered his neck and he spurted into her as she sucked and swallowed and filled herself with him. And when she was sated the others took her place.

* * *

Father Benedict's body lay crumpled and empty on the floor of the meeting room. He was drained before he could share in their special Communion. He would not rise again. Ellen, the last of the creatures to fall upon him, stepped back from him, a red flush shining out from the pallor of her cheeks.

"So, Ellen, what do you make of his rantings?" Diego had not partaken. He had been deep in thought while the others attended the priest.

"Insane," said Ellen. "They are all insane." She wiped at a dribble of the Jesuit's blood at the corner of her mouth.

"Of course," agreed Diego. "But whatever their reasons, which in truth I cannot understand, they seem as determined to kill St. Clair as we are. It would be a shame to waste such holy dedication."

"What are you thinking?" asked Madeline. Still naked, she sprawled back in a chair, her body relaxed and languorous. She was gorged.

"I think a message to Rome is in order. We'll use this priest's name and tell them where St. Clair has landed. It should be a few nights, at least, before they miss him. And just in case Mr. King's human is not as capable as he appears to be, we shall even tell them that the human is one of her familiars." Diego smiled. Everything was falling into place perfectly. "Then we shall be saved the bother of eliminating him ourselves and with the Jesuits so inexperienced in these matters, it's bound to be a messy affair. It shall be amusing to see how they contrive to stay out of the humans' newscasts."

The others joined in Diego's amusement. The Jesuits were such fools.

"And then," said Diego, "all that remains is to find out why they think there is a connection between St. Clair and Washington." And to find out if she knows about the Final Plan, he thought.

"Couldn't she have contacted them?" asked Ellen. "Wouldn't they have the facilities she was seeking?"

"No, she wouldn't trust them. She would be afraid of

their military and the uses they might have for her. No, I'm certain of it. She would not contact them.'' Unless she knew what the Conclave planned.

''Would they have somehow contacted her?'' The question was unthinkable but Diego was glad Madeline had asked it.

''For the sake of the Conclave, it cannot be true. But that is what we must find out.'' Or had the Americans, with all their industry and science, stumbled upon it for themselves? That could explain it. They knew the horrible future waiting for them. They saw St. Clair as an ally. And she would be. Alone among the *yber* and the humans of the world, she could destroy the Final Plan, preserve the humans' future.

Diego waved his hand to the larger of his two familiars. The youth began to unwrap the black cloth from his neck as he approached his mentor.

First Lord Diego would feed. And then he would arrange the message to Rome. It must be a message which could not be misunderstood. It must enrage them. The Conclave must stop St. Clair at all costs. Even if it meant somehow collaborating with their hated enemies the Jesuits.

She could destroy everything, Diego thought as his fangs slipped into the willing flesh of his familiar.

I wonder if she knows that?

The blood was warm and satisfying. He thought of the message he would send the Jesuits.

And he knew it *would* enrage.

Eight

Major Anthony Weston, United States Army, examined the documents and photographs on his desk without really seeing them. He knew there were other, more pressing matters to attend to, but an immobilizing inertial block made him sit at his desk, unable to begin anything new, until the phone call came that would tell him that the location had been determined.

With a great effort of will, he forced himself to at least straighten up his desk. He began to slide the papers back into their gray metal file container. For the last time he looked at the glossy eight-by-tens of the three hundred and forty rats that had been suffocated by a rapid rise in temperature in their lab at Berkeley. They were meaningless to him. He had far worse things on his conscience than the deaths of rats.

Included in the documents was a photocopy of his letter refusing a reallocation of funds to enable the experiment to be restarted. He knew that he would have to answer to that young doctor he had had placed at the Haaberling Institute (he couldn't remember his name), but that would come later. The experiment had been stopped. That was all that mattered for now.

Weston looked far older than his years. Since he had been assigned the directorship, he had aged incredibly under the strain. This is what happens to presidents, he thought. They enter the Oval Office, eyes bright, faces fresh, and then the briefings begin. The quiet, somber men begin to call. They whisper their secrets to their new commander, and in months the burden shows. Conditions and situations the quiet men have dealt with for years enter the presidents' lives in moments. In four years they age ten. Nothing would ever be the same for any of them. But Weston had never been in the Oval Office. There were some secrets in Washington which could not be trusted to someone whose power rested in his appeal to the people. That kind of power base was too unstable. The real power of the government was not subject to such transitory conditions. Weston and his people held their secrets alone.

He locked the documents in the container. Their classification would be non-existent. They would never be filed where someone not connected with Weston and the Nevada Project could get at them.

Weston stared at his office wall, thinking about what lay beyond it—the fragmentation that was growing through Washington like cracks on thin ice. So many pieces floating away on their own. How many files like his were there in that city? What other unimaginable secrets were hidden away under only one key because no one could trust the central filing systems? Sometimes, late at night when sleep eluded him, he found himself thinking that perhaps there was another project like his operating out there. A project just as shrouded in secrecy so that no others knew their work was being duplicated, but a project different from his. That other project would have the answer.

Weston knew it was a dangerous thought, and he knew what was behind it.

He had been forced down too many blind alleys. He had had to order too many repugnant solutions. Hasty, panicked, murderous. Some solutions had been easily bought. Like the young doctor with the rats who had ended up in Stockholm. He had not even known he was being bought off and his experiment stopped. But some of the others, the older ones especially, who could not be easily dazzled and diverted, were much more stubborn. Fatal car accidents were being arranged in an almost regular manner. The loss to the country's scientific potential was enormous, especially now that it was so desperately needed. The moral cost was something Weston had stopped thinking of long ago.

With the directorship had come the understanding that certain actions were to be considered necessary in the extreme. Years ago, he had accepted that. Everything flowed from that decision. Recently, that decision had been coming more and more to mind, but he kept thrusting it from him. Now was not the time to reconsider.

He coughed. The pain seared through him, making him tense up. His deeply etched, lined face contorted. He was alone in his office so he was allowed that. Never before his people. The pain settled to a dull ache in his chest. He resisted the urge to cough again. It was after him all right. He had gone after it, but it had zeroed in on him first. The country wasn't the only thing running out of time. At least he wouldn't be around to see it end. He would be spared that agony. And out of everything he had been faced with in the last fourteen years, that thought was the one thing that really scared him. *It would end*.

But not today. Today his lungs worked and the country was secure in its ignorance. In a matter of weeks that security would inevitably erode and crumble and he would be forced to go to someone. Certainly not the President. Certainly not anyone he could think of. Everything hung poised and motionless waiting for his phone to ring.

Eventually, it did.

Weston's agent on the other end gave the location.

"The contact is Leung. She's in Toronto."

Weston's mind broke free of the stagnation of waiting. If she had contacted the primed doctors in Washington or Chicago or any of the other major American cities, it would have been the end of it. The field was far too open and she would be dead before the proper arrangements could be negotiated. But Canada meant there was a chance the Nevada Project could be first. His mind raced with the possibilities.

He spoke quickly. "How soon can we have a team operating there? Can we get a consular expedience order to bring in the Mounties?"

His agent responded. "We've got Davis up there now making the final negotiations with Leung. Davis is sure he's going to cooperate fully. Everyone will be in place for the first moves tonight. Davis says not to bring in the Mounties." The agent paused, wondering how much he could say even over a secure line. "Someone's already brought them in."

Weston had half-expected that, but still he was surprised. Rome had also made the location. The others wouldn't have bothered with the Mounties. But how had they done it?

His men would now be operating in a friendly nation

without sanction. But a diplomatic incident would only bring it all to a head a few weeks earlier. There was, in the end, nothing to lose.

"Set up for surveillance and protection. I'll be there within twenty-four hours for the initial contact." There was a silence.

"Jack," Weston said finally, calling the agent by his first name. "This is it, you know. There's nothing else."

"We'll do it," was all the agent said. The line went dead.

Weston switched to another line and began to make his travel arrangements.

Everything rested on this last effort.

If they failed, nothing else would matter, ever again.

Nine

The plane was half-empty and Helman sat alone in his row by a window, staring sightlessly out over the night darkened water. The flight from LaGuardia was almost over. The atrocity he must commit would soon begin.

They had told him his victim's name and then they had told him little else. What Adrienne St. Clair had done to them, what one person could possibly do to them which would make them react this way, he had no way of knowing. He could only guess that her actions had been devastating, because the conditions of this closing were the most vicious he had ever agreed to.

"An example must be made, Mr. Helman," one of the black-masked ones had said. "She has gone from our ways onto another path, and any who might be tempted to follow her must know what reward is waiting. The conditions must be met *exactly*!'' The last had been a hiss, like an animal spitting its rage, and Helman had felt the first tendrils of a nightmare disorientation; an intense feeling that things were somehow wrong, like some cloudy manifestation from the pit of his mind. Those people could not be *real*.

The No Smoking/Fasten Seatbelt light chimed on in the cabin and Helman returned to the present as he watched the lights of the city grow closer. The plane banked and began its descent. He wondered if it would somehow be better this time if it crashed.

Four years earlier, Helman had spent a month in Toronto on ''standby.'' Power plays influenced by criminal organizations from the predominately French city of Montreal had threatened the stability of a Toronto family's control over a Canada-wide development industry. Helman, and he believed, at least five others in a similar line of work, had been brought to Toronto as a show of force and as insurance, in case the conflict spread from Montreal and obstacles had to be removed.

As the situation had developed, a carefully orchestrated accident involving a well-known political figure occurred in Montreal. The details surrounding the accident were enough to destroy the politician's career. He had immediately seen the possibilities and capitulated that same evening. Certain elements of the planted evidence were removed from the scene of the accident and when the story broke, even the newspapers were sympathetic to the politician in their reporting.

The politician's future was secure, important concessions had been made, and five days later a fire bombing in a Montreal night club eliminated the final holdouts to a settlement. The threat had been contained and Helman and the others were free to leave Toronto, paid well for their month of waiting.

Helman had heard that two years afterward, an investigative reporting team came across disturbing evidence that a concentration of ''hired guns'' had existed in Toronto for that month. The reporters explained it away by saying it was part of an attempt by motorcycle gangs to consolidate their control over drug trafficking in the area.

Helman had never been sure if that story showed that the Canadian police and press could be bought off easily, or if it had just shown how stupid they were. Either way, he had not liked his stay in the city, and he did not like the fact that it was going to be his killing ground for the closing of Adrienne St. Clair.

Customs clearance and baggage claim took minutes. Helman walked out of the enclosure directly to a wall of pay phones. This was the first chance he had had to be alone since he was picked up in Times Square. After his briefing, Mr. King had again reached up to Helman's neck and Helman had been unaware of anything until he woke up in a car in the LaGuardia airport parking lot. Mr. King, who was beside him, accompanied him to pick up his ticket, and then saw him off in the departure lounge. Finally Helman was free to call his sister.

He put through a collect call. The phone was answered in the middle of the first ring and he heard Miriam accept the charges.

He said hello and Miriam began to cry.

''He said you were all right but I couldn't be sure.''

''Who said I was all right?'' Helman had to press his hand against his other ear to hear what his sister was saying. ''Who were you talking to?''

''The man who called the night before you left.'' Miriam's voice was tinny and sounded far away. Helman realized a tap was on her phone. Either it was an old, unsophisticated, direct link that was drawing far more power than it should from the line, or it was purposely designed to interfere so that Helman would know that his every move was anticipated. The group in New York had reached out to him again. If he told his sister to take her children and run, he doubted if she would make it out the door. She was the group's insurance, and their assumption was correct. He would do anything before he would let harm come to them.

"Well, he was right," Helman yelled into the phone. "Everything's just fine. I should be back in a couple of days. How're the boys?" Desperately hè thought of something he could say to her. Some way to warn her, to tell her to run. But he had never involved his sister in his work, except for that first time. He had no codes to tell her, no plans had been worked out in advance.

They were all of them locked into the fate of Adrienne St. Clair. Her death alone would buy their freedom.

The rest of the conversation was brief and meaningless. Miriam sounded calmer when she said goodbye, relieved that Helman was alive and soon to be home. She had no idea of the part she was playing. For that Helman was grateful. If anything happened to her or her family, Helman knew he would destroy the group in New York, no matter what the cost.

A man in a long, black leather coat came up to Helman at the hotel's registration desk, and Helman knew immediately the man was his contact from New York.

He was tall and slender and had the same perfect teeth that King had shown. He must have been waiting outside for Helman's arrival because his hands were startlingly cold when he reached out to shake, as though they were two business associates about to conduct a meeting.

That close to the man, under the bright lights in the high ceiling of the lobby, Helman saw an out-of-place discoloration on the man's shirt collar. It was make-up that had rubbed off the man's neck.

"Good evening, Mr. Osgood," the man said, using Helman's 'drop' name and pumping his hand. "I'm Mr. Rice. I'm sure your office told you to expect me."

Helman nodded. Mr. Rice's face was covered in make-up. Not effeminate, not as a new men's fashion, but like theatrical make-up, accentuating what tone and shadow already existed. Helman was sure the man wasn't wearing it as a disguise, but could think of no other reason.

In the more subdued light of the elevator, the evidence of

the make-up was impossible to see. Rice looked as if he might be a brother to King or in some other way related. But Helman did not question him. The less they thought he knew about them, the more likely he was to be left alive when he had finished their work. If they had not already made up their minds to kill him.

Helman tipped the bellhop and the two men were left alone in the room. It was the typical North American box design: bathroom on the right forming a small entrance hall to the rectangular area with two double beds, two chairs, and an assortment of chests and tables. In the summer, the room would be more expensive because of its sliding glass doors onto a balcony which overlooked the outdoor pool three floors below. But the pool was covered in tarpaulins and the balcony adrift with snow.

Rice spoke first. He threw his attaché case on the bed. "These are the final details, assassin. We will study them."

Another incongruity. Rice's voice was different now that they were alone. It had gone from a nondescript flat accent to the drawn-out hissing whisper of King and the group in New York. Were they subjecting Helman to a particularly sophisticated form of subliminal conditioning? Planting any number of false clues, seemingly related suggestions that would lead nowhere, in case he were captured? Or were they actually that *strange*?

Helman slipped off his coat and pulled a chair over to the corner of the bed. The attaché case was cheap plastic, embossed to look like grained leather, and brand new, as if Rice had never had use for an attaché case until he was told to deliver material this evening. Even so, Helman didn't touch it. "Is there a certain way to open it?" he asked.

Rice reacted with impatience. "We have no need to play the games that you do, assassin. If we do not wish to have documents looked at, then they are never placed in a situation where they can be looked at. Our briefcases don't explode." He opened the case. There was one large brown envelope inside. Except for a manufacturer's tag looped around the inside pocket closure, there was nothing else.

Rice opened the envelope and slid the contents out. The top item was an eight-by-ten, black-and-white photo of a woman. It was a copy print of what Helman took to be an old passport photo. The woman's hair was dark and swept up in a stiff style popular years before. Probably the early fifties, thought Helman.

"This is the woman, Adrienne St. Clair. Study the image carefully. You will not be allowed to keep it. Or any of this," Rice said, indicating the rest of the material on the bed, "except for the map."

Helman held the photo close. The woman was attractive, despite the awkwardness of her hair. Her chin and mouth were small, her eyes a bit too far apart, and her face was stretched by either flat cheek bones or puffiness around her eyes. He couldn't tell which. Something about her made him think she was British. He was sure he could recognize her when he saw her, but her hairstyle was old fashioned.

"It's a clear photo for identification, but it looks about thirty years old. What does she look like today?"

Rice sighed. "The photo is much more recent than that. Her hairstyle and make-up were applied for a particular assignment she was to carry out. She looks much the same today. Her hair is red when it is not disguised, and cut short." Rice picked up a sheet of paper that had been beneath the woman's picture and read from it. "The woman is about thirty years old, five foot five inches in height, weighing approximately 100 pounds. She is ambidextrous, and, as you were told by my associates in New York, trained in a variety of the so-called 'martial' arts. If you get within arm's reach of her while she is conscious, I should not expect you to live more than a few seconds."

Helman nodded, he had been told that. If she had gone through the same training as King, with his ability to paralyze within seconds, Helman could believe it too.

There were many questions to ask.

"You mentioned that her hair is sometimes disguised. Do you know if that is the case now?"

Rice shook his head. "No, she thinks she is well-protected, and has not taken any steps to alter her appearance."

"What does well-protected mean?"

Rice dug into the pile on the bed. He handed two more photos to Helman. The first was of an oriental male. He was wearing dark rimmed glasses and Helman could see a scarf around his neck just above the picture's cropping. A cloud of exhaled breath streamed away from him. The background of the photo, an open courtyard, or something similar, with some small bare trees, was compressed, showing it had been taken with a telephoto lens.

"That was taken a month ago. He is Doctor Christopher Leung. He is on staff at the University of Toronto Medical Facility. The woman is staying with him in his house in the city."

The second photograph, from a reflection in the corner and some blurriness, obviously a shot from a moving vehicle, showed a row of five townhouses. They were four stories high, very narrow and modern looking. Half of a much older, larger house showed at the edge of the picture, indicating the townhouses were built in an older neighborhood.

"Dr. Leung's is the middle one." Rice paused. "Tell me your plans, assassin, and I shall tell you anything additional you need to know."

Helman stared at the photos of the doctor and the woman. They seemed an unlikely pair to have such attention paid to them.

"What is the woman's relationship with the doctor? Are they lovers?"

Rice looked indignant. "That is quite impossible."

"How do you know?" Another anomaly presented itself.

"You will take my word for it, assassin. I am only to tell you what you need to know to carry out your work."

Helman took care not to raise his voice in the thin-walled hotel room. He pointed to the photograph of the house. "Look, these top rooms are most likely bedrooms. If they're lovers, I'll only have to penetrate one room with an explosive or a gas. If they're not, I'll have to attack several rooms at once."

"I see your point, but they will have separate sleeping accommodations, you can be sure. The woman will most likely be in a basement room."

"And again, you won't tell me why. I'm just to accept it."

Rice smiled. "That is correct, assassin. Accept it."

Helman sat back in his chair and rubbed his face. He tried again. "What *is* their relationship?"

Rice sighed again. Helman wondered if he always did that before he gave his most dubious answers.

"We believe that the woman has contracted a rare disease. Most likely tropical. Not fatal. Disruptive at best. Paralyzing at worst. We believe she has made an arrangement with the doctor to begin treatment. Each evening she accompanies the doctor to a research facility at his university. When the disease is controlled, she will be free again to work against us."

Helman was sure Rice was lying. "So while she's here, with the doctor, she is not actively working against you?"

Rice leaned forward, seething. "Her existence works against us!" The chair arm his hand was gripping cracked suddenly. Helman felt his own chair arm. It was solid.

Rice sat back. "Think, assassin. How shall you rid us of her?"

"I'll need a day. I need to see the townhouse. Possibly the lab they go to. Make contact. Check the neighborhood. For myself."

"If a day is what you need, then by all means take it." Rice stood up and went for his coat. "The townhouse address is marked on the back of the photograph. The university building also. You may keep the map of the city. I shall take back everything else."

Helman removed a standard folded map from the pile and checked the address on the photo. Rice gathered the rest of the material together and placed it back in the cheap plastic case.

"I shall see you tomorrow evening. I trust you shall have your plan ready by then so we are not forced to turn to someone else."

Helman said nothing. Rice took the case, and left.

Helman stood under the shower for half an hour, alternating between steaming hot water and straight cold. Too much had happened to him in the last forty-eight hours. The package and phone call in New Hampshire. The useless cat-and-mouse game ending in New York. And now the two briefings by the oddest people he had ever dealt with—and the most dangerous. Men who wore unobtrusive make-up for no particular reason. Black-masked people who were addressed as "Lord." His mind swam with the confusion of it.

Finally he lay back on one of the beds and thought about the closing. Demolishing the house with explosives would be ideal in any other situation, but not appropriate for Adrienne St. Clair. *The conditions must be met exactly!* they had told him. One way or another, Helman was going to have to get himself close enough to Adrienne St. Clair to decapitate her.

Sleep, when it came, was not easy. And it ended in screams.

Ten

Silently, it had slipped up through the open stairs and wrapped wetly around his ankles. In that instant of transcendent terror, the darkness below him vanished and he saw clearly what waited for him in the basement.

Their masks fluttered from their faces like black flying

things. Their make-up rippled and dripped like melting wax. They were all together, waiting for him, down there. They were smiling at him and he *saw* . . .

It was his own screaming that woke him.

Helman thrashed at the sweat-soaked sheet wrapped up and twisted around his feet, and sat upright, trembling. He was in the delicate transition between sleep and consciousness. His brain held the secret of King and Rice and whispered it to him. He shook with the knowledge of it.

But the sun was streaming through the slightly open curtains and traffic noises growled somewhere near. The knowledge fell away like dust, leaving only its warning, its feeling of dread.

Helman showered again and dressed. He had one more phone call to make. His broker, Max Telford. The person the people in the masks had referred to, but never named. The anomaly must be checked.

Two months ago, after the Delvecchio closing, Helman had told Telford his decision to retire. Telford had taken it well. Helman felt the old man had a type of fatherly feeling toward him. On one hand, he had complained about how short-handed Helman was leaving him; how difficult it was to recruit professionals instead of kids who had seen too many movies and wanted to be hit men—"torpedoes" Telford called them, disparagingly. Telford thought they'd be better off being mercenaries in Africa or Central America, so they could blast away to their hearts' content and never have to worry about witnesses, or killing civilians. Yet, on the other hand, Helman felt Telford was glad to see him quit the business alive. Telford had handled twenty of Helman's twenty-three closings. Helman had no precise statistics on the rest of Telford's crew, but he felt his success rate was a record. Even so, Helman had learned long ago that feelings were not to be trusted. Perhaps three months ago, Telford did feel like a father to him. But Helman knew how quickly situations could change in his business. Telford might have felt pressure from one organization or another, and as a result, turned over his "insurance" on Helman to representatives of the group from New York.

Everyone in the business had "insurance." A secret cache of information, names and dates, that would implicate and endanger as many associates as possible in the event of an untimely, unwarranted death. Telford kept it on each of his crew. Helman kept it on Telford. It was an accepted and acknowledged fact of the business. And necessary. An assassin without insurance represented a final, easy-to-take-care-of loose end. An assassin without insurance was a dead man.

Helman sat on the edge of a bed in his hotel room and placed a long distance call to a restaurant in Miami. Telford owned several seafood restaurants there, and operated his "brokerage" from the offices at the back of the largest one. Tourists came and went as Telford plotted murder above the kitchen. If Telford had released his insurance about Helman, an action usually taken by lawyers upon a client's premature death, Helman would see to it that the release had not been unjustified. Feelings were not to be trusted. He would have another closing to attend to after he finished with the St. Clair woman: Max Telford.

The phone rang five times. Helman heard the receiver being lifted. On any other phone line into the restaurant, a voice would identify the restaurant by name and ask what the caller wanted. On the line Helman had called, the voice said only, "Go ahead."

"This is Mr. Bryant. I want to make a reservation for next Wednesday at 8:45, for nine. Actually, there will be at least six of us. We may be joined by up to five more. However a reservation for nine should be about right." Helman waited for the voice to respond with the second phase of the signal.

"Our pleasure, Mr. Bryant. Is there anything else the *maître d'* may prepare for you?"

"I'd like it charged to my card, number 416—"

The voice interrupted, as it should. "That's quite all

right, Mr. Bryant. I'm sure we have it on file. Is this a party?''

''A surprise party. We'll be bringing a special cake.''

''Wonderful. We'll expect you Wednesday then. Goodbye, Mr. Bryant.''

Helman hung up but kept his hand on the receiver. It had been the most urgent message he had ever placed into the system. If the situation in Miami was normal, Telford would be informed of who called, the urgency, and the phone and room number that Helman had given in the reservation information, within minutes. The return call should be immediate.

Two minutes later, Helman lifted the receiver in the middle of the phone's first ring. The situation in Miami was normal. Or was arranged to appear normal.

Telford's rasping voice was on the other end.

''So what's the big 'surprise,' Granger? You coming out of retirement?'' His voice was friendly, perhaps even happy. But Telford was a professional, too. Feelings, as well as appearances, were the same.

Telford had also called Helman by name. That meant the call was being routed through at least three other phone lines in the Florida system. Two of them would hold a scrambler system. Helman could not be sure if his motel phone was secure, but no one would be able to trace or tap a thing from Telford's end. Telford would assume that since Helman had given his number, the line was safe.

''I've been forced out, Max.'' Helman paused. Letting the seriousness sink in, provided Telford wasn't the man behind it in the first place.

''Go on.'' Telford's voice had changed. A clinical edge had crept in. He understood the implications. It was the reaction Helman had expected, and hoped for.

''It appears my insurance was cashed. I'm hoping it was a policy I didn't know about.''

''Screw it, Granger. You retired. I put the lid on your file. Are you being pressured? You think I've sold you out?'' Telford was clearly agitated. Some of it was because Helman seemed to think Telford had betrayed him. Most of it because, if Helman did believe Telford had turned on him, Helman would have no option but to release his own insurance on Telford. Things could get messy. Telford had had to do it before, but he hated to assign a closing on one of his own crew.

"I hope not, Max. I'm going to give you some details and I want you to tell me where I've gone wrong. Because if it's not me, it's got to be someone else." It's got to be you, Max, he thought.

Telford stayed quiet on the other end. His whole operation depended on what Helman said in the next few minutes. If some of his other crew ever turned on him the way Helman was threatening to, it would cause trouble. But Helman he knew, could, and would, destroy him.

In coded words, Helman quickly told his story: the insurance in the package, the offer to purchase in New York, and the closing in Toronto. When he had finished, Telford jumped in immediately.

"Think it through, Granger. You never told me how you got the Delvecchio woman out of the house. I never even knew you *did* get her out of the house. I thought you probably decoyed her while she was driving some bloody place or another. How could I know about the fish or the milk?"

Telford could have arranged surveillance of Helman during the Delvecchio closing. If it had been carried out by the New York people who met him in Times Square, Helman knew he would never have been aware of it. But the desperation in Telford's voice was convincing him that his ex-broker had nothing to do with it. At least knowingly. At some point, Helman knew, he was going to have to take a chance to get out of this. He decided to follow his instincts.

"You're right, Max. I knew that. But I had to hear you say it."

The relief in the old man's voice was evident.

"So what can I do for you, Granger? How can I help?"

"I need information on the group in New York."

"Mafia?"

"That's what I thought at first. They seem too sophisticated. Possibly a European organization. Remember, they want a *ritual* killing. See if you can get anything on that. And Max, I need someone to check out my sister and her kids. I'm sure they're being watched. I think they're the guarantee on the closing."

"Jesus, Granger. What's it coming to? Getting family involved?" In many ways, Max Telford was a very old man, belonging to a simpler time, when there were rules. "I'll get someone out there to check around right away. And I *will* get that information. Count on it."

"I will, Max. When will you get back to me?"

"Later on this morning, Granger. I'll get this stuff started right away. Then I have to take care of some of my own business." Telford laughed. "Hey, Granger. I'm a solid member of the business community down here. I've got three restaurants. City politicians want to meet with me. Can you believe it? The guys I have to see this morning are two priests or something. Want me to support a daycare center. Help the kiddies."

Granger smiled at that. Every sign of normalcy strengthened his belief in Telford's innocence.

"Good for you, Max. Good luck then. I'll be waiting for your call."

"I won't let you down, Granger. Face it. You're one of the special ones, okay?"

"Thanks, Max."

Helman felt relief. The last of the night terror had left him now that he knew he was no longer in this alone.

He ordered breakfast through room service and read the morning papers, disappointed that only one had a worthwhile crossword. Then he lay back on the bed and waited for the phone to ring.

The housekeeping maids woke him just after one. They were knocking on the door, asking if they could make up the room.

Helman sent them away. He phoned the desk, but there were no messages.

Telford had said he would phone back in the morning. It was the afternoon. The tenseness returned.

Helman phoned the special reservation line in Miami again. It rang five times. It rang ten times. Then he heard a metallic click and the phone began to ring again, sounding farther off, as though the circuit had been forwarded.

This time it rang three times. Then a flat computer voice said, "The number you have dialed is not in service. Please check your directory and dial again."

Helman was certain he hadn't misdialed, but he tried once more. It happened again.

He called the restaurant through a regular line. It rang fifteen times before it was answered. Helman recognized the man who answered as the same one who had answered the special line earlier that morning. But his voice had changed. There was panic.

"I want to speak with Max Telford," Helman said.

There was a pause. It sounded as if the receiver had been covered and people were talking. Something was happening in Miami. Helman felt it the same way he had when he had seen the van pull away from his sister's farm in New Hampshire.

"I'm sorry, Mr. Telford is not in the office this morning. May I take—"

"I've already talked to Telford this morning. I—"

The man on the other end turned his head away from his receiver and shouted out to someone else.

"This may be one of them. Get the extension."

The line clicked. A second voice began.

"Who is this?"

"I want to talk to Max Telford. I've already talked to him once today and . . ."

"That's impossible." The voice was abrupt. Final. "Telford's dead."

Helman froze. Just hours ago Telford had offered him help. Telford had made him not be alone.

"*Who is this?*" the voice repeated.

"I'm Bryant," Helman said, using his code name. "Mr. Bryant. The first man to answer the phone took a reservation from me today. This morning. Max called me back. He was fine. *What's happening there?*"

The receivers were covered again. More muffled voices. Helman felt helpless, a pawn of the tenuous link of the phone wire. A new voice came on the line.

"Talk fast, Helman, or you're going to be closed so fast you won't see tomorrow. The number's been traced and we've got the alert on right now."

Madness. "Who are *you*? What are you talking about?"

"I'm the last person you may ever meet in your life, Helman. Telford gave me some bullshit story about checking up on an organization commissioning ritual closings. He said you told him about it. Decapitation he said."

"*What's going on there?*"

"So after he talks to you he goes into his office and we find him half an hour later. Jesus Christ. The fuckers took off his head with a wire, Helman. A fucking wire!"

"Who? The priests?" It was preposterous, but it was the only thing he could think to say. Max had told him: He was going to meet with two priests to talk about a daycare center. It had been a sign of normalcy.

"That's it, Helman. Who told you about the priests? Why'd you turn on him, Helman? What could he have done to you to deserve this?"

"Believe me. I don't know. I asked for information. The same people are after me—"

"That's not all who's going to be after you, Helman. Telford's been *murdered*. When his insurance goes public you're going to have—"

Helman heard another voice shout out in the distance. He heard the receiver fall to the floor. More scuffling sounds and shouts. Orders. Then he was sure he heard the deadly whisper of silenced guns, followed by heavy thuds. He was listening to insanity.

He heard the Miami receiver being lifted. A new voice.

"Mr. Helman? Nothing to worry about on this end."

The phone went dead.

Helman trembled.

He had placed one phone call to an old friend, and now that man was dead. His head squeezed off by a garrote used by men disguised as priests. Another phone call, and he had heard at least three others shot to death.

The madness snared him, twisting him around. He had reached out for help and found himself deeper in the maelstrom with still no bearings; no way out except to continue with the St. Clair closing.

The most brutal shock hit him then, as he realized with horror that all this had already happened, but the closing had not yet even begun.

Impassively he put on his heavy coat and boots and left the hotel to check the conditions around Dr. Leung's townhouse. He ignored all his training and did not anticipate the results of his planned moves. He had nothing sane to base his conjectures upon. He could not imagine how things could be worse.

He felt positive, however, that they would be.

Eleven

Major Weston was cramped and cold in the back of the surveillance van. But he was happier to be there than in a warm Washington office. It was the same as the feeling he had about flying and driving. There was a far greater chance of being in a car crash than a plane crash, yet driving always felt safer. In an airplane, he was just along for the ride, a victim of happenstance. In the car, he felt the semblance of control over the situation, however insecure that control might be. He felt the same way now. The van was parked across the street and three houses down from the townhouse of Dr. Christopher Leung. Across the street and three houses down from Adrienne St. Clair. He felt a semblance of control.

A second van was parked twenty feet away from Weston's van. It was one of the decoys. Both vans were orange and white, the colors of the local cable television company. The owner had been most cooperative when the situation had been explained to him.

A master circuit had been taken out of line at the cable company's main switching board. A six-block grid, which included Leung's townhouse, lost cable television reception. It was a Friday night. "Dallas" was interrupted. The office was flooded with calls within minutes. Eight installer/repair vans were dispatched immediately. The drivers were instructed to check every connection in the affected area; a three-day job if necessary. No one in the area would think anything of the cable vans being in the neighborhood while the service was interrupted. The vans would be invisible.

With that accomplished, a ninth van was prepared as a surveillance station. Again the owner had been cooperative. Cable companies were monopolies. They needed as much favorable publicity as they could get. The ninth van had been stripped of equipment cupboards and installer's gear and completely reoutfitted by Weston's advance team. Microtelevision cameras peered at small mirrors angled in concealed holes in the van body as well as the corners of the windows in the driver's section. The cameras were equipped with Startron intensifier CCDs and presented clear images in almost total darkness.

One of Weston's team, arriving in a legitimate repair van, had climbed a telephone pole near the front of Leung's townhouse, ostensibly to check the cable line, and had wired in an inductance phone tap with an FM transmitter. Every call into or out of the townhouse was narrowcast to the receiver in Weston's van.

A green telephone truck, also a closed van, had been street parked since Weston's arrival. The cable installers had, at their foreman's request, asked the cable customers whose homes they entered if they were also experiencing problems with their phones. No one was. The telephone truck was a second surveillance unit. Weston had run up against the Watcher Section, Section I, of the Royal Canadian Mounted Police; Canada's equivalent of the FBI. Weston knew their presence could only mean the Jesuits had discovered St. Clair's whereabouts.

Weston's team had told the owner of the cable company a totally fictional story about needing his company's cooperation to crack an international drug smuggling ring. Weston wondered what story the Jesuits had told the Mounties. Whatever it was, Weston knew they could no more have told the truth than he could have.

Four other RCMP Watchers had been identified so far today. There were definitely others which Weston had been unable to spot. The Watcher Section was notoriously good. It was comprised of people who, for some reason or another, had been unable to qualify as regular Mounties. Sometimes because they didn't match the physical requirements; sometimes because of a criminal past. No matter, at some point in the rejection process they were earmarked for Watcher Section. Their divergent physical appearance meant they were never immediately identifiable as law enforcement officers, and the knowledge that their assignment was the only way they could serve the Mounties made their dedication border on the fanatical.

The intelligence community in the United States had long used "deviant" surveillance agents as they were known, but had never systemized the practice the way the Mounties had. Partly because there was a resistance to change in American intelligence groups that became particularly strong when faced with suggested alterations from foreign countries. Mostly because it was common knowledge among American intelligence officials that two of the top-ranking Mountie officers were KGB moles. Americans would never accept an operational change that originated, as they perceived it, from the Soviets. As a result, the Canadian Mounties were never seen as a legitimate ally by the United States. They were simply a funnel for feeding misinformation to the Kremlin. All the Americans had to do was allow the Mounties to participate in a few border drug seizures from time to time to keep them in line.

That was the real problem with the American intelligence organizations, thought Weston. They felt, justifiably, so powerful, and so assured of their purpose, that everyone else, Canadian Mounties, British MI-6, or even American citizens, were contemptible in comparison. The image of Washington shattering like thin ice came back to him. This time the ice grew and he saw it as a glacier breaking up: giant, crushing icebergs drifting ponderously in their courses, blindly, pushing forward until the all-encompassing sea had consumed them, leaving no trace.

Weston didn't want his fragment, the most important fragment, consumed. The Nevada Project *must* survive for anything else to survive. The only possible answer lay three doors down, in a townhouse basement.

"There's another one." Davis, sitting on the small bench beside Weston, pointed to a walking figure on one of the four television screens on the camera surveillance console. "Let me get him on zoom." The image expanded. The man's face filled the screen. His eyes moved ceaselessly between the vans and the townhouse, but his gait was relaxed and his posture indicated disinterest.

"Look at his eyes go. He's taking it all in. Pretty slick."

Weston studied the man's face. He didn't look familiar.

"How do you know he's with I Section?"

"He was by about an hour ago in a taxi." Davis scanned a log book on the console's desk ledge. "There it is," he said, reading from his notes. "14:27: red and orange taxi, Volaré, Metro Cab, licence Delta Young Baker three three zero, southbound, approximately 5 miles per hour. Driver female, Caucasian, short dark hair. Both hands on wheel. One passenger. Male, Caucasian. Light hair, blue parka.

Appeared to be checking house numbers. Reference number two two five nine seven."

Davis ran the video recorder deck back to the log number. The image on a second screen broke up and then solidified as the shot from earlier in the day when the cab appeared on the streets came on. Davis held it on fast forward until the passenger's face came into close-up view. He froze the image.

"See? Same guy." Both faces on the two screens were identical.

Weston said, "Okay, that's number five. Cook, you want to get a look at this one?"

The third man in the van turned away from his bank of monitoring equipment at the front of the compartment. He leaned over and looked at the faces on the screen.

"Jesus. The Mounties have brought in a mechanic."

"What do you mean, a contract man?" Weston was concerned. The Jesuits of the Seventh Grade used others unmercifully to gather information, but generally they kept the killing to themselves. The involvement of soldiers at Heathrow was, so far, the one bloody exception.

The third man squeezed his eyes shut. Concentrating on the past.

"I'm sure of it. At Langley. He was in the system. 'Domestic Operations'."

Davis reacted for them all. "That's crazy. You've confused the file code. Or his face." Langley meant CIA headquarters in Langley, West Virginia. The CIA were forbidden to operate domestically but no one in the van doubted for a moment that they did. What was crazy about Cook's statement was that the CIA would maintain a file—evidence—that was in a position to be seen by an operative of another agency.

"No, I haven't." Cook looked defensive. "He's freelance out of Miami. Anybody can have him. And it looks like either the Jesuits or the Mounties do."

The camera had pulled back to a medium long shot. The

man was passing by the van. In less than a minute, he would be gone from the street.

"Or else he's still working for the CIA," Weston said. He turned to Cook. "When were you in Langley? And why?" Cook had been in the Nevada Project for seven of its fifteen years. Weston had to know why one of his agents had been in contact with another agency. Jack's statement might have been a slip revealing a different set of loyalties.

"Two years ago, Major." The agent looked surprised. "When we were having labor problems with Malton Chemical. You were going to go yourself. The file that guy was in," he said, pointing to the diminishing figure on the screen, "was offered as one of our options. He had done that kind of work before."

Weston remembered. He felt shock that the tension of his assignment had led him to make an error of recall. Malton Chemical was one of the main sources of Nevada Project's operational funding. It had begun as a Delaware corporation—a CIA front—at the height of Vietnam. Agents were infiltrated into most major munitions manufacturers throughout the world by being hired away from Malton Chemical. The subterfuge that had created the company was so successful it was turning a profit. The company had been reassigned to the Nevada Project in 1969. Most special agencies received their funding in this way. It meant millions of dollars earmarked for covert or classified operations never had to be approved by Oversight Committees. The Nevada Project was, theoretically, responsible to no one for its operating budget.

Labor problems two years earlier had threatened profits. Since the CIA had set up Malton in the first place, Cook had gone to them for advice. Assassination of one of the union officials had been one of the options suggested. Weston could not remember how the problem had been resolved.

"I want him brought in. We have to know who brought him. If it's the Jesuits or the Mounties, okay. But if the CIA has somehow tangled itself up in this, we've lost it. Consider him armed and dangerous.''

Davis flipped a toggle on his console and spoke into a small microphone.

Down the street, Granger Helman turned the corner and disappeared from the camera's sight. A minute later, Cook followed him, closing quickly.

The Watchers in the telephone van had been unable to determine the identity or the allegiance of the man whom, they too, had spotted twice. When they saw the American agent follow him, they knew something important was happening, but they had no idea what.

The wait for Cook's return, for the crews of both surveillance teams, was tense. Eventually, both teams realized it was also useless. Cook was found shortly before sunset. His right index finger had been ripped off, presumably when he was disarmed, and his neck was broken.

Granger Helman had disappeared.

Twelve

The voice had said, ''*Nothing to worry about on this end.*'' And at least four people on that end, in Miami, had been killed. By whom? Helman had no clue, no concept. Somehow it was linked to him, the killer who was to kill no more. Four were dead in Miami. One in Toronto. But he had no worries at that end. Just here. Just now. Especially from the man in the hotel room chair opposite him. Mr. Rice had returned.

''What am I to do with this list, assassin?'' Rice looked up from the sheet of hotel stationery Helman had given him.

His voice was more gutteral, harsher, as though he had no more patience to control his natural way of speaking, regardless of whether or not Helman could understand him.

"I had no time to prepare. Those are the items I require to fulfill my contract with your people. You said yourself I shouldn't use my bare hands." Helman had the feeling Rice was suppressing an urge to snarl, literally snarl at him.

"I fail to see how guns, fertilizer, and children's toys can fulfill your contract."

Helman fought hard to control his own anger. He had no patience for the man he must deal with. His disgust at having slept that morning while waiting for Telford's call—something he had never done in the past, and no professional could condone—and his experience with the man who had followed him that afternoon, had left his nerves raw. But he was familiar with the penalty for not showing respect.

"Mr. Rice, your people have come to me because of my abilities and experience in this field. One of the reasons I have that experience is because I have been successful. And I have been successful because I do things my way, on my own, with no accomplices, and no witnesses. I don't care that you 'fail to see' how I can fulfill my contract. I don't care if you can't read a word on that bloody sheet. All I care about is me doing my work and you doing yours. And if you can't do yours maybe New York better send up someone who can!" Helman's voice had risen in anger. He was close to screaming.

Then he was halfway across the room, slumped beside a bed, his head ringing and his eyes exploding with red and black flashes. He hadn't even seen the blow. Rice was back in his chair.

"The next time, assassin, you shall not be able to regret your foolish behavior because you shall be dead."

Helman tried to struggle to his feet. The left side of his body was useless. Rice had connected with a pressure point, paralysing his arm and shooting molten tendrils of pain through his rib cage, into his neck and leg. He had never experienced anything like it. He sagged back against the bed.

Rice spoke again. There was no trace of gloating in his gutteral voice. "I am unfamiliar with the various specifications which you may require from some of these items. I propose to provide you with currency to obtain them yourself."

Helman shook his head, slowly. His jaw ached and it was difficult to form words. "Must get me guns," he managed to whisper.

"You forget the conditions, assassin. Guns are not required."

"Not for her. Her bodyguards. One tried to kill me today."

For a moment, Rice looked surprised. "Today, assassin? During the day?"

Helman nodded yes.

"What did you do?"

"He had a gun. Got too close. I took it away from him. Broke his neck. Left him by a house. I need those guns for her bodyguards. I don't have the contacts for buying them in this city."

"What was he wearing, assassin?"

Helman was furious. He was incapacitated, at the mercy of a maniac with a hair-trigger temper and an unbelievable knowledge of what seemed to be a type of karate. And he was being asked about the clothes of a man who had tried to kill him.

"Ordinary. Open coat. Suitjacket. Brown, grey, I don't know."

"Did he wear anything around his neck, assassin?"

Helman was incredulous. "He had a tie on. I don't remember seeing the label. Why is this important?"

"It's not important, assassin. Just interesting. You'll have the guns and the money before sunrise."

Rice put the list down on the broadloom beside Helman and left the room. It was two hours before Helman was able to stand.

In another hour, the message light on his phone began

flashing. There was a parcel for him at the desk. Helman had it brought to his room and opened it on his bed.

Five thousand dollars in Canadian currency, five times what he estimated he would need. And the guns.

He had specified two: a Smith & Wesson .44 Magnum and, as back up, a slim, five-chambered .44 Bulldog, easily concealable in the small of his back. Fifty rounds of Keith semi-wadcutters—bullets that could solidly pass through cars yet mushroom fatally in body hits—were included, as well as Alessi concealment holsters and silencers for each weapon. Despite himself, Helman was impressed with Rice's ability to deliver.

He worked with the weapons for a while. Loading and unloading, adjusting the holsters, until he felt as confident as he could without actually test firing them. Then he lay down on the bed and stared at the ceiling. He didn't even attempt to sleep. He knew it would be useless.

Helman thought only of the day after tomorrow. The day when it would all be over. And he would present the head of Adrienne St. Clair to Mr. Rice. Or he would be dead.

Either way, it would all be over.

Eventually, he did sleep. And in his dreams, the things in the basement were telling him he was wrong.

Thirteen

The detonator was warm in Helman's hand. He had four minutes left until he would press the transmit button. It would take an additional forty-five seconds to run up the stairs and into the lab, and anywhere between thirty seconds to two minutes to decapitate the body, depending on her location when the charge went off.

At one minute before detonation, he would attach the auxiliary antenna that ran up the side of the university building which contained Dr. Leung's research facilities. The antenna ended at the third floor window of the lab that Leung and St. Clair worked in during the night. That placed the antenna within six feet of the charge. Even the child's toy car remote control which Helman held would be sufficient at that distance, and unlike high-powered and sophisticated radio control equipment which was available from only a few outlets, no one could ever trace the purchase of one of thousands of similar toys, available anywhere, to Helman.

Leung and the girl had arrived eight minutes previously in the doctor's TR7 and parked at a meter in front of the building. Helman was giving them ten minutes to establish themselves in the lab.

What Helman assumed to be her bodyguard's car, which had followed them from the townhouse, was parked across the street from the building. There were four lanes of traffic and two sets of streetcar tracks between them and the stone front steps of the building. With his head start, Helman would be able to lock enough fire doors to slow the bodyguards down to give himself the time he needed. The confusion added by the students who were constantly moving into and out of the building would also help.

One minute. Helman, hidden in the shadows at the side of the building, connected the auxiliary antenna.

The university building was at least a hundred years old, and looked it. Helman had studied it the previous afternoon, after his encounter with the man who tried to kill him. It had been perfect for his needs.

Old buildings were constantly undergoing repairs and renovations. The granite-blocked university structure, covered in the bare, brown ivy vines of winter and stained black by years of traffic exhaust, was no exception.

Three doors down from Dr. Leung's lab, which was

deserted in the daytime, plumbing was being replaced. The work crew had left their acetylene welding outfit locked in the room. After five o'clock, Helman had taken fifteen seconds to open the lock. The two tanks of acetylene and oxygen were now chained to a radiator pipe beside a hole Helman had made in the wall of Dr. Leung's lab. Helman's charge, composed of untraceable chemicals derived from a fertilizer available at hundreds of nonregulated stores, and the radio detonator adapted from a toy car's radio control, was strapped tightly to the bottom strut of the welding cart, hidden by the tanks' bulk. It would shatter the bottoms of both tanks, causing the gases to mix violently and trigger a second, far more powerful blast.

By the clutter of personal papers in Leung's lab, Helman assumed that he had worked at the University for years. Leung should not be surprised at discovering his office was in the midst of unscheduled renovations.

Ten seconds. Helman adjusted the straps of his shoulder holster through his new winter coat, a non-descript olive drab—the kind worn by repairmen and outdoor workers—and checked a final time that his machete was securely in place. He kept his eyes on the seconds as they counted down on his digital watch. For the last few seconds, the mist of his breath no longer obscured the watch. Everything seemed silent.

He pressed the button and a dull whumph sound accompanied the crash of shattered glass as the lab's window blew out above his head.

Before the glass had fallen to the ground, Helman was running around the corner of the building and up the main stairs, pushing startled students out of his way.

He charged up the stairwells, using the old style pin locks to jam the fire doors on each floor. At the third floor he pulled down a red fire alarm panel. The glass rod snapped and a strident ringing echoed through the halls. Students and staff on the main floor milled about, uncertain if the fire signal were a test or the real thing. But on the third floor, where Helman saw the explosion had blown the lab's fire door off its hinges, there was panic. He was unseen as he moved against the crowd of escaping students.

Smoke filled the devastated lab. Flickers from a handful of small fires lit it eerily. Helman held the end of his scarf to his nose and mouth, slid the machete from the sheath strapped against his chest, and entered in to fulfill his contract.

A draft was created between the shattered window and the open door. The smoke swirled out like a mist clearing from a dark hidden valley. Helman saw a bloodsoaked form crumpled against the base of a cabinet unit. The unit was crushed. The shrapnel from the exploding gas cylinders had been devastating.

Helman held the machete ready to strike, and turned the body over. A jagged section of cylinder metal was imbedded in a flattened hollow in the forehead. The face was covered in blood and small solid particles sprayed out from the skull. It was the doctor. Beside him, his glasses were unbroken.

Helman lowered the machete, stood and turned to examine the room for the woman's body. Part of him continued counting off the seconds. The bodyguards from the car across the street would be breaking down the first floor fire doors to the stairwells by now. He had a minute at most.

A cold swell of wind billowed the smoke in front of the window and carried it out the door. There was a moment of clearing in the far corner of the lab, well lit with the growing intensity of the fires. A bulky refrigeration unit appeared untouched by the blast. And then he saw her.

Impossibly, she was alive. Her clothes hung in tattered remnants, exposing pale, unmarked, undamaged flesh. Her hair was scorched. Part of her scalp was bald. But she lived, untouched by the deadly, explosive spray of metal fragments. She lived!

Helman froze. The impossibility of it screamed in his mind. The smoke and fire and destruction around him, the sound of far away sirens, all collapsed in on themselves, shrinking away to nothingness beneath the awesome reality of what he saw. She lived. And she saw him. And she was coming at him.

Her hands were like claws, arched and deadly. Her face was twisted into animalistic fury. A high pitched whine came from deep within her. She lived, and she was attacking.

Bent over, looking as if she were preparing to jump the fifteen feet to where Helman stood, she picked her way through the rubble toward him.

Every warning given him by Rice and his people rushed through Helman's mind. He stepped back, slowly, judging the distances between the woman and himself and the doorway. He held the machete before him and reached carefully inside his coat for his magnum.

Out in the corridor, he heard the crash of the firedoor being forced open. Then shouts. Then gunfire. *People were shooting at each other outside the lab*. The woman stopped her advance, still whining in ragged breaths, and looked toward the door. Helman drew the magnum, but held his fire. If he killed her now, with hostiles so close, he might not have a chance to get her head.

A sudden flash of motion shot through the open doorway. An arrow appeared, imbedded in the wall near Helman. *Who was outside the door?*

The woman jerked her head as though she had seen the arrow in flight and followed its flight. Her whining stopped. She spun, ran to the window, and was gone, down into the night.

Helman felt he was in a dream. Nothing made sense. More shots echoed in the corridor. He ran to the window, hoping to follow the woman's escape route.

There was nothing outside the window to hold on to. No ledges, no outthrust bricks. And there was no body on the ground below. Adrienne St. Clair had vanished.

A man dressed in black appeared in the doorway to the corridor. He carried a crossbow. It was aimed at Helman.

Helman turned at the sound of the gunshots that ripped through the man's body. The crossbow released its bolt into the wall as the man spun around and collapsed.

Without knowing the reasons, Helman realized two groups, somehow connected to St. Clair, were battling outside the ruined lab. If the one side was using only crossbows against gunfire, it was only a matter of time before the other side achieved dominance of the corridor and the lab.

Helman ran to the hole he had started in the wall near the welding tanks. It was larger. The walls were made of drywall over soft fiber insulating blocks. The blocks had splintered, absorbing most of the blast force. They were held up only by a warped drywall on the other side. Helman knew the room on that side of the lab had been locked after five on the night of his reconnaisance. He would have to risk that it hadn't yet been taken over.

With three kicks he had enlarged the hole. There was nothing but darkness on the other side. He squeezed through. The door was still secure. Inside the next room, he slid a filing cabinet in front of the hole to obscure it from the other side. He had to do everything he could to buy time.

Now the sirens were coming from directly outside. Firetrucks had arrived. The fighting in the hall seemed to be over. Helman crouched in a corner behind a desk and kept his gun trained on the doorway. He would not risk stepping out into the hall. His plan was to stay in position and try to walk out as the building was opened in the morning. He heard firefighters running through the corridor outside and the hollow whoosh of chemical fire extinguishers from the lab. It seemed unusual that he could hear no shouts about finding a body.

There was a loud noise from the door to the room Helman hid in. The doorknob dropped off. Helman aimed at where a man's chest would be. The door swung open.

A firefighter in a rubber coat and respirator, carrying an ax, paused in the doorway. Helman held his fire. The firefighter ran a rubber-gloved hand over the wall by the doorframe until he found the light switch. The blue fluorescents flickered on; their power lines hadn't been severed. Helman crouched lower. The firefighter walked over to the wall shared with the lab and began examining it. He started pushing at the filing cabinet.

Helman got up quickly and quietly and swung the door shut. Then he flicked off the lights. The firefighter looked up at the light fixtures then slumped onto the floor. Helman had connected with rigid fingers behind the man's jawbone.

Outfitted in the firefighter's equipment and protective clothing, respirator mask in place, Helman went into the corridor.

Another firefighter down the hall yelled, "Hey, Gerry, is that room secure?"

Helman nodded and made a thumbs-up sign. He continued down the opposite end of the corridor. There were several other firefighters wandering into the blownout lab, but there was no body in the hall. Whoever had been shooting it out a few minutes before were efficient as well as deadly.

Helman walked out of the building through a back parking lot exit. There appeared to be no surveillance. In deep shadow, he removed the firefighter's gear, and cut through three adjacent parking lots before emerging onto the street. Nothing seemed unusual.

He walked to the building several blocks away where he had hidden his bus station locker key. It was still buried in the frozen dirt of a raised concrete flower bed in front. He took a cab to the bus station and retrieved his wallet and identification. He wouldn't risk returning to the hotel and Mr. Rice until he had a more definite story to tell him. He did not want to confront Rice's temper with the idea that the woman he was supposed to kill didn't seem to be human. She had probably been protected behind the refrigeration unit that had been in the lab. Regardless, Helman knew she couldn't get far without clothing on a cold night. She had only one place to go, and he was going to meet her there.

He waved down another cab. The night was not yet over.

Fourteen

There was no such thing as coincidence. Helman slipped the slim, easily concealed form of the .44 Bulldog into his hand the moment he saw that the four street lamps closest to Leung's townhouse had been extinguished. Somewhere on that street was someone who wanted the cover of darkness.

The cab that had let Helman off passed by him as he stood on the corner of Leung's street. It continued along the residential street to cut back onto a major road. As it rounded the bend its headlights shone onto the front of the townhouse. The door was open. There were no lights on. Either the woman had returned or the house had been penetrated by the groups from the lab.

Helman crouched over and ran up to the front of a house fifteen doors down from the townhouse. He knelt in the dark cedar bushes, observing. The cable television and phone company truck were still in position. He had assumed the day before that they were bodyguards. Now he could not be certain. But he did know that they were somehow connected to St. Clair.

He ran silently across two front lawns and pressed closely against a stone porch. The street was still. The only sound came from a radio being played too loudly through an open window. A glint of light from the phone truck attracted his eye. He looked off to the side of it, letting the more light-sensitive areas of his eyes concentrate on the obscured details. The glint was a reflection from a streetlamp down by the corner. It was caught by a jagged piece of glass hanging from the truck's windshield. It was almost totally blown out. All of the glass in the driver's section was smashed. Helman looked over to the cable TV van across the street. Its windows were intact. One group had won.

Helman moved through the shadows to the closest house to Leung's to have a streetlamp in front of it. Nothing had moved or made noise in the direction of the townhouse. The radio playing through an open window stopped abruptly. Helman turned to the absence of noise. The light in the room went out. He could see a figure come to stand in front of the window. There was a tinkle of glass down by the far corner of the street. Another streetlamp was extinguished. Helman had heard no shot. The guns in the night were silenced.

Suddenly light from the porchlamp flooded over him. The porch door opened. A man in his early twenties, the look of a student about him, peered out at the unilluminated street. Helman dropped closer to the ground, the protection of the shadows gone. The man saw the movement.

"Hey, what the hell's going on?" The man leaned over the porch railing, looking directly at Helman. Helman's response was swift. He had to rescue his position. Control the situation. He shot his hand out, flipping open the wallet from his jacket pocket. It opened randomly on a credit card. His other hand was just as fast. It held his gun.

"Police. Get down. Get the light off. There's a sniper."

The man saw the gun, ignored the wallet. The misdirection had worked.

Then, incredibly to Helman, the young man turned to look for the sniper. Helman shouted to him again and an arrow tore out of the night.

The barbs caught in the soft flesh of the student's right cheek, splitting his face open and ripping the skin back to his ear. The arrow splintered against the bricks by the porch door. In an instant the man was down, clawing madly at the open wound of his face, his screams turned liquid by the blood filling his mouth.

Helman shot out the light above the door and rolled away from the porch. A flight of arrows rushed above him, sparking against the bricks and clattering down around the writhing figure.

A woman came running to the door and stopped in a moment of horror as she saw what lay on the porch. She crouched and pushed the door open for the wounded man to drag himself through.

Helman detected motion in the bushes of a house across the street. More glass clinked softly in the distance. There was one streetlamp left on the street. Soon the night would be impenetrable, except for the soft city light glow of the low clouds. Helman rolled off the front lawn onto the driveway which ran beside the house, stopping as he turned the corner.

He held his gun ready, pointed straight up by his head, and took five deep, measured breaths. Then he spun out from behind the corner, swinging his gun to waist level. The man with the crossbows was two feet away. Helman saw his face, young and frightened in the muzzle flashes of his gun. The man was down instantly, one leg twitching by the unfired crossbows at his side.

Helman moved back behind the corner. The police must arrive at any second. They would provide the confusion for Helman's escape when it became necessary. He rejected the option of immediate retreat and pushed on through the backyards in the direction of the townhouse.

Two houses from the townhouse block, he inched his way along a side wall so he could observe the street again. Nothing visible had changed. He could not see the watchers he knew must be there, but he knew they would see him if he attempted the seventy-foot run to the open townhouse door. He decided to wait for the others, the mysterious others armed with crossbows, to show themselves. The first mistake would be theirs.

Five minutes passed and Helman decided the police were not going to arrive. Whomever he faced, the influence they wielded was respectable. Then he realized, Rice would have that influence; Rice and King and New York. Had they controlled the situation to enable Helman to fulfill his contract? Could he simply walk across the front lawns of the townhouses and go after St. Clair, protected by the power of New York? His mind raced with the details. Had he ever been actually threatened? Or had he simply been too close to attacks on others, as he had been to the man on the porch?

Helman reviewed. There were two forces: the group with guns, the group with crossbows. Which were the bodyguards? In the lab, the woman had stopped her advance at the sound of the gunfire in the halls. But she had fled when the arrow appeared in the wall. A threat or a signal? The key had to be the crossbows. Anachronistic. Like decapitation. They were part of some ritual method of killing. Rice had gone for a "sweep."

Helman was not the only assassin contracted. Other assassins from New York hid in the shadows. Helman had killed one of them. The people with guns must be her bodyguards. But the risks were still too great. Helman stayed close to the wall. One of the other assassins could try to run to the townhouse door. Helman would wait.

There was movement in the backyard of the next house. Gun or crossbow, Helman was exposed against the side wall. He held his gun ready. He would try an alliance with the crossbows. He would try to outshoot the guns.

"King," he whispered to the unseen presence in the yard. "Out of New York."

The movement stopped. A long silence followed. Was he drawing aim, or considering? Then a whisper came back.

"Nevada."

Did it mean there were agents operating out of other places? Helman held his fire. He whispered back, "Nevada."

More movement. The figure emerged from the deep black of night shadows. He carried a gun aimed straight at Helman.

Helman slid slowly over from his own protective darkness. The glowing clouds lent a hazy halflight to the driveway between the two houses. To eyes accustomed to the dark, it was enough for recognition. The figure smiled.

"We've been looking for you, *Phoenix*." The figure kept his gun trained on Helman. Helman stayed silent. He had no idea who Phoenix might be, but if the confusion of the man with the gun was keeping him alive now, he wanted to do nothing to dissuade the man.

The man spoke again, gesturing with his head, being careful not to let his gun deviate from its killing aim.

"Listen, Phoenix, we can cut the suspense and waste each other right now, or we can hang around like this for another minute or so and let the Jesuits do it for us. Or we can get back there and meet with Marker One." He nodded back toward the pitch black backyard.

Helman heard the names, but none of them registered. Phoenix. Jesuits. Marker One. All code names he assumed. Nothing.

The man was becoming impatient. His eyes kept darting nervously toward the street. "Come on, Phoenix. We know all about you. Marker One wants you. For a few questions. We'll pay you off just as well as the Mounties or Langley or anyone. And then we'll help you out of here."

"Langley" registered. Someone had confused him with a CIA operative. Helman thought he had spotted the first mistake. He moved on it.

"Tell Marker One to put questions through Langley. I can't be interfered with."

The figure's brow knotted. "There's no time for Langley. Jesus, Phoenix. We'll admit it. Anything you want. Anything Langley wants. We shouldn't have sent our man after you yesterday. It was unfortunate, but understandable. Langley didn't brief us. We're not going to try anything like that again. You work for Langley, you're golden. Okay? Now if we don't move, one of the Jesuit's arrows is really going to start interfering with you."

Shadows moved across the street. The nervous man saw them. Helman willed himself not to follow the man's gaze. Now was not the time to fall for a trick from the movies. He had to know where his charade would take him.

The man's gun wavered between Helman and the street. "They're coming, Phoenix. Jesus, let's—" He jerked around sideways. An arrow hung limply from his coat. He fired blindly towards the street.

Helman looked down the driveway. Three, now four, five shadows with crossbows were converging on him. More arrows hit the man who had questioned him. Some hung from his clothing. Others bounced off him to the ground. The gunfire was silenced, and only muffled whispers of rushing air were heard above the clatter of the advancing archers. The man's gun clicked empty. He turned to Helman, desperation colored his voice. "For God's sake, help—"

An arrow took him in the throat, jerking his head over like a hanged man. He crumpled against the opposite side wall. Two figures had been dropped by the dead man's firing. Three still advanced.

Helman stayed close to the wall and aimed carefully. An arrow sparked above him off the bricks. He fired. His silenced weapon spitting harshly in the narrow space between the houses. He saw the closest attacker stumble. He drew aim on the next. Another hit. The third also. But the first had gotten up and he *continued*, crossbow coming up, aiming at Helman.

Helman fired twice more. The first attacker slumped forward and was finally still. The two others, also hit, came on. He pulled the trigger. There was no recoil. The gun was empty. The archers, clutching at the wounds Helman knew they must have, drew closer. Mortally wounded, they would not stop until they had reached their target.

Helman fumbled in his jacket for his Magnum. But it was too late. The closer one had dropped to his knees and was lifting his weapon twenty feet from Helman.

Then the archer was lifted into the air by a blinding stream of white as explosion after explosion burst off the brick walls. Helman felt the echoes sting through his shoes and clothes. The smell of cordite was strong and thin blue smoke was illuminated in the flashes of the automatic rifles fired by the two men who had appeared at the back end of the driveway.

The attacker farther away had begun to fall when the first volley hit him, pushing him back up and making him twitch like a crazed dancer down the length of the driveway where he finally toppled over and settled in a formless heap.

Then there was silence. One of the men with rifles walked over to the body of the man who had talked with Helman. The other walked toward Helman.

"You hit?" he asked.

Helman shook his head. He couldn't hear what the man had said but could understand the movements of his mouth. The echoes of the gunfire still rang in his ears.

The man held out his hand to Helman. "Let's go down to Marker One. I think this was the last of them."

Helman stood up on his own. He had seen arrows bounce off a man. Others with crossbows had walked into gunfire, and had continued. A wave of desperation threatened him. None of the rules was working. He fought it, and walked in front of the man who had offered to help him, the man's weapon pointed at his back.

As he passed the body of the second archer a bloodsoaked hand stretched out, grabbing him. Helman froze. Half the man's body had been blasted away, yet he moved, he talked. At least his mouth was moving. Helman heard a voice, but it was far away, buried amongst the explosions. It did not sound like English.

The man with the rifle saw what had happened. He said something to Helman. Helman shook his head and pointed to his ear. The man yelled louder. "Confession. He wants a final Confession. The Last Rites." Then Helman placed the language. The torn apart body which clutched him in an iron grip, was speaking in Latin. Half his guts spread out over a frozen driveway and he would not let go until he had had Confession. Helman knew then what kind of men they were with the crossbows. Fanatics. The ferocity of it was terrifying.

The man with the rifle knelt in front of the dying archer who gripped Helman's foot. He whispered into the man's blood-drenched ear. Helman could not be sure, but it too sounded like Latin. The dying man talked in gasps. Pink foam frothed at the corner of his mouth. Helman knelt, struggling to hear anything at all that might help him. He leaned close to the man. Some words did break through. They were all meaningless.

Then the dying man opened his eyes. For a moment, things had cleared for him. He stared at the face of the man he had thought to be his confessor, and tears began to form in his eyes as he realized the hoax that had been played on him. Then his eyes turned to Helman and the face changed immediately. Hatred took over and the one bloody hand on Helman's foot and the bullet blasted finger stumps of his other hand rose up like pythons and constricted themselves around Helman's throat.

Helman's eyes bulged. It was unbelievable. The strength, the hatred, were staggering. The dying man was going to win. And then Helman saw the man's face disintegrate as the man with the rifle fired into the side of his head. For an instant, the seething eyes glowed, back lit by the bullet's explosion. Then the face collapsed. The image of those eyes burned into Helman as the rigid fingers slowly fell away from his neck.

Helman knelt for a moment longer. Rubbing his neck. Catching his breath. Trying to conceive what could cause the maniacal fanaticism necessary for such determination. Then he saw it. Like a shining clear pool in the dark blood that thickened around the neck of the dead man. *He was wearing a cleric's collar.* Helman struggled to his feet. The men with rifles gave him room. Helman turned over the body of another dead attacker. He wore a collar also.

Five bodies lay torn and steaming in the frozen night air. He checked them all. All of them in black with the patch of white at their throats. Madness lay about him.

His hearing was clearer. He approached one of the men with rifles. "Why are they all disguised as priests?" All pretense of his Langley charade had gone from him. He only wanted answers. "Why?"

The man looked concerned. "You're mistaken, Phoenix. They aren't *disguised* as priests. Those are the Jesuits. They *are* priests."

Fifteen

The yellow Emergency Task Force police van drove slowly down the middle of the dark street. Only its parking lights were on. The driver had been instructed to see as little as possible.

One of the men escorting Helman to the TV truck turned to the police van. The van stopped. The driver, not in uniform but in a plain suit, got out and walked away, still keeping to the middle of the road. Though the man with the rifle had said nothing, the driver left with his hands in a half-raised position. At the end of the street, he ran.

Helman watched in awe as the man ran away. Who were these people to control the police? He waited by the back doors of the TV truck. More figures with guns had emerged from the shadows. Three watched him, their weapons ready. Others dragged bodies, some from inside the townhouse, toward the police van. In the silence and the night, it was a nightmare image of ghouls invading a graveyard, carrying off their carrion plunder. The winter evening was cold. Helman shivered. "Jesuits" was not a code word. They *were* the bodies of priests. Priests who fought gunfire with crossbows. Priests who walked into a Miami restaurant and sliced Max Telford's head from his body with a wire garrote.

The door to the TV van swung open. Four men were inside, seated on a bench in front of a console of television screens and radio equipment. Helman had been right about the surveillance role of the van. He had also been right in his other assumption.

A man with a telephone company employee badge clipped to his open parka was bound hand and foot in front of the console. One sleeve of his parka was ripped away, exposing a bare arm. A rubber tubing tourniquet was wrapped around the arm above the elbow. The man sitting beside him held a hypodermic. The people in the telephone truck had been the losers.

A voice from the back of the truck spoke. Helman saw the barest outline of a face weakly lit by the green glow of the console. "Now give them the clearance for the first police van. Tell them to send an ambulance next."

The captive man spoke a string of code words into the microphone. Whoever the people in the telephone truck had been, they were the ones who had controlled the police. But now the men in the cable truck controlled the man with the code words. Command was too fragile a thing when placed in the hands of faceless people and whispered words which carried too many meanings. Leaders could change instantly, and the people beneath them would never know. Helman knew it had happened before. It had happened again.

By the conversations crackling from the radio equipment, Helman realized the whole area of Leung's neighborhood was under police cordon. Anything could happen in this area. Only after the evidence had been eradicated would the local authorities be allowed in to piece together some sanitized version of the truth. Anything could happen. Helman began to plan his escape.

The green-lit man spoke again. "Tell them they can move in when the ambulance and this van leave. The operation is terminated."

The captive man complied. The figure with the hypodermic waited till he was finished and an affirmative response came through the speakers. Then he plunged the steely tip of the hypodermic into the neck of the captive. He shuddered once. His already drug-glazed eyes gave no indication of the passing of life. Then he slumped forward.

The man with the hypodermic caught him and pushed him out to a guard waiting beside Helman.

"Put him in the police van. Keep the civilian for the ambulance."

The bound, lifeless body was dragged through the street to the yellow van. It seemed filled with bodies. The clean up was extensive. The battle had been savage. Helman felt trapped in another century. He mentally ran through his escape attempts. None were feasible against so many men with guns.

"Is that Phoenix?" said the green-lit man, pointing to Helman. His guard nodded. "Marker One's in the basement. Hold Phoenix till he comes out. We'll have a police escort to the airport by then."

The door to the van swung shut. Most of the armed men were clustered around the police truck. An ambulance with only its parking lights on rolled silently down the street. The men by Helman were distracted and he reacted instantly.

His flattened palm drove splinters of the closest man's nose up into his forebrain. His heel caught the second above the kneecap with a dull crunching sound. The second man jerked forward and Helman's elbow drove into the top of his unprotected skull. The third man had time to realize what was happening and back stepped, swinging his rifle stock up in a killing blow. Helman pushed his hand along the whistling stock and diverted it from his chin. The man's arms swung up, leaving him open to Helman's crushing punch below the sternum. The man faltered backward again, the rifle spiralling from his hands. His breath had left him in an explosive rasp. Helman connected on the man's jaw with his foot. The man slammed against the side of the van and was down. Footsteps clattered behind him. Helman grabbed a rifle and ran to the front of the van. He fired a wild burst from the protection of the engine compartment, then zigzagged to the closest house. No shots rang out behind him. The footsteps stopped. He was free.

Back in the shadows of the darkened houses around the townhouse, Helman put down the rifle and freed his magnum from the shoulder holster gone awry.

He cut through the backyards. No one seemed in pursuit.

Maybe the thought that he was from the CIA had scared off the followers. Maybe they thought he could not escape the police barricades. If they did, they were wrong.

Police were police. He had no trouble slipping by them. Their attention was focused on the wooden barricades and congestion of cars which had formed around the closed off streets. There were crowds of curious residents and passersby. Many had gathered around a film crew from a local television station. Helman moved into them, moved through them, and was gone.

The man on the driveway, the man whom arrows had first bounced off, then killed, had said that they knew all about Helman, thinking he was someone called Phoenix. If they knew about him but had not tried to locate him at his hotel room, then they did not know everything. There was one place in this city where he would be safe. He headed for his hotel. He did not reflect on what had happened. He could not bring himself to believe it.

Standing in the hotel corridor, peering through the darkened doorway, Helman could tell that his room had been altered from the way he had left it. It might have been the maids. It might have been a penetration. He did not reach up to turn on the lights. He slipped in quickly, holding his magnum exposed, and shut the door behind him so he would not be a backlit target in the doorframe.

There was no movement from the room.

He took two steps down the short hallway and pushed the bathroom door open with the barrel of his gun. The bathroom was empty.

Two more steps and he was around the corner. The curtains to the balcony window were half open and let in enough city light for Helman to see that the room was clear. He walked warily into the middle of it, checking between beds and at the end of the long, low dresser. The room was secure.

He holstered his magnum and slipped off his coat, throwing it to the middle of one of the beds. Slowly the events of that evening came to him. He had shut them out of his mind as he had returned to his hotel, concentrating on the telltale signs of a follower. He knew what would happen if he stopped to consider the confusion and the senselessness of the explosion in the lab and the fire fight in the residential street. Now, safe in his hotel room, sanctuary from the violence of the night, it happened to him. He sat on the edge of the bed, staring without sight at the floor, his mind reeling. Nothing he could think of, no scenario he could imagine, could explain the conflict he was involved in. There was far more to it than a group in New York hiring him to commit a murder; far more than a woman with a tropical disease. Somehow, someone believed him to be an operative of the CIA and accepted it, as if someone from the CIA *should* be involved. And the Jesuits. Priests with crossbows who *killed*. Nothing could explain it. He was desperate for answers; desperate for some grain of sanity for his impossible world. He would phone his sister. Hear her voice. Be transported to the reality of a farmhouse in New England, far from the madness of things which did not seem real.

Desperate for peace, desperate for answers, Helman reached for the phone on the night table between the beds. There was a movement on the balcony. The answer had arrived.

Hand on the phone, his head jerked up as the flicker of a shadow swept across the floor, and he saw her, Adrienne St. Clair. Her look of hatred was unimaginable. The sense of power in her eyes froze him.

In that long, silent moment she pressed her black-clad body tight to the glass balcony door. Her face deformed against its flatness, her palms spread like dough against the glass. Her eyes seemed to grow, coming at him, coming for him. And the silence was broken by the first crystalline splinter of glass as a delicate web spread first from one hand, then from another, cracking through the length of the balcony door like jets of water. Then the door exploded in a blizzard of glass and she was in and coming for him. She whined, high pitched and angry. She came for him.

The crash of the glass freed Helman from his paralysis. His instincts took over. He threw himself backward off the bed, springing to his feet and drawing his magnum. He held it on her.

"No more or I'll fire." His voice was almost inaudible. Terror constricted his throat.

Adrienne St. Clair still moved forward. Her whining stopped, replaced by a deep rattling wheeze. She was growling at him.

Helman fired. The magnum bucked violently, silently, in his hand. He saw the black cloth against her skin erupt and shred. He saw the drapes behind her billow out as the bullet's shock waves tore through them. He saw her white skin untouched.

Adrienne St. Clair still moved forward. He fired again and again till the hammer clicked empty and her black clothing hung in shreds. Still she came toward him.

He was backed against the wall. Her hand reached out and took him by the neck. Small and delicate he saw in the heightened awareness of time-slowing panic. She's just a girl, he thought. What harm can she do?

The small and delicate hand of the woman who had just taken six point blank hits of a weapon designed to deliver a fatality with each body impact closed around Helman's throat and slowly lifted him into the air, pushing him against the wall, leaving his feet to dangle inches above the carpet.

Black stars exploded at the edges of Helman's vision. His neck felt as if it would burst beneath his ears. His lungs burned for air but his struggles could not bend the thin arm an inch from its hold upon him. His movements slowed, a red haze filled the room. The woman spoke.

"I shall make this offer once. You will agree to tell me everything about what has brought you here to me or I shall continue holding you against the wall until you finally suffocate. It should take twenty minutes. And I shall see to it that it will be very unpleasant. Do you agree?"

Desperately Helman tried to signal his answer. Nothing

would come from his throat. His head was immobile in her grip.

"Do you agree?" she spat at him, loosening her grip for an instant.

Helman bent his head forward, straining against the pressure of his hanging body. He gasped out the word yes as best he could. The woman released him. He slid to the floor, incapable of protecting himself.

He touched his own throat, gently massaging, trying to gauge the damage she had done to him. He stared up at her, his vision slowly swirling back to normal. The hatred still burned in her eyes.

"You shall have a moment to compose yourself, and then you shall tell me everything I wish to know."

Helman nodded. His eyes moved to the fallen magnum. His instincts judged the distance.

Without looking she kicked it away from him, under a bed.

"Don't even consider it," she said. "You already know it is useless. Nothing you are capable of can harm me. I am already dead. Do you understand? I am *yber.* What you humans call vampire."

The answer had arrived.

PART TWO

THE DEAL

One

Vampire. The word rushed through Helman's mind until it became disjointed and meaningless syllables. The word that replaced it, the word that he wanted to use, was "impossible." But he didn't know if he meant it for the idea of Adrienne St. Clair being what she said she was, or for the idea of her being shot six times by bullets designed to tear ten-inch holes in people, and surviving untouched. He had seen the destroyed body of the doctor in the lab. He saw Adrienne St. Clair, unmarked. Helman didn't know if anything were impossible anymore.

He watched her intently as he got up from the floor. She stood so that the soft flashes of city light played against her face as the drapes billowed in the draft from the shattered glass door. Her face was pale and sunken. What he thought had been puffiness in the photograph that King had shown him was the smooth prominence of striking cheekbones. She looked as though she might be thirty as King had said, but the structure of her face was the kind that would not change throughout the years. She could be almost any age.

Her body offered no clues either. It was thin, but not fragile looking. One small breast was visible through the black sweater she wore; the sweater which had been torn apart by the bullets. He did not find it erotic. Adrienne St. Clair could kill him instantly.

Helman was alive now because she needed information. If only he knew which information it was.

She spoke to him as he sat down on the edge of the bed farther from the balcony door.

"Are you ready?" Her voice was drawn out. A whispered hiss, like the voice on the phone. Like the group in New York. Helman made the connection and the jumbled pieces worked together.

"Are there others like you?" he asked. He knew what the answer must be, but had to hear her say it.

She narrowed her eyes at him. She made no move to change her standing position in the middle of the room. He could tell that she was fighting a powerful urge to kill him immediately. But she needed information, and decided to cooperate, for the moment.

"Like me? No. Which is why I think you are here. But there are other *yber* most certainly. Thousands perhaps."

"*Yber?*" he asked. She had used the word before.

"It is our word. An old word. We are a people and that is our name. We kept it *yber* amongst our own. Humans took it and changed it. Today, in this language, it is vampire."

"Are King and Rice and the group in New York *yber* also?"

"I do not know those names. That is what I wish to find out. What is their *group* in New York?"

Helman told her about the meeting in New York; being taken, unconscious in the limousine, to the expensive, windowless room; the eleven people with voices like hers, and cloth masks to hide their faces.

She nodded as he described them.

"Were they *yber*?" he asked. Then he realized why they wore the masks, not to disguise their faces but to hide their mouths. He looked at St. Clair's mouth. Her teeth were flat, white, and perfect.

"You have no fangs." As soon as he said it, he felt like a

fool. The concept she proposed was ludicrous. Why was he going along with it? He thought about the bullets.

"No, human, I don't have fangs. I cast shadows. I have a reflection. And Holy Water doesn't burn me. But the group in New York have fangs. And they will use them to rip out your throat when they find that you have failed them. Tell me more. What did you demand as payment?"

"Nothing. They were blackmailing me."

"How? For what transgressions?"

"Another crime. A murder." He called the Delvecchio closing by its proper term. "They had evidence that they could turn over to people in authority. I had no choice."

St. Clair considered Helman for a moment. "Were you guilty of the crime they had the evidence for?"

"Yes."

The woman, still standing in the position she took when she had walked away from Helman, said, "Tell me *everything* they said to you. Each word you can remember."

Helman complied, reciting the conversation with the masked group. Then he came to the point when King seemed to slip and almost called one of the masked people "Lord."

St. Clair broke in immediately. "You're quite certain? 'My Lord'?"

"That's what it sounded like. He corrected himself quickly. What does it mean?"

St. Clair turned to the balcony and looked out into the night. The sky was still a dark glow of low clouds.

"Listen carefully to what I am going to tell you," she said. "When I'm finished, you're going to have to make a decision which could mean your death. Whichever way you choose."

Helman nodded. Adrienne St. Clair began.

Helman was not in a unique position. Other people had been coerced into fulfilling certain roles in the same way as Helman had been. Likely individuals who might someday be of service to the *yber* were first located and observed.

Usually this observation netted information which would provide leverage for other actions.

In Sussex, England, in the late 1940's, an *yber* had broken from the Ways and become a maniac. The discrete killing and feeding patterns developed over the years were abandoned and humans whose blood had been drained were being discovered at a terrifying rate. Investigations intensified. The entire network of *yber* operating in England was threatened with disclosure. They had banded together and destroyed the offender. It was called the Final Death. But the investigations continued. A sacrifice had to be made, and it was.

A quite ordinary man named Sussex, one who had been noticed years before as fulfilling certain requirements, received visits in the night. Voices spoke to him. *Yber* came to his bedroom and enticed him, offering him the beauty and the life of blood. The man was John George Haigh. With the aid of the *yber* he committed two more murders of his own, drinking the blood of his victims though he was not *yber* himself and could derive no nourishment from it. Then he was given to the police. All the evidence implicated him. During the trial, he spoke of the voices which had come to him, but it was obvious to all that the man was insane and no one took notice. Gruesome, vampire-like murders had occurred. A murderer was provided whose mental state explained the nature of the crimes. The investigations were closed and the *yber* were free from exposure.

"High profile-low profile," said Helman. "When a crime has to be completed for an operation to be successful, a high-profile suspect is provided to draw suspicion from the real perpetrators. Politicians who don't comply with a couple of the big lobbies in Washington usually end up being beaten by 'muggers.' It's called a hi-lo."

"We call it survival," St. Clair replied. "We have called it survival for years."

The same thing had happened in Hanover in the mid 1920's. Fritz Haarman had been provided. He had been executed. The *yber* survived.

In Montparnasse, in 1849, the French Army had gone so far as to hide guards in graveyards and place armed men at all entrances. Disdainful *yber* had used all their powers and special knowledge to slip by them and raid the tombs of the newly dead. It was a scandal. Investigators from around the world were coming to learn the truth. Some had actually seen the *yber* at their work. Discovery was threatened. And then Sergeant Victor Bertrand was visited by the voices: visited by women who slipped through his barracks window; women who delighted him yet no others could see.

Sergeant Victor Bertrand was shot one night in a graveyard. He told the same stories at his trial as would Haigh and Haarman. It did no good. It never did. The investigations closed and the *yber*, once more, were safe.

"And I was to be like those men? A sacrifice? A cover-up for the murders you commit?"

"What murders?" St. Clair asked. "I don't murder. *You* were to kill *me*: the Final Death for one who has already died. Quite possibly it would result in the deaths of humans close to me. As it did. Undoubtedly you would be killed yourself, afterward. The evidence would point to you. They would have you. And no one would look any further. The same as all the other times. The *yber* would be protected."

Helman shifted his position on the edge of the bed, rubbing at his neck. The pain was dull and throbbing. "So I'm trapped in a plan set up over a hundred years ago, kept going by the same organization."

"Not the same organization, human. *The same individuals*."

"What do you mean the same people? The ones who set up the French Army sergeant are the same ones setting me up a hundred and thirty years later?"

The woman shouted at him. "You're not listening. You're not accepting any of this. We are *yber*. We are vampires. We drink blood to live. And as long as we keep drinking blood, *we live forever.* All the things you know about us, all your superstitions, their details are wrong. But their origin is in the truth. If you want to live, human, you must accept this."

The woman was right. Helman had not accepted it. He had already begun convincing himself that the bullets had never hit her in the first place; that she had been protected by the refrigeration unit in the lab explosion. How could he accept that the things of nightmares, the things that lived only in the basements and cupboards of children's homes, could actually be true? This was the world of space shuttles, heart transplants and television. Faced with the unknown, the sure knowledge of something that had no place in his view of the world, Helman had chosen to ignore it. What else could anyone do?

"How can I accept what you're telling me? It's ghost stories, old movies. Such things can't be true?"

"Then *you* tell me how I survived the shrapnel of the explosion you caused in Chris's lab. You tell me how I went out that window on the third floor, how I found you here, and how you shot me six times," she held out her bullet-ripped sweater. "And then picked you up and held you against the wall. Tell me another way that could be possible."

Helman spoke very slowly, very softly. "There is no way any of that could have happened."

"Except my way. Listen to me, human. You are in great danger. So am I. The *yber* you met with in New York have great power, and great influence. One of them, the one Mr. King referred to as 'My Lord' is from the Conclave."

Helman remembered the Jesuits. Their crossbows lying beside their steaming bodies. He dismissed her statement. "That's something to do with the Pope in Rome."

"It has nothing to do with Rome. It has everything to do with Rome. It is an insult. The Conclave is the name given the ruling council of *yber*. They have provided organization and stability for us for more than two hundred and fifty years. Understand me, human; Europe was becoming civilized. There were newspapers, more education. Science was replacing superstition. The *yber* had to become civilized, too, or they would have been discovered, hunted down, and eradicated like the natives of other countries the Europeans invaded. The Conclave was formed and the *yber* became organized. Methods of hunting, of feeding undetected, of fully using our constantly growing powers had always been passed down through the generations of mentor and prey. The Conclave collected that knowledge. They imparted it to all. The Ways of the *yber* have enabled us to survive in the modern world. Without them, *yber* would be both a superstition *and* memory. Gone like dust in sunlight. Yet they demand a price.'' And Adrienne St. Clair told Helman about the Conclave, and that price.

The early history of the *yber* was one of constant conflict with their only food supply, humans. The *yber* came at night to drink the blood of their victims. Sometimes the victims would succumb to the horrific condition and become *yber* themselves. All humans knew this to be true. All humans feared the night and the teeth and the unprotected throat. The stories made their way into the mythologies of all cultures.

As cities and civilization expanded, the *yber* who moved with the new population invariably were discovered and put to the Final Death. The *yber* who stayed in the more rural and remote areas flourished. Knowledge of them passed from being a certainty to all people to being a story told by the backwater peasants of small farming communities. The *yber* were safe, protected by the superstitions of humans. Eventually they came to accept those superstitions and the Conclave perpetuated them by including them in the Ways.

The Ways said the *yber* were the spawn of Hell; minions of the Devil. Their enemy was God and the Kingdom of Light. All other things came from this; all *yber* acted on this.

Most of the organization of the *yber* was taken from the Church to ridicule it. The Conclave, which ruled the *yber*, took their name from the gathering of Cardinals who selected the Pope, thus ruling the Church.

The Conclave provided identities for the *yber* who must move among humans. Thus Adrienne's last name, St. Clair. Wherever possible the Church was mocked. Even the creation of new *yber* was called Communion.

The drinking of blood by an *yber* did not automatically

cause the victim to become one, too. If that were so, a single *yber* who needed one victim every night, would create more *yber* within five weeks than there were people in the world because each new *yber* would in turn require a victim of its own. Instead, *yber* could drink a small amount of blood from a number of victims who could survive unharmed. New *yber* could only be produced by the act of Communion.

The mentor *yber* would first drain the prey almost completely of blood. Shock from loss of blood had to set in. While the prey was in that condition, he or she had to be made to drink the white blood of the mentor. Only then was the condition passed. Only than was a new *yber* created.

The Conclave had seen to it that the *yber* had always a ready food supply by creating a special role for humans in the structure of *yber* affairs—the familiar.

Familiars were humans who were specifically chosen by *yber* to become *yber* themselves. But first, a period of servitude had to be undertaken. One *yber* might have five to ten familiars. Some higher ranking ones, like the Lords of the Conclave, might have dozens. The familiars tended the *yber's* sanctuary from the sun, took care of the business and financial transactions that must be handled in the daylight and offered up their blood in small and regular amounts to their mentor. After a suitable time of such service, familiars could be presented before a smaller gathering of *yber* and take part in Communion, becoming *yber* themselves.

The group in New York had been one of those smaller gatherings. A meeting of *yber* bound as a geographical unit to pool their financial resources, keep their actions coordinated, and provide mutual protection. St. Clair was certain the New York group had been a high-ranking group of *yber* because of the cloth masks which hid their mouths.

Of the many changes which occurred when a human first became *yber*, one of the most immediate and apparent was the growth of fangs. The canine incisors fell out within hours of the transformation. During the next two nights, tertiary incisors erupted through the gums and grew rapidly to become half-inch-long, needle-tipped fangs. These fangs overlapped the lower lip and were impossible to hide.

Yber who were protected and served by their familiars needed to do nothing about their fangs. They served as a symbol of their power and special nature. However, some vampires had to move among humans. For them, the incisors were filed and capped. Every few months, the continually growing fangs had to be altered, but in the meantime, there was nothing visible which could distinguish *yber* from human.

Helman thought of King in New York and Rice in Toronto. Their teeth had been perfect, like St. Clair's. He asked her about the two of them.

"Sometimes it's hard for humans to tell the difference between some *yber* and their familiars because the familiars quickly adopt the manners and the appearance of their mentor. Since you never saw this Rice or King in the daytime, and their attacks on you were so fierce, it is fair to assume they were *yber*."

There was a long silence as Helman stared out past the billowing drapes. The temperature was below freezing and he had put on his coat. St. Clair still stood in the same position, dressed only in her tattered sweater and black pants. She did not look the slightest bit cold or uncomfortable.

Helman shook his head violently. "No, no. It's ridiculous. How can I believe this?"

St. Clair's face reverted to the animalistic fury she had shown when she had burst through the glass doors. Her voice dropped to the chilling, sibilant whisper.

"How can you *not*?" she spat at him.

There was a brittle silence, primed to explode. Helman broke it softly.

"What is the decision you want me to make?"

At last St. Clair moved. She walked over and stood in front of him, staring down into his eyes. Seeing her face close up for the first time he was struck by its total lack of color. An image of Rice came to mind: he had worn make-up. Even her lips lacked darker coloration; they were the same color as her skin. The nipple of her exposed breast was just the same, pale white as the skin of the rest of the breast.

"Do you know who it was you killed this evening in the lab?" she asked.

Helman forced himself to look her in the eyes and said, "Dr. Christopher Leung. The doctor you were staying with."

St. Clair nodded, almost sadly. "He was a fine human. A fine man. He was also my familiar. My only familiar in North America. The last familiar I had in the world. The Conclave killed all the others at Heathrow airport when I escaped from England. My familiars pretended that I was being transported in a coffin after they had secured me in another container. They died trying to protect that empty coffin so the Conclave would be tricked by the diversion. All of them, dead." She paused, letting the conclusion of what she would say slowly dawn on Helman on his own. "An *yber* cannot survive in this world without aid. Chris provided that aid and you took him from me. I am asking you to replace him. To become my new familiar."

Helman felt his stomach contract. It was one thing to be able to admit that what St. Clair had told him was the truth. It was completely different to become a part of it himself. He remembered what she had said when she had started talking to him. *It could mean your death. Whichever way you choose*. He knew what would happen, immediately and painfully, if he refused her. Once again, the doors were closing all around him, only one path was open. Since the package had arrived in New Hampshire, he had been nothing but a pawn. First to the Conclave, and now to her. His anger and frustration grew with each decision he was forced to make. But what else could he do? Above all else, he knew he must live. At some time the moment would come when he could create his own options and make his own decision, striking back at the forces which controlled him. But it wasn't now.

"Does that mean you will drink my blood?" It was

insanity. Nightmares come true. What had happened to him? How could such questions even exist?

Adrienne St. Clair shook her head. "I've told you, human, I don't murder. And I don't feed on the living blood of humans."

She looked out at the night sky. There was no change yet. The time of departure had not yet come. She turned back to Helman.

"There are better ways for *yber* to survive. And that is why the Conclave want me dead."

Two

Adrienne St. Clair paused as though considering what she should do next, then sat down on the bed opposite Helman.

"Somehow, human," she began, then stopped. For the first time, Helman saw her expression soften. The rock hard intensity of her angry scowl faded for a moment. Perhaps she came close to a smile. "I'm sorry," she said at last. "Sometimes I forget everything of my first life. What is your name?"

Helman told her; his real name. He did not want to face the consequence of her learning he had told her a false one.

"Somehow, Granger, you have been thrown into all of this unaware. The Conclave have chosen you, as they have chosen the others, because of your past. And whatever else is in that past, there is also ignorance. They counted on that. It made you easier to control. The lies about my tropical disease would explain my aversion to the sunlight and my association with Chris. The lies about my knowledge of martial arts would keep you from getting within my reach.

The lies about wanting to make an example of me helped justify their demand that you decapitate me. In fact, that is one of the few ways to give me the Final Death. An instruction to drive the traditional stake through my heart might have been too obvious a clue."

"They didn't have to justify themselves to me. My sister's life and the lives of her children are in their hands. I was in no position to question any of their demands."

"They are clever, Granger. Most of them have had centuries to study the way the human mind works. Without the justification they provided, even if it were nothing more than one or two subconscious hints, you would have followed through with the physical actions they demanded of you, but your mind would be rebelling all the way, looking for a way out. With the stories they told you hidden in the back of your mind, those actions would be more acceptable to you. Your desire to rebel would be lessened. You would be more apt to simply complete the assignment just to get it out of the way."

Helman realized she was right. Not only had he been manipulated overtly by the threat to his sister and her children, he had also been manipulated covertly by the false details they had fed him. He was impressed with her reasoning.

"How long have *you* had to study the way the human mind works?" he asked. Part of him feared the answer she might give.

"Not that long, Granger. I'm only 67. Barely a lifetime."

He stared at her. Sixty-seven years old. She looked no more than thirty. She seemed to smile again, at his expression of shock.

"Keep telling yourself it *is* true." Her voice had lost some of its harshness. It almost sounded reassuring. "We don't age in the way that humans do, after our Communion. The infirmity of age never touches us. And we *do* live forever. Or at least we have, as far as any of us knows, the ability to do so if we wish."

She was sixty-seven! She could be one hundred and

sixty-seven. One thousand and sixty-seven? *Immortality.* The word eased into Helman's mind and floated there, glowing. It was unbelievable. But if everything else she had told him were true, why not this also?

"How long is forever?" There was awe in his voice.

"There are legends among us of certain caves in Greece, where elders from our people's dawn still live. Our dawn is thousands of years ago, Granger, thousands. But they are just legends, even to us. None of us knows for certain. What I do know is that my friends from my first life, before Communion, are now weakened and frail, if not dead. And I am still as I am; as I was at the moment of my First Death. And always will be."

There was just the cold flapping of the curtains in the hotel room. There was nothing Helman could think to say. The things she was telling him filled his mind and froze it.

"I am also in this by accident, Granger. The Conclave has survived with exceptional stability because it has been able to choose its members with great care, observe their behavior over the years of their servitude as familiars, and only then allow them into full blood membership. And the original leaders do not die to be replaced by new, younger ones, with new ideas. Immortality leads to stable government. But I am an exception. Years ago, I believe they wanted to put me to the Final Death because I was not chosen. But they relented. And now I suppose they regret their first decision."

"If you weren't chosen, how did it happen? How could it happen without another vampire—*yber*?"

"There *was* another *yber*, Granger. But it was a time of war, and even the organized structure of the Conclave could not hold completely against it."

And Adrienne St. Clair told Helman her story. The hotel room seemed to disappear from around him, and he felt he was there; a witness to the accident which had brought her into the nightmare world of the *yber*.

* * *

1944, and the current of victory flowed across Europe, sweeping against the Nazis on both fronts. In the west, in France, Adrienne St. Clair was there, part of the massed army, growing stronger each day past D-Day, pushing toward Berlin.

She was a nurse in a British field hospital, following behind the front lines; patching the wounded, cleaning the dead for their final journey. Her unit stayed close behind the fighting.

In the vicious counterattacks where positions would creep forward and back like the edge of an amoeba, she found herself unexpectedly in the front line more than once. And one day, the last day of her first life, a brutal shelling and savage attack destroyed the line and forced a retreat. In a Red Cross truck full mostly with dead and some of the living, she was cut-off from the rest of her retreating unit behind the enemy's advance. To be a soldier, and captured, was bad enough. To be a woman, and captured, was more than she could bear to imagine. The terror began to mount in her. She realized the jerking green truck with the large Red Cross emblazoned on the side would be no protection against the forces which had created the misery she had tended in the weeks before. And then the truck was gone, twisted into shellholes on a fragmented road and lurching to its side in a gutter. She was thrown from the truck to the side of the road. When she had awakened from her blackout the few groans from the living cargo in the back had long stopped, replaced, instead, by the distant chest rumbling of *panzers* and the hollow pops of gunfire.

Adrienne limped to the collapsed metal and canvas confusion of the back of the truck. The bodies were hopelessly twisted, limbs bent in ways that nature did not allow. To her horror, she realized she was glad that her charges were dead. Glad that her duty would not force her to stay with them, until the enemy arrived and she was taken. With her soldiers dead she was free to save herself. She cried as she ran into the trees by the road, the rumbling of the *panzers* growing louder in her ears. She was glad they were dead and felt shame in her eagerness to live.

The sun was blood red and setting, swollen and rippling on the horizon behind the farmhouse in the small, barren field.

She could hear soldiers shouting to each other in the woods. Were they following a trail she had trampled through the forest or were they just scouting, hoping for a prize such as her?

She ran for the farmhouse. Straight across the field. She had never been given the training to be aware of the target she made of herself. The farmhouse was something removed from the war. It meant protection. That was all she considered. If there were watchers in the forest, none fired. Perhaps they simply noted her position and planned to save her for later, after the officers had declared the region secure and gone on. Perhaps then they would go after the English woman who hid in the farmhouse. But for that moment, under the harsh and crimson light of a setting battlefield sun, Adrienne St. Clair burst through the freely swinging wooden door of the farmhouse and felt herself safe from the soldiers. And she was right. The thing stirring in the root cellar would see to it.

The farmhouse had seen other occupants since the farmer and his family had left. Empty ration cans, British and German, were heaped in a far corner. Shell casings lay like animal droppings near the windows. Except for a large, rough wooden table lying on its back and the splintered ruins of two chairs and a bedframe, the farmhouse was bare.

Gasping for breath, her mind on a fine line between reality and unthinking animal terror, Adrienne stumbled about the farmhouse, looking without thinking for anything more which would offer protection. She thought of standing in the stone fireplace, body up the chimney, feet hidden by scraps of wood. It was foolish but she gave up the idea only when her scrabbling at the chimney showed her it was too small for her.

Her hands were blackened with the soot from the fireplace. Some of it streaked across her face where she had brushed at her hair. The rough green fabric of her uniform trousers and jacket were caked with mud and thick clumps of burrs. She stomped back and forth across the farmhouse floor, desperately searching in the quickly fading light.

Finally it entered her consciousness. The floor was wooden and her heavy, bootshod footsteps sounded hollowly across it. There was a cellar beneath the floor! A dark, protective cellar where she would be safe from the soldiers.

She crawled around the floor, her breath in desperate gasps, feeling for the trapdoor she knew must be there. She couldn't find it! She went to the table, lying on its back. She pushed against it, scraping it against the floor. She strained until it hit one of the stone walls of the farmhouse, but the rumbling it made as it moved along the wooden floorboards did not seem to end when its movement stopped. She listened for a moment, holding her breath. The *panzers* were coming closer.

She clawed at the floor. Rotting splinters dug into her fingers and under her nails. her hands felt cold and numb. She felt the indentation of a row of floorboards ending at the same point. The light was almost gone. She had found the entrance to the cellar.

A knotted rope was tied through a hole in the trapdoor. She pulled on it and the section of flooring swung up and fell over with a dull and ringing smash. If they're outside in the field, they'll have heard that, she thought, and her heart raced even more.

She stared into the darkness of the root cellar. No light penetrated it at all. How deep was it? She pushed her head close to the edge, staring hard, yet could see nothing.

She lay against the floor. Her head and arm overhanging the empty darkness of the hole into the cellar. Frantically she waved her arm around in the nothingless searching for a ladder. She could almost feel the thick wet smell of damp earth and rotting things well up from the darkness. The scent was warm and humid, as if she were reaching into a pit that held an immense animal whose fetid breath had seeped into everything, warming it, then dissolving it. Her arm tingled as this thought came to her and she imagined her arm swinging inches above the outstretched claws of something in the cellar. But the *panzers* still advanced, and they were an evil she could comprehend.

Then her hand hit it, off to the side of the hole. It was rough and wooden. She swung her hand against it again to determine its position. Something thin and sharp and cold wrapped itself around her wrist. Instinctively she wrenched her hand backward. For a heart-stopping instant, she was trapped, held back. She screamed breathlessly through clenched teeth and wrenched again. There was a snapping sound. Her hand flew out of the cellar doorway with something dangling from it, sparkling like fish scales in moonlight. Adrienne was rigid in her terror. In the almost total darkness she could see vivid images of snakes. But the object slowed its swinging and cautiously she reached out for it with her other hand.

It was cold and metal. Her hand recognized its shape. It was a crucifix. Someone had, for some reason, hung a crucifix from the top rung of the ladder leading to the cellar as though it were in a position of watchfulness, of protection. She shook her hand and the broken chain fell away. She tossed the crucifix into a far corner, and reached back into the darkness for the ladder.

The ladder descended for eight rungs before her foot sank into the damp cellar mud. Dirt from the slam of the trapdoor, when she had pulled it down above her, covered her face in irritating little particles. Standing with both feet sliding into the oozing floor, she blew and sputtered and rubbed her face with her hands till she felt able to open her eyes again. When she did, there was nothing to be seen. Not even the ladder directly in front of her face.

She ran her hands along the outside of her trouser pockets. She and most of the other nurses always carried matches to light the cigarettes of the soldiers who could smoke. Where were hers? She found them in a jacket pocket. There was at least half a box left. She felt her panic subsiding.

In the light of the first match she was able to determine

the size of the cellar. It was small, taking up perhaps half of the floorspace of the farmhouse above her. The beams of the floor overhead were silvery with spiderwebs. The walls of the cellar were simply earth with a few retaining timbers spaced regularly around. The wall farthest from the base of the ladder looked as though it had fallen victim to years of winter run-off. It seemed to have collapsed, sloping up and away from what would have been its original position. The earth from the washout had collected in a rough pile at the base of the wall, piling out along the floor. She also saw a box in a corner away from the mound of earth. She dropped the match to the damp floor. It sizzled for a moment and was extinguished. Then she walked carefully toward the box, no more than three or four feet away. Her boots slurped each time she lifted them from the muddy floor. She tapped the edge of the box with her toe. It was time to light another match, and open the box. Perhaps, she thought, there was food.

The lid creaked oddly as she lifted it. The dull jumping light of the match barely seemed to penetrate the darkness within. Then she froze. The light picked out the form of a small figure, like a child, lying down in the box. The eyes were open but dull. Adrienne held a match closer, trembling. The figure was an old doll, paint flaking from its porcelain face, lying on a folded set of mildew spotted sheets. The cloth body fell away as she lifted the doll. The head tumbled into the chest and disappeared as the second match burned toward Adrienne's fingers. She dropped it into the mud.

At the very least, the box was a dry place to sit. And that's what she did, leaning forward on her knees to keep from touching her back against the damp wall.

Sound was effectively muffled by the moist earth surrounding her and she realized she would have no way of knowing if the Germans were right outside or if they had passed by. She decided she would worry about that later, when her watch said it was morning. For now she would rest and not worry about the darkness or the dampness or what could be lurking in them. She thought of whoever it had been who had laid the doll away, so long ago, so carefully; whoever it had been who had placed the crucifix on the ladder.

Then she heard the first plop of earth fall into the damp floor. Rats she thought. The matches would save her. She lit another. No gleaming rat eyes stared out at her in the orange flicker of the match light. The match dropped into the mud. The earth shifting sound came out of the darkness. Another match, and there was nothing. Or was the mound of earth somehow different? The match sizzled on the floor. There was a long, liquid sucking sound as though something was lifting itself out of the clinging mud.

Another match. Silence. She threw the match to the floor and lit another immediately after. The mound of earth *was* changing; pulsating like some enormous earthworm turning in on itself. Another match and another. Like a strobe light, one flicker after another revealed a sudden jump in appearance. Adrienne was standing, the rush of her heartbeat filling her ears as she watched *something* trying to push its way out of the earth.

And then the first of it was free. Something white and maggoty and rising up out of the dirt on its own. More of it lay below, throbbing to the surface.

The match burned into Adrienne's fingers. She gasped and scattered the open box around her. One match remained. She fumbled with it. It lit. The thing in the earth was a foot! The toes spread wide, stretching the clinging dirt and making it fall to the side.

Another foot rose beside it and the forms of legs could be seen pushing through the earth in front of them. Then two arms. And a torso. And a hideously mud-caked head like a golem come to life.

The match flickered closer to her fingers. The head turned slowly towards her. Eyes were somehow operating beneath the dirt which encased it. Then the dirt fell away and Adrienne was left staring at a man's slug white face with eyes like black wounds untreated for days. And a gaping, sucking mouth that had fangs—

The match went out. Dead against the blistered skin of her thumb and forefinger.

She screamed then and flung herself headlong toward where she thought the ladder should be. In the darkness, she missed it, and collapsed into the clinging mud. Her screams turned to gurgling. She waved her arms frantically in front of her. She hit something solid. It was the ladder.

Instantly she was crawling up it. The mud had soaked into her uniform and had weighted her down, making each movement seem ten times slower as if in a bad dream when she just couldn't move fast enough. Her head banged against the solid trapdoor. Her grip slipped and she nearly slid back down. She threw up her hand and grabbed at the end of the knotted rope. It steadied her. She pushed her forearm against the trapdoor. It creaked slowly open. Too slowly.

Adrienne gave it one last push and it swung up and over, crashing into the floor. Her head was above the level of the floor. Her waist. The hand grabbed her by the ankle and pulled.

She screamed, shrieked, thought left her. She shook her leg, savagely kicked and connected, and was free.

She jumped up from the ladder, cracking both shins against the hard edge of the trapdoor opening and rolled across the floor, sobbing hysterically.

It was night. Moonlight cast soft shadows through the unshuttered windows. The interior of the farmhouse glowed faintly. The head appeared above the level of the floor. It saw her. And smiled. The fangs glistened in the moonlight.

He rose slowly, smoothly, as if his body were not touching the ladder at all. He continued upward, hands by his side, until his foot stepped onto the floor and he walked toward her. His footsteps made no hollow echo on the wooden floors.

She felt weightless in his arms as he lifted her. Her voice

was gone from the moment he had stared at her in the moonlight. Her body would not move to protect her.

Adrienne's mind was like a person trapped on the bridge of a sinking ship. Everything was clear. The outcome was inevitable. And there was nothing to be done.

In her mind she screamed, long and hard. But it did not drown out the ripping sound his teeth made as they sliced into her neck.

She felt him nurse from her torn artery. Felt the insistence of his lips as they ringed the wound, slowly sucking up the flesh around it, then relaxing, letting the surface of her soft, white neck fall back. His tongue felt smooth as it swirled around the hole he had made, coaxing the blood out in its rhythmic spurts. The pain of the bite gradually eased. The warmth of her body slowly faded from her arms and legs, concentrating in the warmth which grew in her neck. She could feel the strong contractions of his throat as he drank from her. She felt herself spinning, round and round. The only focus was her neck where he sucked on her. She was melting, flowing into him. Faster. Faster. The swallowing stronger, the contractions of his throat more intense. Her vision fell away into tunnels of shifting sparks. One red point was fixed in the swirls. And it grew. Pulsating over everything else. She wanted it to come closer, to swallow her completely. Closer and—

The spiralling was real. He had thrown her through the air to land limply near the trapdoor. Dimly she saw that the farmhouse door had burst open. Men in grey uniforms, moonlight glinting off the barrels of their weapons, talked in German. Their voices were slow and far away.

One of them swept a light through the farmhouse. She saw him stop it suddenly, his face twisting into an expression of horror. The three other men raised their weapons and smoke and fire flared through the farmhouse. Adrienne pushed herself over to look toward the other side of the room. The thing that had fed from her was pinned against the stone wall. Chips of stone and clouds of dust leapt from the wall behind him. His mud-stained, already ruined clothing danced around him with the bullets' impact. But when the weapons clicked on empty, he attacked.

His body, pockmarked with small dark punctures where bullets had entered and left, glistened with a white shiny liquid that seemed to coat his skin like the gelatinous slime of snails. It highlighted the rippling of his lean muscles as he leapt fifteen feet across the farmhouse and onto the soldiers.

Adrienne watched the butchery in slow motion. With her own blood streaming from his howling mouth, the creature tore into the soldiers as if they were no more than the rotting doll in the cellar chest. Arms and heads flew. Three were dismembered almost instantly. The fourth, the one who had stood well back with the flashlight, ran screaming from the farmhouse.

The creature did not give chase. Instead he gathered the pieces of the first three soldiers and carried them, oozing and dripping, to the trapdoor. Vaguely, Adrienne was aware of the sound and vibrations of approaching tanks. She wondered if this thing knew about tanks. Then he picked her up, again without the slightest strain, and threw her down into the pit of the cellar. Adrienne felt herself float through the damp cellar air. She had no sensation of impact. The bodies of the dismembered soldiers had cushioned her.

She lay on her back, staring up into the farmhouse through the trapdoor. The creature stood at the edge. He looked down at her. His mouth working like a fish. Gaping, sucking. Adrienne wanted him to come and finish her. He looked away. The tank noises were louder, then gone, swallowed by the thunderous crash that roared through the farmhouse, turning the moonlit interior into brilliant day.

The shell must have entered through the door or window and exploded on the far wall. Jagged stones ripped through the air. The creature was impaled upon them, caught by the explosive wind, and blasted down the hole in the floor. Adrienne watched him fall toward her. In the half second more that he existed she saw his body ripped and split by shards of stone. She tried desperately to raise her arms to him, to welcome him to her. But he was gone. Dissolved. Dust in the sunlight. The rocks fell lightly around her. Their velocity absorbed by their impact with the creature's body. And Adrienne was covered with the thick cascade of what was left of him. The white blood of life. The blood of *yber*.

It smeared across her face, dripped into her mouth and she came alive. Movement returned to her limp arms. The taste of the thick liquid was indescribable and made her ravenous. She trembled with the touch of it on her tongue. She wiped it off her face into her mouth, off her hands and arms and body. From the ladder rungs. And then, it led her to something even more wonderful, more satisfying, where it had dripped from her to what lay below.

It led her to the soldiers' bodies. And their blood.

This was Adrienne St. Clair's Communion.

Three

Helman was silent. The creature who sat across from him—the undead, the *nosferatu*, all the names he could remember from the stories—trembled with the telling of her story. She stared at the floor of the hotel room. Her shaking hands clasping each other on her knees. Helman reached out as if to take her hands, as if to comfort her. But he hesitated, and she looked up, and the moment was gone.

"More than thirty years ago that happened. Sometimes when I wake up, it still feels as though it happened just the night before, and if I open my eyes I'll see nothing but darkness, and feel the bodies of those soldiers beneath me." She looked away from him, staring into the darkness of that long ago cellar.

"What happened to the thing, the *yber* that attacked you?"

She took a deep breath. "The stone shards from the exploding wall acted like a stake through the chest. One of them must have penetrated his heart. It was the Final Death for him. The First Death for me. His body dissolved. Just like in the movies, Granger. Upon the Final Death an *yber's* body decays incredibly rapidly. The longer we are *yber*, the faster the decay is. Had I been given the Final Death the next night, my body would have looked like any human's body. If it happened today, I'd be gone in seconds." She shrugged. The personal part of her story which had been exposed in her as she told it, had dropped beneath the surface again. It was now a technical discussion. Helman regretted not taking her hand when the moment had seemed right.

"What *did* happen the next night?" Perhaps by going back to the story, the personal side would surface again. A key to understanding her.

"I'm not sure. I think I stayed in the cellar for several nights. I was very weak. Human blood does not sustain us if it has been dead for more than a few hours. But I didn't know that then."

"Did you know what had happened to you?"

"Oh yes. Most certainly. I was a vampire. I had heard the stories. Stories for children and make-believe, but I knew them. It was quite obvious. I had had my blood drunk by a thing with fangs that couldn't be killed by bullets. I was a vampire. Or I was insane."

"You don't feel insane now?"

"Not for a long time, Granger." Finally she smiled at him. "This is my life." Helman could not share in what she thought was the humor of the statement.

"How did you meet with the Conclave? You said they wanted to get rid of you."

"Long after I left the cellar. In the beginning, we are protected from our ignorance by a set of strong new urges and drives. We become sluggish as morning approaches.

Our minds fill with thoughts of darkness and refuge from the light. Our self-protection is like a new set of instincts. We follow them blindly. Later, as we mature, the drives lessen. But our intellect has taken over for us by then. Anyway, I roamed the front lines looking for bodies of the newly dead. I sickened myself many times feeding from blood gone bad, but I could not bring myself to feed from the living.

"I tried the blood of animals, also. For a time, it worked. But the nutrient composition is different. After a month or so, human blood is necessary or starvation will follow.

"On one foray, months afterward, I met another *yber*. He was experienced in the Ways and knew another had been hunting in his territory. He said later he was prepared to kill me to defend it. But he followed me for several nights and decided I was infringing by ignorance and not design. He became my mentor, as the *yber* in the farmhouse should have been."

"Mentor. The *yber* who would teach you in the Ways?"

"That's right. He helped me develop my new senses, my new powers. Taught me to be undetectable by humans and identify other *yber* at great distances.

"He took me to Geneva as the war was ending. That was where the Conclave based itself, until the reconstruction. They were alarmed that there were so many like me; the Unbidden, they called us. Many *yber* were created without agreement from a governing group or Meeting during the war years. Many were given the Final Death. I was protected because I had a mentor. He saved me more than once." Her voice sounded wistful, caught up in pleasant memories.

"Were you in love with him?" Helman was at the point where he did not think it odd to ask this creature who could not be killed if she could love.

"Yes, I was in love with him. I do love, Granger. That's the whole conflict. The Conclave says we are the children of demons. Devil's spawn. They rule the *yber* with the old superstitions of damnation and the fight against God and the Church. And they're wrong! I am *yber*, yes. But I am also human. There is nothing evil about me. I am not cursed by Heaven.'' She leaned forward, staring intently into Helman's eyes. ''Granger, all that is different about me is that I have a disease.''

Immediately everything became acceptable for *yber*. What he had witnessed had been presented to him in terms of the supernatural. Vampires. Night creatures. Things that his rational mind could not accept, even though the evidence had played itself out before his eyes. But a disease. That was rational. No matter that the evidence presented was the same. A disease spoke of medicine, of science. A disease he could accept. Science was his modern superstition, and when the proper words were said, Granger Helman could believe.

''A rare disease,'' Adrienne continued. ''Communicable only by ingesting the living blood of one who is infected and only then when your body is in a state of massive shock. A disease that alters the nutritive needs of the body, speeds the metabolism incredibly, and does away with the side effects of aging. I've studied it for years. Chris Leung was going to help me. Had helped already in letters and research he'd conducted on his own. Vampirism is a disease. It *can* be controlled.''

''And that's why the Conclave want you dead. Because if it is a disease, their supernatural hold over the *yber* is without basis. They lose all their power.''

''Exactly, Granger, exactly. They knew I thought these things long ago. Because I wasn't chosen as the others had been? Because I had had medical training in my first life? Who knows? But I was warned not to discuss those things. I was a heretic they said. I risked the Final Death if I continued.''

''But you do continue.''

''I must continue.'' She looked away. ''For Jeffery's sake. As well as my own.''

Helman looked puzzled at the mention of Jeffery.

''He was my mentor, Granger. The man I loved.''

''What happened to him?''

He saw the answer in her eyes before she spoke.

"Six months ago, they came for me. Emissaries from the Conclave. Jeffery protected me. Just as he had helped me in my research." Her voice became tight and strained. "To teach me a lesson, they took *him* instead. They chained him to an outcropping of rock near the villa which held our sanctuary." She whispered, her voice barely audible. Helman could see tears. "They faced him to the east. To the sunrise . . ."

Helman reached out and this time did not hesitate. He took her hands in his to try and comfort her. They were like ice, like death. But the cold air through the broken glass door had chilled his fingers and he did not notice.

Adrienne took a deep breath and sat up. She squeezed Helman's hands a moment, as if to thank him, then moved them from him.

"That night I went to the outcropping. The chains were loose around the rocks. His clothes scattered around the ground, blown by the wind, like Jeffery. The ring I had given him lay buried beneath the chains. Can you know what it's like, Granger? Humans may fall in love and have decades at most. Death takes mere years away from you. But for *yber*, the Final Death takes centuries, eternity away. Not even his body to kiss goodbye . . ."

Memories of love lost, decades stolen, rose up in Helman. Is this what it comes to? he thought. Roselynne Delvecchio was dead from the moment she met Helman in the parking lot, so long ago. In her last moments, he had given her new life. A mistake had been made, he had told her. And life had flowed into her seconds before Helman took it all away forever. It had cost him, that final closing. And now he was faced with the same situation. The woman before him was already dead, a vampire, an *yber*, but Helman once again could act and give her new life. He could offer her protection. Perhaps it could be a way to make up for the past? But there was no making up for the past. It was gone. His rational mind had no superstition of godly retribution for past sins. He had only the superstition of science, and the far more powerful one of conscience. When she first had made her offer to him, that he be her familiar, he knew he would accept, if only to prevent his immediate death; to preserve himself so that he might still save Miriam and her children. But now he knew he would accept Adrienne's offer for a new reason, a stronger reason. Finally, he would act. He would accept her offer because he wanted to. For Helman, the difference was enormous.

"Adrienne, I will help you, be your familiar, whatever you need. I'll do it."

"The Conclave will do everything they can to stop us."

"They'd do that anyway."

Adrienne checked the sky again through the fluttering drapes. It was growing lighter. How was her knowledge of the Ways going to serve her if she found herself talking like this? Of things best hidden away from her heart.

"What should we do first?" Helman asked. She was the one with the experience. He would trust the opening moves to her.

"First I must get to my sanctuary. It is almost dawn. The sun is deadly." Helman nodded, thinking of Jeffery.

"But you can't go back to the townhouse, your people didn't defend it from the priests, it's not—"

Adrienne's face went rigid. "What do you mean, 'my people'? My last familiars were butchered by the Conclave at Heathrow. I have no 'people.' And what do you mean by 'priests'?"

"The Jesuits with crossbows. Your people with guns. It was a bloodbath. It started at the lab after the explosion and by the time I got to your townhouse, it was all up and down the street. The leader of the people fighting the priests was 'Marker One'."

"Jesuits of the Seventh Grade." Her eyes were wide, her nostrils flared. "I thought I had eluded them long before I reached England. Their sources are better than I had thought."

"Why are they after you?"

"They're after all *yber*. They're as caught up in superstition as the Conclave. Who knows why they're after me."

"But the people who fought the Jesuits . . ." Helman suddenly realized what he had said. "Jesuits? How can Jesuits do those things? Killing? It's ridiculous."

"They're Jesuits of the Seventh Grade, Granger. I don't have time to explain. The sky is getting lighter. I don't know who it could be who was fighting with them. The Conclave has skirmishes with them from time to time but I don't see why they'd be trying to protect me from the Jesuits. Find out for me before this evening." Adrienne got up and moved to the balcony door.

"But what if the Conclave contact me? What about my sister and her kids? What should I tell them?" Helman reached out to touch her arm. She pulled away.

"Tell them that what happened to my first mentor, in the cellar, happened to me. They'll accept that for now. As long as they believe it, your family will be safe. I must go, Granger. This evening I'll come back. Be ready to travel."

She walked out to the balcony. He came after her. "Where will you go? Wouldn't you be safer in a closet or something here?"

The wind pushed at their hair. Helman saw that when he spoke, his breath condensed and swirled away. Nothing swirled away from Adrienne.

"I have other sanctuaries they won't know about. I'll be safer at one of them than here. Now go inside. Rest for this evening."

She turned from him and slid over the balcony railing, headfirst.

Helman gasped her name and ran to reach after her. His hand held empty air. He leaned over and saw nothing. Her voice came to him through the cold air.

"Go inside. Rest."

He peered in the direction of the voice. Perhaps there was a shadow moving down by the pool. Perhaps it was the wind rustling the tarpaulin. Adrienne was gone.

Helman stepped back into the room. He straightened up the evidence of the initial fight and then phoned the front desk to tell them that a sheet of ice, or something, had just shattered his balcony door. There was glass all over the inside of his room and he wanted to be moved.

When he was in his new room, a duplicate of the first, but without a balcony and sliding doors, Helman collapsed on the bed. He would sleep through the morning. This time by choice and not by accident as he had the day Max had been killed by the Jesuits. Oh God, had they killed Max because of his connection with Helman? Then the Jesuits must have known about Helman's contract on Adrienne days ago. And who had said *"Nothing to worry about on this end?"* Were familiars of the Conclave told to kill Max disguised as priests? Then dispose of witnesses? To ensure Helman could work for them?

No, the Jesuit on the driveway by the townhouse had *recognized* Helman. That's why the dying priest had tried to strangle him. But for what purpose? Because he was working for the Conclave, trying to kill the woman?

Circles wheeled within circles, none would interconnect. There was not enough information for him to follow it any longer. He must sleep. He must be rested for the first part of the bargain with Adrienne.

Who were the people who had tried to protect her from the Jesuits? And who was Marker One?

That morning, as Helman slept, there were no dreams. The basement was far from empty, but it was well lit.

Four

It was an abomination.

The doctor had dealt with the bodies of those who had died by fire and violent car crashes. He had performed autopsies on bodies of the drowned which had been recovered days afterward, swollen with the gases of decay, flesh puffed and stretched from bones no longer held by cartilage and tendons. He had cut into those bodies, explored the unrecognizable dark masses of rotted organs, felt the liquids which were not blood ooze up around his hands as his knife delved deeper, and he had not been as affected as he was now. The body before him had not achieved this form by chance and the inevitable corruption of nature. This body had been *made* this way; a will and conscious thought were behind its destruction. And his scalpel trembled in his hands as he contemplated such a will, and the creature who would exercise it thus.

Outside the doctor's surgery, Father Clement sat and brooded in the darkness. The outrage that had seared through him earlier was now subdued. Once before, long ago in the time of the suppression, the officers of the Society had felt such outrage, and had decided that there was a time when prayer and Holy guidance were not enough. At such times there must be actions. Those officers, tricked by the Enemy into the near destruction of their order, had taken the Fifth Vow of the Society of Jesus. And action *had* been taken. A Pope lay dead. Another learned the lesson. The Society was restored.

Since that time, the Fifth Vow, unknown to the world, save by rumor, unknown to all but the very select of the Society itself, had existed. Those who professed it were those who took action. Action that was necessary in extraordinary times. Such as now. When the Realm of Darkness and the power of America were to join as an unholy prelude to the End Days. When ten feet away from him a doctor probed the last remains of what had been his brother in the Holy Cause: Father Benedict.

The phone call had come late that evening; the whispered voice had been explicit. A message from Helman could be found in the garden of the Holy Father's house. The Society was to see the price of interference with the woman, St. Clair.

It was a challenge, and it would be met. Father Clement sat in the darkness and planned action.

When the doctor emerged from his surgery into the waiting room where Clement planned, he was pale and still shaken by what he had seen. The Jesuits had told him of such things when he had made his vow of personal obedience to Father Clement, but his rational mind had not truly accepted it.

At first there had been hints that the Enemy he swore to fight for the Society of Jesus was literal and existing on this earth. Then the hints had become stories, and the stories became training. Still he had not believed it. Until tonight, when the ruined body of Father Benedict had been brought to his office, long after hours, and that body had been drained entirely of blood. The wound that the blood had been drawn from had been made in the left carotid artery. It had been made with a *human* mouth. The horror of that knowledge far outweighed any consolation held by the knowledge that most of the other atrocities had been committed after death. Any torture would have been preferable to that first hideous wound.

Father Clement waited patiently for the doctor to compose himself and give his report. There would be no more mistakes like Heathrow. The battle had been enjoined, and the victory would be the Society's. So it was written.

The doctor spoke.

"Cause of death was shock brought on by massive hemorrhage. The blood was removed from the wound in the neck. The presence of capillary damage, skin indentations, and . . . and saliva traces indicate that the method of removal was . . . was as you . . . suggested." Sweat rolled down the doctor's forehead. A detached part of him wondered if he would faint.

"His blood was sucked by vampires, Doctor Biller." Father Clement's voice was cold and flat. "We must not hide from the Enemy. Use the words that must be used."

"B . . . by vampires." Twenty years of medical discipline, twenty years of faith in science, disappeared from him as he said that word. The apprehension of it clutched at him like an icy hand brushing his shoulder in an empty, unlit room. The detached part of him wondered about heart attacks.

He must continue. Reduce it to the known, the manageable. "Aside from the superficial mutilations of the face, apparently caused by . . . claws, and the traumatic excision of the left eye, the other mutilations occurred after the subject . . . after Father Benedict had died."

"Detail them, Doctor Biller. Come to know the Enemy."

His heart raced. Far away he heard his voice speak, but he clearly heard his heartbeat pounding in his ears. How fast can it go? How much can it stand? "The most apparent mutilation is the massive destruction of the chest caused by a large wooden crucifix which has been thrust through the sternum, cracking the lower ribs on each side, destroying the heart, and exiting through the spinal column between the seventeenth and twentieth vertebrae. The tongue has been split along the medial axis, again, it would appear, by claws. Also, the septum appears to have been removed in the same fashion." The room spun. He prayed he would faint before his heart had reached the limits of stress. Father Clement listened impassively.

"Go on, Doctor. All of it."

"The massive destruction of tissue makes it impossible to tell if his genitals have been excised or just shredded unrecognizably." Sweet Jesus, take those images from his mind. "The mutilation has been caused by sharp imple . . . by teeth and claws, oh God, Father—" The doctor's mind broke before his body. He collapsed into a sobbing, quaking form, unintelligible words bubbling from his mouth: deep, resonating sounds of unbearable anguish.

Father Clement went to him and held him; rocking the man back and forth to comfort him. The doctor was one of the lay brothers of the Society who had kept their vows a secret from the world. Such agents of influence were necessary to the Society's work when unobtrusive access was needed to the secular seats of power. Such agents within the Washington bureaucracy had first alerted the Society to the initial contact between the Americans and the woman, and had discovered the link between the assassin and the death merchant in Miami. Occasionally these brothers were chosen by the professed of the Five Vows—the Jesuits of the Seventh Grade—and, bound by their oaths, the lay brothers would join in the necessary actions. But always, when faced with the horrible shadow reality that lay under the façade of the modern world, the reaction was the same. The people of the middle ages, the savages of the world today, none would question the truth that had reduced this doctor to hysteria. Humanity had set its task to isolate itself from horror, and it had succeeded too well. Unknown, unwatched, ignored, the real horrors grew until their slightest touch could devastate. Centuries of progress and enlightenment vanished in that awesome moment of recognition when humans looked into the darkness and saw that the half-seen things that scuttled within it were *real*.

Father Clement had spent his life in that darkness, fighting with those things. Some would say the darkness existed only within his mind. He would call those people possessed of the Enemy. Forty years ago he had reached out and almost embraced that Enemy. More than any other of his order, he *knew* the attraction and the power of the Pit. That knowledge drove him. That and the secret fear that the darkness might once again reach out to him, and this time, he might not be able to resist. Father Clement comforted the doctor and prayed for forgiveness for the contempt that he felt toward him.

Father Clement got into the gray Plymouth Fury that had waited for him outside the doctor's office building. Around him as the morning brightened, the traffic grew; great lumbering creatures roared through the obscuring mist of the steaming sewer openings, bellowing at their mindless near-collisions. His driver accelerated from the curb, pushing them into the monstrous herd past 79th then through the park, to escape from the island hell.

"Is it done?" the driver asked. His eyes never left the maneuvering of the cars surrounding him. He was young. A scholastic still in his first ten years of service, but he had been trusted with the organization of the New York House.

"Yes," said Father Clement. "He will prepare the proper documents to show he is the physician of record. The death certificate will state heart attack. Father Benedict was old. No one will be alarmed."

The driver was silent.

"You have word from Toronto?" Clement continued. "Did something come through while I was with the doctor?" His voice took on a harsh edge in his question.

"We have lost," the driver said.

"Everything?" Clement was incredulous.

"Two of the novices escaped. Everyone else is gone. Even the Mounties."

"But how could they? There were ten of us, the Mounties, the police—"

"We didn't face just Helman and the woman. There were Americans, armed with guns. Protective clothing that our arrows wouldn't pierce."

"Americans? Familiars of the Conclave?"

"No. Inquiries are being made now. It is believed they are agents of the government."

Father Clement held his hands to his face. Not now. Not so soon. "So they have joined already. The power of the Americans has been added to the evil of the Conclave."

"Father Clement," the driver seemed apprehensive. He stole a glance at the man beside him. "We may be wrong about that."

"How do you mean?" There could be no mistakes in this war.

"The novices followed St. Clair to the Chinese doctor's facilities. There was an explosion. Helman was there immediately—"

"To protect her," Clement said.

"The novices don't think so, Father. They say he had a machete. In any event, the explosion was deliberately caused."

"What are you trying to say? That Helman is trying to

kill the woman? That's impossible. He's an agent of th
Americans.''

''Father Clement, forgive me, but I have been investigat
ing him. It's true that at certain times in the past, he's bee
associated with the Americans. Late yesterday, inquirie
were made about him in Langley. The lay brother we hav
there indicated the request came from a friendly source; tha
is an American agency in a foreign location. That could b
the team in Canada. I think it might mean that Helman i
being employed by someone other than the Americans
Otherwise, why would they be checking on him?''

''To confuse us,'' Clement said. It was weak, but ther
was only one other conclusion, and he couldn't see the logi
behind it. ''Or else he is being employed by the Conclave.'

''To kill Adrienne St. Clair.''

''But to what purpose? She is their link to the Americans.'

''Perhaps the Conclave don't wish to be linked with them.'

Clement stared out at the rushing landscape. ''Then thi
entire operation has been for nothing? Is that what you'r
saying?''

The driver shook his head. ''I don't know what th
answer is. The only thing I'm sure of is that Helman is *no*
working for the Americans, and the Americans are trying t
contact St. Clair, *and* learn the truth about Helman them
selves. We are trapped in the middle.''

''The middle of what? What are you daring to suggest?'
Clement's voice was raised in anger.

''It *is* a suggestion, nothing more, Father. We know th
Americans want to contact the woman. What we don'
definitely know is whether or not they intend to use her as
conduit to the rest of the Conclave. We know that Helman i
involved with the woman. What we don't know is how. I
he an agent of the Americans assigned to protect her? Is h
an agent of the Conclave assigned to kill her, and fail, as
ploy to confuse us? Or is he truly intended to deliver her t
the Final Death? If we act against Helman we may b
stopping him from accomplishing something which both w
and the Conclave may desire: her death. However, we ma

be playing into their hands by concentrating on Helman, as they have planned, while the joining of the Americans and the Conclave goes forth, hidden from us by our zeal to attack the most likely target."

"Very complex. What do you *suggest* we do?"

The driver drew a deep breath. "That, Father Clement, I must leave to you. I don't know."

They drove a while in silence.

"What *I* know," Clement said, finally, "is that someone, some*thing*, did what we both saw to Father Benedict. It was the work of the Conclave, attributed to Helman. Both are our enemies. We shall destroy them. The Americans are involved with one or another or all three. They shall destroy them. The woman, the Conclave, Helman, all will fall before us. And if the Americans intercede, we shall destroy them too, as we did the cursed dealer in murder in Florida. We are the professed of the Five Vows. We shall act. And we shall destroy them."

The car sped along the freeway. The course was set. An ending was inevitable.

Hands clenched to the steering wheel, the scholastic prayed to God that it would be the ending the Society worked for, and not the other, terrifying alternative.

Hell must stay where it was. It could not be allowed to spread over all the earth.

But there were men in Washington who knew that it already had.

Five

Along the street, behind covered windows, in hedges, on roofs, they waited. Adrienne St. Clair had been seen entering his hotel room. Three hours later, dangerously close to the first rays of morning sun, she had been seen leaving. Inquiries were made through the front desk. He had asked to change his room. He was alive.

Phoenix would return to the street, and they waited for him.

Weston had taken responsibility for letting Helman go. The Jesuits had been the first to storm the townhouse but were easily repulsed. They were trained to meet the emissaries of the Conclave; emissaries who retreated before crucifixes, blistered at the contact of Holy Water and fell beneath the bolt of a crossbow. The Jesuits were no match for the agents of the Nevada Project, with their impenetrable Kevlar body armor and devastating Uzi submachine guns. Weston knew the outrage of the laboratory would not go unpunished by the woman. She had methods of tracking which Weston's people had never been able to quantify. Phoenix might be able to escape from the Jesuits. He might be able to escape from Nevada. But he would not escape her. Weston had gambled and Weston had won. She was desperate for help. Phoenix was experienced, undriven by any loyalties to one side of the conflict or another, therefore he was suitable to be her familiar. She had let him live. That meant she would be in contact with Helman again. Weston had lost Christopher Leung. Soon he would gain Helman.

Weston knew Helman would have to return to the townhouse so he waited for the assassin there, in the basement. The carnage of the Jesuits had been cleaned up, if not obliterated. St. Clair's sanctuary had been repaired and replaced in the false wall under the staircase.

The condition of her sanctuary was further proof to Weston that he had chosen the right target. She was so unlike the others. Her sanctuary in no way resembled a coffin. There was not even the obligatory handful of soil from her native country scattered in it. It was much more like a bed, padded softly, and light tight. She was not a victim of the superstitious nonsense of the Conclave. She was the Nevada Project's last hope.

Earlier that day, Weston's second-in-command had placed a coded phone call to his Toronto station. *Lancet* had accepted an article by a physician working out of a small clinic in Omaha, funded by the multi-millionaire, Daniel K. Ludwig. The research definitely pointed to airborne transmission, possibly viral in origin.

The researcher had not published in years, and never in this field. A small fish had slipped through the net. Other journals would see the article and pay closer attention to the other reports that Weston's people had skillfully maneuvered them into avoiding throughout the past years. One by one they would begin to publish. Within a month or two, the professional circles would be full of speculation. Within three months, the science reporters would have carried the rumors to the feature pages. The country would be in an uproar before the summer was through. And tomorrow, Weston thought, the world.

A small buzz of static crackled through the silence of the basement. Weston turned to look at the speaker.

"We've got a make on Phoenix. Coming up the street behind the backyard. He is armed. Does not appear to have spotted any surveillance."

Weston reached over for his microphone. "Keep low. He's coming right to us."

Static, then nothing.

Weston waited in silence. Phoenix was coming.

The townhouse's street was quiet today, there was no evidence of the grisly battle from the night before. The television crews had left. No doubt the reporters would still be questioning confused residents, but nothing would come of it. The Jesuits had used their influence on the Canadian Mounties; the Mounties had used their influence on the Toronto Police; and Weston's people had then taken over from the Mounties.

As far as the police knew, they were helping the Mounties capture a group of Red Terrorists who were trying to use

Toronto as a base of operations. The Mounties, backed by orders from the highest government sources, had forced the Toronto police to relinquish authority over the operation. The police had reacted bitterly. There were rumors of Mounties pulling guns on police officers during the confusion of the previous night. Inquiries would be held, but nothing would be made public. All that mattered was that when the power had been required, it was there. In emergencies, certain structures existed to bypass all the laws and systems. The police could rant and rave, the newspapers could fume, but the secret channels of power were always open. All anyone would ever learn, as had happened so many times in the past, was that the Mounties were in control. And, as far as the Mounties knew, their special Security Service team was still in position and undercover, with instructions not to report until the complete operation was finished. As far as Weston knew, all those Mounties were dead.

Somehow, he didn't feel badly when an agent of an intelligence group died in action. They were like soldiers. It was part of the job. They all knew it. Most accepted it. Especially the victors.

What made Weston feel bad was killing scientists. Especially now, with the *Lancet* article about to appear. Maybe it had all been for nothing. He struggled to avoid coughing. With Phoenix so close, he couldn't risk the disorientation of pain.

Weston heard a short surprised grunt from outside the backyard basement window. It ended quickly in what sounded like a drawn out stacatto of hiccups. Phoenix had arrived and Phoenix had been captured.

He was brought downstairs. His arms and legs twitching, eyes rolled up.

The yellow-and-blue-striped body of the battery dart had imbedded itself in his left leg. It was sending intermittent pulses of 40,000 volts of DC current into his central nervous system. It was an offshoot of the Taser pistol, except it didn't need a wire to connect to a battery in the gun and could be fired over a much longer distance. And depending on the size of the battery, and how long it remained in the victim, it could be fatal.

The two men who brought Helman downstairs, lowered him into an easy chair. The chintz-covered chair did not belong to the concrete-walled unfinished basement. It had been brought from upstairs. Weston was uncomfortable sitting in front of unprotected windows.

He went over to Helman and withdrew the battery dart. Helman still twitched. He would for several minutes more. One of the men soaked an antiseptic fluid onto the pant leg above the wound. The other presented Weston with Helman's collection of weapons.

Eventually, the worst of the shaking left Helman. He directed his eyes to Weston, and Weston spoke.

"I'm glad to finally meet you, Phoenix. I'm impressed with your artillery." He gestured to the magnum and the Bulldog the second guard held. The first guard held the battery dart rifle, aimed at Helman.

"I take it you're 'Marker One'," Helman said.

"That's right," Weston agreed.

"Well, someone with a gun called me Phoenix last night. He was wrong. And you're wrong. I don't know who Phoenix is." Helman found it hard to speak without his teeth chattering, it sounded somewhere between having a chill and a stutter.

Weston held his hand to his eyes, shutting them as if reading from a file he kept written on his eyelids. "Code designation Phoenix. Domestic Sector. Terminal operations, etc., etc. Operative designation: Helman, Robert Granger. Used effectively in March '74, December '75, January and April of '77, and November of '80. And so on and so on."

The dates were familiar to Helman, but he couldn't understand their context. "I'm Granger Helman, yes. I don't know Phoenix. I don't know those dates." They were all months in which he had handled closings. Were these people from the Conclave?

Weston sighed and turned away. The second guard handed

the pistols to him. The other guard with the battery rifle moved silently off to the side so he would have a clear field of fire.

The second guard, face thin and intense like a long distance runner's, stood in front of Helman holding a small black case. "Well, the Central Intelligence Agency knows those dates. Now stop fucking us around, Phoenix, and answer a few questions before we turn your brains to jelly. You were there last night. You saw what happened to that asshole in the TV van. He was a professional, Helman. Tougher than you, by God. And it only took us eight minutes to get the code responses from him. You know why we killed him? Injected him with a lethal overdose of barbituates?" The guard screamed into Helman's face. Spittle clouded from his rapidly moving mouth, covering Helman in spray. Helman could not react. But he could remember the man with the phone employee's badge and the drugged eyes. The man they had killed with a needle in the neck. "Because it was the fucking humane thing to do to him. After the other drugs we loaded him with, he would have been a fucking vegetable."

The guard squatted down in front of Helman, opening the black case. There were vials of clear liquid. And a hypodermic needle. "But you know what, Phoenix? We really killed him because we respected him. We respected him enough to give him a clean death. But not you, you fucker. We'll load you up with the same drugs, you'll tell us everything we want to know. And then we're going to leave you here to wallow in your own shit until the neighbors complain about the smell, because you're not going to have enough brains left over to stand up and fucking walk to the can."

Helman's face was red. He willed his arms to rise up and rip at this maniac's throat but none of his nerves were in sync. Nothing worked. He could only become more enraged and sputter.

The guard held up his hand and snapped his fingers.

"Major, help me hold him down. There's only one way this asshole's going to talk."

Weston grabbed Helman by the shoulders, pushing him deeper into the chair. The first guard held a vial from the case upside down and plunged the hypodermic through the rubber seal. He withdrew the plunger, filling the cartridge. Helman desperately tried to struggle, but except for an abrupt shudder, his body still would not obey him. He spoke hurriedly to Weston as the guard forced the drug out of the tip of the needle, expelling air.

"You haven't even asked me to talk yet. I've told you, I'm Helman. I admit it. Ask me questions about anything. But I tell you I don't know anything about Phoenix or the CIA. Ask me."

Weston looked directly into Helman's eyes.

"Did you speak with Adrienne St. Clair last night?"

Who were these people? thought Helman. Why does everybody know so much more than I do?

"Yes," he said. The guard swabbed an area on the side of Helman's neck. Helman thought the swabbing to prevent infection was hideously gratuitous.

Weston put out his arm to stop the guard from injecting the needle.

"Let's just hold off on that for a while. See what we can get from him while he's cooperative."

The guard protested. Helman could see the anticipation in his eyes.

Weston calmed him. "We can *always* use the needle, son. *Always*. You just keep it ready. It might be that he can be a bit more cooperative with us while he's alive. Or at least while his brain is still functioning." He turned to Helman. "You better make this good. Once that stuff's in you, there's not a whole lot we can do for you. Understand?"

Helman nodded. He concentrated on his fingers. They clenched when he told them to. Weston saw the movement. "And the next dart in that thing over there," he pointed to the guard with the battery rifle, "will paralyze your heart before you hit the ground. Let's not be a martyr."

Helman sank back into the chair. He was boxed in again. he had the sinking feeling that he had just fallen for the classic "good cop-bad cop" routine played out between Marker One and the guard with the needle. If he could, he felt like holding some people up to the wall by their necks to watch them slowly strangle, too.

"So Adrienne St. Clair wants you to be her familiar?" said Weston.

"If you bugged the room, why do you need me to answer questions?"

"We didn't bug the room. St. Clair is in a very precarious position. Two very powerful organizations are out to kill her. The Final Death I believe they call it. You took away her only chance of escaping."

Helman's eyes narrowed.

"Do you know who it was you killed in the lab explosion?" Weston asked.

"Christopher Leung. A doctor. It was unfortunate."

Weston looked worried. "Unfortunate that you had to kill him? Or unfortunate that he died?"

"I didn't have to kill him. The lab was the only place I could get at the woman."

"My God, you were trying to kill *her*? Not Leung? Why would the CIA want her dead? Why—"

Helman screamed at him. "I'm *not* with the CIA. I don't know *anything* about the CIA. I'm working for the *Conclave*!"

Weston was pale. "Do you know what the Conclave is?"

"I do now. Do you know what Adrienne St. Clair is?"

"Of course. That's why Dr. Leung was working for me. That's why we lost four men protecting this sanctuary for her last night, in addition to the one you killed two days ago. Adrienne St. Clair is a vampire. And that's precisely why we want her. Now I want you to tell me everything you can about the Conclave. The guard is very eager to use the needle, and I'm not going to be able to hold him off unless we start hearing why you're involved."

Helman fought to keep from screaming again. He saw the

guard with the needle standing near. A single, quivering drop of liquid shimmered on the needle's tip.

He told all he could.

Weston paced to take the stiffness from his legs. They had been at it for more than two hours, and Helman had to be back in his hotel room by sunset to await contact by St. Clair *and* the Conclave.

Helman looked exhausted. Motor control had returned to his body but the shock of the battery dart had taken its toll. The sandwiches and coffee one of the guards had brought in had gone down all right, but they hadn't seemed to do much good in steadying his insides.

Weston spoke. "Okay. You're a hit man. Retired. The Conclave gave you a contract on St. Clair. Why? We're not sure. St. Clair says it follows a pattern they have established over the centuries. You were going to be their hi-lo. Your sister and the kids are their insurance. We know they don't have many 'emissaries' in North America. They keep a very low profile. Probably they couldn't get a team together fast enough. It's not as easy to disguise a murder here as in Europe. So they chose you as a local expert. Someone who could be caught if you made too big a mess of it, and killed, no doubt, before you had a chance to talk. Killed in any case, even if you had gotten away with it."

Granger had been sitting with his eyes closed. He opened them. "They told me I was to go free after I had completed the deal."

Weston twisted his mouth. "I suppose you still write letters to Santa Claus, too. You don't understand those things, those creatures. All the people we know about who have dealt with them, usually through business associations, are fine, as long as they have a use. As soon as the use is no longer required, they disappear. It's no accident that vampires faded to nothing more than a myth. They've worked hard for their anonymity. It's their strength. How can anyone fight against something they don't believe in?"

Helman jerked to his feet. The man with the battery rifle swung it around to cover him.

"Miriam and the boys! If I'm expendable—"

Weston signaled to the rifleman to lower the weapon.

"Listen," he said, "if their lives were the Conclave's bargaining position with you, they can be ours, too. I can arrange protection for you. We have special weapons, specially trained agents. Your sister and her kids will be fine. All you have to do is cooperate with us now."

"How?"

"By doing what you're doing for the woman. You killed her familiar. She's turned to you to replace him. Her familiar was also my agent. I want you to replace him, too."

"Why? Who are you to want a vampire? And why do you need me to do it? You can follow her. Why not approach her yourself?"

"She'd be too wary of who we represent. She won't trust us. We've already made overtures. There were three prime contacts she could have made when she escaped from England. We had a man in Chicago, a woman in Washington, and Dr. Leung in Toronto. We made her initial contact with those people such that she would have no reason to suspect Chicago or Toronto was linked to the American government."

Helman's eyes widened. "You're from Washington? The government's behind this?"

"Parts of the government know about us. Very few know about the *yber*. And only my group knows about St. Clair."

"No wonder she didn't want to be contacted by Washington. Who are you? Pentagon? Or just Army? Bacteriological warfare? Create a soldier that can't be shot down and has to drink the blood of the enemy?" Helman's face was scarlet. What was going on in Washington that such things could actually be *considered*?

"Calm down, Helman. I don't represent the Pentagon. Or any military agency. That's why I'm concerned about your CIA link."

Helman protested again. Weston cut him short.

"We don't have to go through it again. For now I'll

accept your story. You've never had any contact with the CIA that you can recall. But you're still carried in their files as a domestic assassin, code-named 'Phoenix,' and I intend to find out why. If I thought you were willfully connected with Langley, operating under their control, I wouldn't be keeping the needle from you and you'd be babbling like a two-year-old by now. Let's leave it at that until I get some more reports in."

Helman clenched his teeth and remained silent.

"Better," said Weston, and continued. "The other reason we have to approach her covertly is because she is being observed by the Jesuits. They've been waging their own little war with the Conclave for about two hundred years as far as we can determine. We don't know all that much about them. We've had agents infiltrate the Conclave; it's quite easy because they're always looking for new familiars. But you have to serve thirty-one years on probation to be inducted into the Sixth Grade of the Society of Jesus. And from there, the members of the Seventh Grade are carefully chosen. We've never managed to get even close to them."

"She told me about the Jesuits. She thought she had escaped from them in Europe. She didn't know how they had traced her here. She was surprised. Shocked, actually. But I can't believe it. How can Jesuits do what those priests did last night? It was a massacre. And most of them seemed young. Almost kids."

"Those were the novices and scholastics—training to be Jesuits. The old guys running the show recruit them for special operations. The kids go along with it. Years ago when we learned of the Jesuits' involvement in this, we were shocked too. We assumed they were some insane cult. There was even some evidence linking them to a small bizarre cult in California. Then our agents posing as familiars got word back to us about how long their conflict had been going on. It's true, Helman. And if anyone is capable of what happened last night in the name of God, it's them, and the young fanatics they enlist to fight their Holy war for them. When the Jesuits were formed more than four hundred years ago, the Inquisitions in Spain and Portugal protested to Rome. Can you understand that? *The Spanish Inquisition* thought the Society of Jesus—the Jesuits—would become too powerful, too fanatical. The Catholic Church existed for the glory of God. The Jesuits' creed dedicated themselves to the *greater* glory of God. No one else in the Church felt comfortable with the Jesuits around, but within years they were too powerful to attack.

"They decided to go after the wealthy and the educated, bring the cream of Europe over to the ways of the Church. To do that they became educated and wealthy themselves. They founded some of the best schools the world had seen. Devoted themselves to furthering human knowledge. Something the Church had never condoned. And it worked. Soon they were involved with the wealthiest and most powerful people in the world. They got involved in politics. They created peace. And they created wars. By lying, manipulation, and assassination."

"The Catholic Church involved itself in that? Knowingly?"

"Not the Church, Helman. The Jesuits. And it only took one. Members of other religious orders swear eternal obedience to God. Jesuits make the same vow, *but to other Jesuits*. If a Jesuit's superior orders him to take some action which the Jesuit considers to be sinful, he has the option of checking it out with another Jesuit. If the other Jesuit agrees, that is, if two superiors give the same order, the Jesuit has no choice but to follow the order. That's why the novices and scholastics kill with such fervor. Not only must they *follow* the orders of their superiors, they must make themselves *know*, not merely *believe*, that the action is not sinful. They *must* follow orders.

"During the days of the Third Reich, Goering took a special interest in the Jesuits. He studied them carefully, and kicked them out of Germany. And then he used their organizational plans and principles as the model upon which the SS was formed! This is not a little group of monks we're dealing with. These are fanatics of the worst sort: brilliant, and able to justify any means to accomplish their ends."

Helman felt numbed. Like most people he suspected that hypocrites lurked within any organization, but he had always thought there were limits to the amount of hypocrisy that any one group would contain. It was astounding that such conditions could exist within an arm of a Church that was becoming more and more powerless in the world.

"Are you saying that everything the Jesuits are involved with is just a front for a group of vampire-killers who might as well be wearing swastikas as crosses?"

"No, no, not at all. Not all Jesuits were involved in the actions of the past. Very few are involved in the actions of the present. We are only talking about the Jesuits sworn to save the world from the *yber*: the professed of the Fifth Vow—Jesuits of the Seventh Grade."

"I don't understand."

"As the Jesuits became more powerful and more of a stabilizing force in the world, the vampires began to come under attack. The Church knew about them. Always has. But under the organization of the Jesuits, the battle between the vampires and the Church began to swing in the Church's favor. The vampires did the only thing they could. They organized, too. The Conclave was formed. Its first task was to destroy the group that was giving it so much trouble: the Jesuits.

"The more clever of the vampires, the ones who had been around the longest without being identified and killed, had amassed great fortunes. They could afford to wait a hundred years or more for an investment to pay off. The Conclave consolidated this wealth and put it to good use.

"Two hundred years ago in Martinique, the Jesuit superior, Father Lavalette, was skillfully guided into some complex investments by highly placed familiars of the *yber*. The investments collapsed. The Conclave had arranged it. Several French banks and trading houses were ruined. Noblemen were committing suicide. It was a horrible international scandal and everyone put the blame on the Jesuits. There was a trial. The Jesuits lost. Eventually they were outlawed in France. Because France had actually attempted the unthinkable, and gotten away with it, other countries tried it on several other pretexts, all connected with the financial scandal, no matter how insignificant. Eventually the growing protest could no longer be ignored. The Pope issued an edict disbanding the Jesuits. They were finished. Except in Russia. Catherine the Great allowed them sanctuary. It was there that the Jesuits of the Fifth Vow, the unwritten vow, were formed. And these Jesuits were different. These were the real fanatics. They took the intensity and dedication that had existed for two centuries and directed it to only one cause: the destruction of the vampires. Their first move was to restore the Jesuits in the world. The Pope, Clement XIV, refused their pleas, so the Jesuits killed him with poison. The next Pope was Pious VII. He knew what had happened to his predecessor. He made sure it wouldn't happen to him and issued edicts restoring the Jesuits to their former position in country after country. Finally, more than a hundred and sixty years ago, the final edict was issued and the Jesuits were totally restored. No Pope has interfered with them since."

"That's unbelievable."

"That's history. When you really do retire, Granger, look it up sometime. Names and dates. It's all there. No one likes to talk about it. The Jesuits have their apologists. The only thing missing from the histories will be the mention of the Conclave. And that's because the Conclave is far more powerful than the Jesuits ever were."

"Why don't the Jesuits tell the world? Get everyone involved in this?"

Weston sat down on a chair across from Helman. It was the mate to Helman's chair which had also been brought downstairs. He rubbed at his face and temples.

"We don't know," he said. "It's almost as if the Conclave and the Jesuits have some secret pact with each other, some hold over each other. But up to now, it's just been a case of one on one. The Jesuits fighting for God: the vampires fighting for the Devil. All of them caught up in a supernatural conflict of good versus evil."

Realization dawned on Helman. "Except for Adrienne St. Clair," he said. "She thinks it's a disease."

"Close enough," agreed Weston. "Let's just say that some of her ideas and some of our ideas are pretty close. We'd like them to get closer. But we need someone with personal knowledge of vampirism, who preferably has some scientific background, or at least isn't caught up in the hocus-pocus of the Conclave."

"And you won't tell me why?"

"No."

"But it's not connected to weapons research or the military, even though that's what Adrienne might think?"

"That's right."

"I have to know more."

"Let's just say that the Jesuits are probably right."

"Right about what?"

"The End Days. It doesn't have anything to do with God or the Devil, demons and angels, but the End Days *are* here, Helman. And Adrienne St. Clair may be the only person in the world who can stop them. *If* the Conclave and the Jesuits let her live long enough."

The basement was suddenly very still, very cold. The animation and emotion of Weston's eyes and face had faded, replaced with rock-like seriousness.

Helman felt his stomach tighten the way it did when he accepted a new contract. He realized he had stumbled onto something far bigger than just another closing. There was far more than one death being threatened here. There was far more than Miriam and her children at stake.

He took a deep breath to ease the tenseness of his chest, and closed his eyes. For some reason he saw an image of a basement room, perhaps the cellar of Adrienne's story. It was empty, the corners were clear. But on a far off wall, there was another door, and it was open onto a staircase descending. Don't go down, said a voice inside of him. He opened his eyes and the image and the voice vanished. The seriousness remained.

"What's my part in it?" he asked.
Major Weston told him.

Six

Helman did not recognize the familiars of Mr. Rice as he walked through the lobby of his hotel. They did not recognize him either. They had been given a job to do, and they had done it, unquestioningly, without knowing the reasons for their actions. The results of those actions lay waiting in Helman's hotel room and Helman entered, unsuspecting.

Weston had proposed a series of daytime contacts, chiefly by phone, for keeping him informed of St. Clair's plans and actions. Helman would continue in his role as the woman's new familiar. She had told him to be prepared to travel, so it was obvious that she had a plan, however hastily arrived at, prepared. Weston wanted to know what that plan was.

In the meantime, Weston would dispatch agents to arrange for the safekeeping of Miriam and her children. He would also attempt to in some way determine the intent of the Jesuits. Helman had been outfitted with a Kevlar bulletproof vest. Body armor made up of several layers of the material could stop a bullet from a .357 magnum at five feet with little more than a bruise or a few cracked ribs. It would be more than adequate protection from the comparatively slow moving arrows of the Jesuits' crossbows, unless, as had happened to the agent on the driveway the night before, the arrow struck somewhere other than the area the armor covered. Helman had also taken a jacket for St. Clair. The logic of it baffled him and he wanted her to explain why bullets passed harmlessly through her, yet she needed protection from a wooden arrow. At least she would have that protection. And Helman's protection from the Conclave. Both of them would also have some sort of protection from Weston's men. Weston had said it was risky to have his men follow them in the nighttime when the agents of the Conclave would be out. It was easy to hide from the familiars in the daytime, but vampires had a preternatural sense of when they were being observed. Any watchers must be far away from the actual scene, as they had been the night Adrienne had visited Helman and Weston's people had watched with a Startron night viewer from the tower of an office building, half a mile away.

At least Helman felt he had a bit more control over the situation. He was no longer a pawn. Instead he had a function to perform to aid one of the more powerful players in this bizarre game. And he was relieved that Weston's men would be looking after his sister. The only thing he was worried about, he thought as he slid the room key into the hotel door, was how the Conclave would react to the aborted assassination attempt the night before. Adrienne had told him what to say, but he wondered if they would give him a chance to say it. Even if they did, would they believe him?

He pushed open the door. The Do Not Disturb sign was still in place and he could see by the unmade bed that the maids had not trespassed against it. The room looked empty. He slipped inside quickly and shut the door, locking it. He lay the package containing the Kevlar vest on the floor and reached inside his coat for the magnum that Weston had returned to him. He held it at the ready and checked for intruders.

Everything was clear and untouched. He threw his coat down on the bed and went into the bathroom. He ran the water into the sink and splashed it up on his face. It was refreshing. He thought of swimming with Steven and Campbell in the New England summer. Sometimes it almost felt as if he were their father. He liked the feeling.

Helman looked at his face in the mirror. The stress of the last four days was showing. He looked as unhealthy as the two teenagers he had seen walking through the lobby downstairs, the ones with the high turtleneck sweaters and the pale sunken faces. He would have to be careful if Adrienne's plans included crossing any borders. He looked as if he were strung out on drugs. He thought of Adrienne; he wondered where she was sleeping now. Other thoughts came to him then. Mostly they centered around the look of sorrow that had been on her face when she talked of Jeffery. *All that is different about me is that I have a disease.* A woman with a disorder, he thought. A small one. One that had killed her and kept her alive at the same time. She had been dead, and Helman knew the dead. Yet she was given new life. A second chance. He wondered about second chances, about what would happen to them if they both survived. He thought about things that might happen until he angrily thrust the thoughts aside. He was thinking the impossible. He threw more water on his face and watched it as it splashed against the mirror above the sink and ran down like raindrops, streaking the glass like it had that morning. Streaks on the glass. He felt alarms go off inside of him. He had washed in the bathroom this morning. There had been streaks on the mirror. A crumpled washcloth by the side of the sink. Used soap in hardened bubbles in the sink's indentation.

The bathroom was now spotless. But the bed was untouched. Had the maids straightened up half his room? If they entered despite the Do No Disturb sign, and found the room empty, wouldn't they have cleaned everywhere? He looked around hurriedly. Other anomalies were present. His towel from the shower this morning was still stuffed over the towel bar. It hadn't been replaced. The washcloth in the shower enclosure was also as he had left it. But the sink had been cleaned. He looked more closely at the surfaces of the bathroom. And the mirror. And the counter running around the sink. Had someone been here and spilled something?

Helman was concerned, but couldn't determine any sinister motive for anyone to have entered his hotel room to clean only his sink. And the floor too, come to think of it. The tiles had been wiped clean, the bathmat pushed to one side. The grouting between the tiles looked darker than he remembered, but he discounted that impression. He hadn't been paying close attention in the morning, so it was not a valid observation.

He turned off the water splashing into the sink and moved over to the toilet. He reached down and lifted the lid. And he knew what had stained the tile grouting. He knew what had been spilled and so meticulously cleaned from the bathroom floor and counter.

Blood.

The blood of the woman whose severed head now stared sickeningly up at him from the toilet bowl.

It was jammed into place, lying a bit on its side. Dark hair, soaked with water and blood, snaked across the porcelain like cracks through fine china. One eye was submerged in the dark pink of the water, the other was pushed all the way to the side as though in her last moments she had sought help from beside her. The mouth was open. The water's surface lay still within it. The severed head stared up at him.

And Helman screamed.

For one timeless instant, as his heart literally jumped in his chest and his eyes stretched open and refused to focus on the horror before him, he had seen the face of his sister and his stomach had convulsed and the bile burned in his throat. The scream had come with the shocked recognition that the face was the face of a stranger. And his stomach churned again and he fell toward the sink, his legs collapsing under him and he vomited as if he were exorcising the demons who had caused the monstrosity he had seen.

His breath came in hoarse gasps. But the shock was numbing him, giving his mind back its control. He reached over and flipped the toilet lid down, entombing the horror with the clatter of plastic. He stepped out into his room holding onto the doorframe.

Helman went to the bed and sat upon it. He concentrated on making the shudders he felt diminish and go away. His foot hit something solid behind the bedspread. Something was under the bed. He reached out, grabbed the corner of the spread and pulled.

A hand flopped out. A woman's lifeless hand. Helman knelt at the side of the bed. The rest of the woman was there. The rest of her except her head.

There was a pounding on the door.

"Mr. Osgood! Are you all right, sir?"

Helman said nothing. There was more pounding. Then he heard a key being jiggled in the lock. He hadn't fastened the chain.

"Who is it?" he yelled as he threw the bedspread over the bed, letting it hang down low where the headless corpse was visible.

"House security, sir. The maid said she heard screaming. Are you all right, sir?" The jiggling in the lock had stopped, for the moment.

"Yes, yes. I'm fine. Just a nightmare." It was four o'clock in the afternoon.

"I'd like to make sure you're okay, sir. Nothing broken or anything like that. Will you let me in, sir?"

Helman heard the key in the lock again. The security man was coming in no matter what Helman said.

"Sure, sure you can come in. Just a second." Helman grabbed his magnum from the other bed, went to the bathroom and wrapped a towel around it, and said, "I'm coming. Just a second." He shut the bathroom door and held the towel-wrapped gun against his head as if it were a compress.

He opened the door.

The security man was young. The kind of person who looks scary when wearing a police uniform because how can they give a gun to someone who looks so much like a kid. This kid, noted Helman, was carrying a handgun in a shoulder holster poorly hidden under a gold-colored hotel blazer which hadn't been tailored for weapons. A concealed handgun was unusual for Canada. Helman realized the maid might not have heard him scream at all. He might be in the middle of a set-up.

The man with the gun was young, but he wasn't nervous. He walked in past Helman and moved to the middle of the room. Helman saw his face matched the one on the employee photobadge he wore over the blazer breast pocket. He wondered if vampires could have their pictures captured on film. But the sun was still shining. He had nothing to worry about from the Conclave until sunset. Could the Jesuits be behind this butchery?

The man looked around. His badge said his name was McIlroy. "Windows all okay are they, Mr. Osgood?" he asked.

Helman rubbed the towel against the side of his head. Perhaps he wasn't being set up. Perhaps the hotel was keeping an eye on their peculiar guest who seemed to have broken his glass door from the outside in, the night before.

"No more trouble with ice, if that's what you mean Mr., ah MacKilroy?"

The security man corrected the pronunciation of his name. "That's Mackleroy. You have nightmares at four in the afternoon often, Mr. Osgood?" He was peering around the edges of the beds. Helman rubbed the towel a bit lower.

"Jet lag," he said. "Still haven't caught up." He tried to smile, but he was preparing himself to kill this boy who had a gun hidden beneath his gold jacket.

McIlroy looked straight at Helman. "Registration says you're from Buffalo. Not much of a time difference between here and Buffalo, is there?"

Helman knew the man wouldn't have had time to check the registration of the room between the time the maid called and he arrived. They *were* keeping a close watch on him.

"Just spent a month in Japan. Caught the flu or something. Feel pretty sick, actually," he said, returning McIlroy's stare.

McIlroy started to walk towards the door. "Want housekeeping to straighten out in here?" he asked.

Leave damn you, thought Helman. "No, I'm going to try to catch a few more hours, I think," he said.

"Okay with me." He was by the bathroom door. He noticed it was shut tight. "Mind if I use your bathroom, Mr. Osgood? Haven't had a break in a while."

"I'd rather you—" Helman began, but it was too late. McIlroy's hand was already on the doorknob, pushing the door open.

"Just a second," he said and walked in, closing the door behind him.

Helman frantically unwound the towel from his magnum. The door opened. McIlroy's face was wrinkled up in a bizarre expression. Helman lifted the gun behind the loosely hanging towel.

McIlroy waved his hand in front of his nose. "Whew, you really are sick, aren't you?" Helman's vomit was still in the sink. "I'd put the fan on in there for a while before you go in. It stinks to high heaven."

A split second from an irrevocable act, Helman's finger eased off the Magnum's trigger.

"You can get the house doctor by dialing the switchboard," McIlroy said. And then he was gone through the door and into the hallway.

Helman, his fingers trembling, clicked the door shut and fumbled with the chain.

He stumbled back from the tiny hallway. This time he stayed away from the beds and collapsed in an upholstered chair in the corner by the window farthest from the bed with the body stuffed under it.

He sat there a long time, watching the long shadows of sunset move against the fake grasscloth-covered walls. He held his gun loosely in his hand. Slowly the sun disappeared. Slowly his trembling subsided. He didn't think he had too many of those close calls left in him. Someday soon he felt that he might just start shooting. And shooting.

But for now, he was calming. He sat without thinking.

The sun set.

The phone rang.

This is their time, he thought.

He answered the phone. He recognized the voice.

It was deep, sibilant, and this time it suggested a trade: "a head for a head, Mr. Helman."

This was their time.

Seven

As the sun sank near the horizon, bringing on the lifegiving night, Adrienne St. Clair slowly awoke in her sanctuary. She knew the time instinctively. A few more minutes and the killing radiation of the sun would be safely hidden behind the curve of the earth and she could arise.

Years before, she and Jeffery had worked to determine just what it was about the sun that was deadly for their kind, and how they could be aware of its presence in the skies above, even though they slept in deep basements or caverns. That had been in the good times, when they both were accepted by the Conclave and the community of *yber*. Lord Diego had been their friend. He had even cooperated with them.

His familiars had provided a yacht, and he and they had voyaged off around the world. They had been deliriously happy months. She and her love had walked the beaches of far-off islands, watching the moon sparkle on the crashing crests of waves. They had walked through the brilliantly lit night streets of giant cities in many lands where Diego had had business to conduct with local *yber*. And through it all they had been together. Secure in their love as no humans could be. Because the islands would inevitably sink beneath the seas; the cities would crumble or be torn down and rebuilt until they were unrecognizable; and even, she had heard, the moon would slowly move away from the earth and millennia from now would be no more than a bright star; but she and Jeffery would still be together, walking new beaches, seeing undreamt-of cities, and still they would be in love.

In those days, she did not dwell on the horror of her Communion, nor the nightmare of her first months of night scavenging. Her new life started with Jeffery in Geneva. And until the night they had come and taken him away from her, she had not regretted what her life, and her First Death, had brought.

The voyage aboard Diego's yacht had been a whirlwind of discovery. At first they had thought that the *yber* response to the sun was like a circadian rhythm, the inner time sense that enabled plants to open and close in response to the days, and zoo animals to know when their feeding time was approaching. Such rhythms were thrown into confusion by time zone changes, yet on the voyage, all the *yber* present responded exactly to the setting of the sun, no matter how their time sense had slipped because of the journey.

When, at last, they had returned to Spain and the lands and villas Diego shared with them, she and Jeffery had tried an experiment that both were surprised had not been tried before. Diego had told them why it had not been attempted, or if it had, why the results were not generally known. The Conclave said that since the *yber* were of the Devil, and the Devil had more power in the absence of light, thus the *yber* responded to the night through the supernatural influence of Hell. The *yber* had their answer for the phenomena, there was no need to look further.

The two of them, with an entourage of familiars, had traveled to France and a deep system of caverns. There they had attempted to free themselves from the constraints of sunset and sunrise, and they had succeeded. It was difficult at first, a growing weariness enveloped them as the earth turned toward the sun. And an hour or so after the sun had risen above on the surface, a crushing torpor would seize them and they would collapse into sleep. But after a week of trying, they seemed to have broken the old habits. They could stay awake and function though the sun blazed away outside the caverns. A new dimension had been added to the lives of the *yber*. Even Diego was pleased, though it took a long cautious time before he broached their accomplishment to the other members of the Conclave.

Soon, though, it had become a standard practice throughout the world of *yber*. In Zurich, she knew, whole offices had been built without windows and special light locks were constructed around entry ways. The *yber* who controlled the amassed fortune of generations of investment and accumulation were now able to work during the same hours as the bankers who arranged for the transfer of funds. Fewer humans had to be brought into the suspicious conditions of dealing only at night with pale men who spoke in dry whispers. The *yber* became wealthier, and more secure, because of Adrienne's and Jeffery's work. But the Conclave was concerned about how they would go.

Eventually, she and Jeffery applied themselves only to the analysis of their special talents. Their villa became filled with equipment of science. They requested permission to enlist doctors as familiars. The Conclave turned them down without debate or explanation. Diego came under censure for allowing such activity in his domain.

Then they had taken the risk which had brought their ruin. Despite the Conclave's ruling, they had enlisted scientists. It was impossible to keep that knowledge from the Lords of the Conclave. Diego was furious. He had their equipment destroyed, their new familiars vanished during the day. Diego said he was trying everything he could to keep the Conclave from sentencing them to the Final Death. He wanted them to leave his domain.

Adrienne and Jeffery made up their minds. They were on the brink of miraculous revelations. They knew even more of the changes that occurred in an *yber* body; they had x-rays of their new internal configuration. They were sure the *yber* responded to the sun's disruption of the ionosphere, the same daily phenomenon that altered the transmission of radio waves. And most importantly they were succeeding in breaking down the *yber* nutritive needs. There might soon come a day when the *yber* would no longer require the living blood of humans for survival. With that discovery would come the night that the age-old conflict between hunter and prey could finally end. On that night they could come out of their centuries of hiding and take their place beside the humans from which they had so long ago arisen.

With this knowledge, they approached other *yber*. Word of their heresy spread quickly. Within a week the Conclave had reacted, and in one terrible night, Jeffery was taken from her and bound to the rock to wither before the rising sun. From that moment on, Adrienne was hunted. By the emissaries of the Conclave, and, as all *yber* were, by the Jesuits.

One by one her familiars were sought out and destroyed. She learned that Lord Diego himself, his position precarious because he had originally supported their work, was leading the hunt himself.

Adrienne knew she could not elude him for long. Knowledge of the Ways was imparted in special ceremonies. Most occurred in the first year after Communion, but other ceremonies still remained to come as the new *yber* matured; ceremonies which took place at fifty-year intervals. Adrienne had not experienced even one of those advanced rituals of knowledge. Diego had been through eight.

He had the abilities to track her down no matter where she ran. It was just a matter of time.

So Adrienne set her course. She could not let Jeffery's and her own, inevitable Final Death, be meaningless. She had to find someone to whom she could impart her knowledge. She had to find someone who would help her, in the time that remained, finally perfect the substitute for human blood. Once that was accomplished, she would arrange for the formula to be given to other familiars and *yber*. Perhaps even to the Jesuits who could no longer accuse the *yber* of being blood-drinking monsters. Even if Diego destroyed her and her work utterly, he could not destroy the knowledge she would spread. It would grow through the world of the *yber*. Despite all the Conclave's efforts, their years of rule would be at an end. Even in her Final Death, she would be victorious over them all. And in her victory, she would once again be with Jeffery. Once again their love would be eternal.

All hope rested on Granger Helman.

And that hope gnawed within her as she sensed the sun had vanished and she opened the lid of her sanctuary.

Granger Helman should be her enemy. He had killed the one human she had found who was capable of helping her. There was another she had been in contact with in Chicago, but she felt uneasy about him. He seemed too eager, too accepting of her condition, almost as if someone had prepared him for her contact. And there was the woman in Washington. The woman who was so transparently trying to recruit Adrienne into a research project so she could be turned over to the American government.

Adrienne could not go to Washington, but there would come a time when other *yber* would. There was a debt to be paid for tens of thousands of murders over thousands of years. Someday the *yber* would work with humans, she was certain. As soon as the humans were no longer a source of food, there could be a joining of the two people. *Yber* could work in the oceans, even in space. Wherever conditions might be too dangerous for humans, *yber* could survive. The debt was there, and Adrienne would see to it that it could be repaid. But first she must arrange for her survival, and that meant trusting herself to a peculiar human. One who had tried to kill her, yet was now, somehow, committed to her. She couldn't quite understand it. Maybe she had been too long in the company of humans who were chosen to be familiars. Helman was different.

He had reached out for her, the night before, she was sure, to offer comfort when she had told him without planning to, of Jeffery. He had accepted her, as Jeffery had, despite the fact that to him she must appear a soulless creature. "From beyond the grave" was the phrase from the books. Somehow, he had stepped past the strangeness of her condition and her circumstances, and accepted *her*, as one like himself: another human, despite her disease; or as a woman.

She stopped thinking about him. It didn't matter at this point *what* she thought of him, or what he thought of her. She was his only chance at keeping his sister and nephews free of the Conclave. As long as they believed the story she had told him to tell and considered her dead, she and Helman had a chance at life. And he was her *only* chance to survive the last journey she had to take; the unthinkable journey to an ultimate sanctuary that so few *yber* had attempted before because the price of discovery and failure was too great. But if she did survive, not even the Conclave would dare touch her. There were some things of the *yber* that were even greater than the Conclave. Or so she hoped.

Her sanctuary this day had been in the musty basement of a church not far from Chris Leung's townhouse. She had taken time to scout out the locations of additional resting places the first evening she had gone to the lab with Chris. While he had prepared a series of cultures, she had wandered the streets of Toronto, looking for what she knew every large city had, the church whose doors were always open to receive those who wished to pray.

Adrienne had not been strongly religious in her first life. She had been brought up in the Church of England, but it was not a demanding faith, and the lessons had not burned into her the way she knew they had in others raised in other faiths. As a result, unlike most of the specially chosen familiars who later became *yber* the supernatural teachings of the Conclave had not affected her. She could handle crosses and enter churches without effect. She had seen the effects that Holy articles had had on other *yber*: the burns and blisters and horrible disfigurements that would never heal. She surmised it was a psychosomatic reaction to the teaching of the Ways. She was convinced that some sort of psychic or telekinetic ability was awakened in the mind upon contracting the disease of the *yber*. This talent, which for the most part, worked with the incredibly rapid metabolism to repair wounds within minutes, sometimes seconds, was also responsible for the self-infliction of wounds caused by artifacts with religious significance. Regardless of the actual mechanism, she did not believe and she was not affected. The church she had not believed in in her first life therefore became her literal salvation in her second life. No member of the Conclave whom she knew of would risk entering consecrated ground.

The old steamer trunk she had lain in throughout the day was almost buried with other storage chests in a dark corner of the basement. She refilled it with the items she had removed to make room for herself: mostly old records and hymn books, and two rotting choir gowns looking as if wine had spilled on them ages ago.

She could sense that there were no humans in the basement. Jeffery and she had never been able to establish a basis for that talent, except to consider it a low grade form of telepathy similar to what some otherwise ordinary humans exhibited.

She made her way up the staircase leading to the vestry off the main entrance. It was being used as a coat room for those attending community functions as well as for storing the church's collection of robes.

Adrienne found a woman's coat which did not look too ungainly on her, too obviously not hers. She walked out the door, using the coat to hide her tattered clothing.

She was halfway down the stairs out front when she felt someone approaching her rapidly from inside. She began to rush down the stairs. Then she heard footsteps. A man's voice called, "Ruth, wait a minute."

She turned to face him. He blinked at the paleness and harsh expression of her face.

"Oh, sorry," he stammered. "I thought you were someone else. Same sort of coat, I guess." He smiled nervously and went inside. Adrienne walked quickly around a corner and sped away. She was gone by the time Ruth and her friend had discovered that her coat had been stolen.

Adrienne's first priority was to get money. She needed

some new clothes and some make-up. She would attract too much attention if she left her face in its natural, colorless state. She and Helman would have to pass through the American border tonight. She would have to appear as inconspicuous as possible.

Getting money was simple. A hotel was coming up on her right as she walked the icy sidewalk. It looked modern and new. Several Cadillacs and Mercedes were parked illegally in the front driveway under the watchful eye of a well-tipped doorman. She needed an expensive hotel, and she had found one.

She avoided the main entrance and the doorman by going through a side entrance which led down into a row of shops. She followed the corridor to a flight of escalators leading up to the main lobby.

Adrienne paused in front of the backlit directory showing a man and a woman seated at a table surrounded by smiling waiters bearing overloaded plates. Most of the restaurants seemed to be located on the floor above the lobby level. She rode the escalators up. She noticed a few humans staring at her when they thought she would not be aware of them. Some of them thought she had just had a terrible shock. Adrienne didn't care. She just hoped that none of the watchers were employees of the hotel who might think she needed help. Or who thought she was not the type of person they wanted here. It could be dangerous.

The floor above the lobby was milling with men and women in dress suits and gowns. Some type of gathering was taking place, perhaps a convention dinner. Adrienne made her way to the woman's washroom. A washroom in an expensive restaurant would have been better, but it was difficult to get by the staff. Hotels were far easier to get into.

The washroom was without an attendant. Adrienne busied herself by a sink. She had washed her hands five times before the conditions were right.

The washroom was empty. Then one woman walked in. Her coat had been checked earlier and she wore only a sleeveless dress. She looked at Adrienne, a bit apprehensive at her strange, pale appearance, but then moved straight for the nearest toilet stall.

Then, before anyone else came in, Adrienne was on her instantly. Her hand flew to the base of the woman's skull, thumb and forefinger digging savagely into the pressure points of either side of the spine. The woman stiffened, throwing her head back and gasping in surprise. Adrienne's knuckles descended crushingly on the side of her head. The woman went limp.

Adrienne lifted her effortlessly and put her into the stall. She lifted the woman's purse from where it had fallen on the floor. It was a silver lamé evening bag. Adrienne couldn't be seen walking out with it. It didn't suit her stolen coat and it was too big to slip into her pocket.

She heard the outer door swing open. She dropped the purse on the unconscious woman's lap and backed out of the stall, shutting the door. The inner door opened and another woman walked in. Adrienne ducked her head and went back to the sink. The unconscious woman's stall door swung open, unlocked. The other woman walked over to another stall, deliberately not looking through the open door. When Adrienne heard the other woman's door lock she rushed back to the open stall, opened the bag and jammed the change purse and a wad of papers into her coat pocket. She ripped some toilet paper out of the dispenser, folded it into a small square and held it against the doorframe as she jammed the door shut. This time it held.

She was out of the hotel within a minute. There had been no cries of alarm.

She flagged a cab and asked to be taken to the Eaton Centre: a downtown shopping complex where the stores remained open evenings. Sitting in the back seat of the cab, she pulled out the change purse and checked its contents. If there had been no money inside, the cab driver would not wake up until tomorrow. But there was a twenty dollar bill and some smaller ones inside. Plus a card case with four charge cards and a driver's license. More than enough to get the items she required.

Her first purchase was a pen. Then she sat in another washroom for half an hour, practicing the signatures on the back of the charge cards.

An hour later, she had new clothes, a new coat, and her face looked like any human's. It was time to contact Helman.

Helman sat against the far wall in a dark corner of the bar off the lobby of his hotel. He tried not to think about what was going on in his hotel room. He had told his story to Mr. Rice, just as Adrienne had told him. Rice's voice was so peculiar that Helman was not able to determine by its tone if Rice believed him or not. Finally Rice had told Helman to leave his room so it could be "cleaned." Helman was free to go for now, but he must be prepared for immediate contact at any time in the future. Helman had the feeling that Rice was going to try to kill him that evening, but he had no choice but to wait for Adrienne to contact him. At least the bar was an open, public area. He should be safe from a direct attack as long as he stayed in it. And for afterward, he had already equipped himself. The gift shop in the corner of the lobby had had a selection of religious items. Helman had a cross in each pocket of his coat, one with a figure of Jesus on it, the other unadorned. He wore a small crucifix around his neck. He felt like a fool doing it, and he still felt afraid. Despite what the woman had told him, he had no real conception of the power of the Conclave. The image that he did have was rooted in the knowledge of such things that had come from the depths of his childhood. Part of him felt he was living out a nightmare. But the reality of his fear was that each time he had gone to the pay phone by the bar counter this night, his sister's number in New Hampshire had rung and had not been answered. He hoped it was Weston who had reached her first. He didn't want to consider the other possibility. He hoped his story had restrained them.

Rice had wanted the head of Adrienne St. Clair.

Helman had shut his eyes, and said he didn't have it.

"I saw the lab, assassin. Was she not in it?"

"I think so. I saw her go in. But after I went in, after the explosion, I think she got away."

"Did you see her? Did she see you?"

"I didn't see anything. Except for her clothes, I think they were hers."

"Her clothes, assassin?" Rice's breathing had picked up at that. For the first time in the conversation, Helman had felt he had a chance of getting away with it.

"Yes, her clothes. I don't understand it. They were lying in a spread-out heap by a desk that was smashed in the explosion."

"What condition were they in?"

"Odd. There was a big rod of steel, from one of the equipment stands, stuck through them all, and they were all oily or greasy or something. Covered in something odd."

"Was it blood, assassin?"

"No, it wasn't blood. It was white. Sort of like a jelly. I don't know what happened. Maybe it was some type of flammable substance they kept around in the lab and the explosion sprayed it on her. There were a bunch of small fires. Maybe she got out of her clothes because she was afraid it would ignite. But I don't know where she could have gone without clothes. It was cold last night."

"I'm sure it was, assassin. On such a cold night, why did you not immediately return to your hotel room?"

"I was being cautious. The police, or whoever they were, responded to the explosion a lot faster than the fire department was able to. Almost as if they had her under surveillance to begin with. Maybe connected with that fellow who came after me with a gun the other day." Helman now knew that the man had been Cook, an agent of Weston's.

"Quite possibly, assassin. Quite possibly. The woman is very resourceful. She may have had contingency arrangements. I suggest you return to your home, to New Hampshire. We shall contact you when we have located the woman again. Be prepared to act immediately or there will be the most serious repercussions. Do you understand, assassin?''

Helman understood. And he was quite sure he understood what was going through Rice's mind. Adrienne St. Clair had been impaled by the flying steel rod Helman had described sticking through her clothing. Her body had dissolved, just as the body of that long-ago *yber* had dissolved, when the tank shell had exploded against a wall of stone, sending wicked shards in all directions, including the direction of his heart.

Helman trembled slightly as he reviewed the conversation again. Perhaps he had gotten away with it. But if Rice and the Conclave believed he had completed the contract, what were they planning for him now? Death in Toronto? Were they waiting for him to return to the States so they could get his sister and Steven and Campbell all at the same time? Adrienne would know. He agonized in the wait for her.

At eight o'clock, the time Rice had told him, he left the bar and returned to the room. The familiars, he supposed, had done their job. He was right. The room was spotless. Nothing lurked in the bathroom, nothing hid under any of the furniture. It struck Helman just as he had gotten out of the elevator on his floor that he might be stepping into a trap; Rice might have phoned the police and had them lie in wait for the brutal murderer who kept a headless body in his hotel room. But he reconsidered. That was too messy a way to deal with him. Whichever way the Conclave chose, it would just involve him and them. And there would be no chance to tell his story.

Helman was not sure what to do next. There were no messages for him at the desk or the switchboard. Had they captured her? Killed her already? Why hadn't she contacted him?

He jerked around when he heard the tapping on the glass. He pulled back on the closed curtains and the face of Adrienne St. Clair looked back through the window. His new room was on the eighteen floor. And there were no balconies, no ledges. Yet she was outside his window.

She motioned to him to open the window. It was an older hotel and the windows were the kind that still slid. She poured through the window like a snake. The image disturbed him.

"I thought I'd let you save the window this time," she said. She brushed at white streaks of dust which lined the dark quilted jacket she wore.

"How did you get up here? Where have you been?" Helman had too many questions to ask all at once.

She looked up from her brushing. "*Yber* muscles are very efficient. Anywhere there's a small crack or space between bricks, we can support ourselves with just our fingers and toes. Now you tell me what's been going on in here. I watched them clean out a body. They looked to be familiars."

Helman told her about what he had found in the bathroom. He repeated the conversation he had had with Rice.

"And you feel sure he believed you?" she asked.

"Fairly sure. It's hard to tell. In any case he's given me permission to leave Toronto. It will be at least twenty-four hours before he misses me back where I'm supposed to be."

"Your sister's farm, you mean?"

"Yes. Now where do we have to go? You said be prepared to travel."

St. Clair looked worried. "You mean you don't want to go check on your sister?"

Helman saw the trap he had set for himself. He couldn't say so, but he was leaving his sister in the hands of Weston and his men. If he returned, it might compromise their position. And besides, he couldn't undertake any action that might deter Adrienne from her plans. Knowledge of her plans was what Weston was demanding as payment for protecting Miriam and the boys. He lied his way out of it as best he could.

"I talked with her this morning. She hasn't seen anything unusual. The boys are fine. What advantage would the

Conclave have by killing them now that Rice has released me from my contract?''

Adrienne thought of Lord Diego. He led the hunt for her. It was undoubtedly he who headed the manipulation of Helman. He must succeed to restore his standing in the Conclave.

''I know the *yber* who is directing King and Rice and the group in New York. His name is Diego. Lord Eduardo Diego y Rey. It is a personal thing between us, and Diego is quite fanatical when it comes to dealing with his enemies. You are his enemy now, Granger. He won't just stop at destroying you. He'll destroy whatever you hold dearest, too. He'll destroy your family. And Granger,'' this time *she* reached out her hand to touch him, ''almost all of his familiars began with him as children. He loves children. He says their blood is far sweeter than adults'.''

She felt the tenseness sweep through him like a roaring wave. His face paled. But he couldn't speak to her about Weston.

''I don't believe he'll consider me an enemy,'' Helman said. ''They're going to have to check to see if you really did escape. You could have left your clothes with the steel rod as I described in an attempt to fool us all. If I were them, I'd check on that, I'd keep the human assassin in reserve in case we need him again.'' His head was pounding. Their blood is far sweeter. Dear God, he felt sick. ''I can serve my family best, save them perhaps, by helping you. You said prepare to travel. I hope that means you have some sort of plan because I don't know what to do.'' Far sweeter, he thought, far sweeter.

Adrienne saw Helman was close to tears. She drew near to him, looking up at him. ''They'll be fine, Granger. You're right. Diego won't do a thing until he is certain I'm dead or alive. As long as I stay hidden, they'll all be fine.''

She held him, feeling awkward. Not sure how hard she should squeeze a human. Not sure if it was the right thing to do to calm him. But he had been through so much. So much that was not part of the world he knew. She held him, but she could tell his mind was spinning. He didn't seem to know she was there.

"Granger, did you find out about the bodyguards? The men you said were fighting the Jesuits. Did you learn anything more about them?"

In his confusion, the desire to survive still struggled to remain clear. He must lie to her. He must not tell about Weston. He must lie.

"I caught up with one of them. I questioned him. Rice confirmed his answers. He seemed amused. The Conclave hired other assassins for you. He wouldn't tell me how many. I kept running into them wherever you went." He realized she had wrapped her arms around him. For a moment he accepted it, like closing his eyes for the last ten seconds before the alarm goes off, pretending it will never ring and disturb him. But then the situation won out and he pulled back from her. She released him immediately, embarrassed. She didn't know what thoughts were going through him. Or her. Images of Jeffery came to her.

"Why would they fight back at the Jesuits?"

Helman lied well. "The one I questioned today said he was worried the Jesuits would capture you. He said he had to keep that from happening so he would be able to get at you himself. Decapitate you."

Something in his story, or his answer, didn't ring true to her. But for now she had to accept whatever he said. He was the only one who could get her to the ultimate sanctuary. Perhaps it was the pressure he was under, the tension she had felt in him as she had held him. That was it. Nothing more.

"You do have a plan, don't you?" he asked.

There was almost desperation in his voice. What human had had to face the Conclave before? And lasted this long? She felt sorry for him. He was caught up in things he might never understand. But he was so important to their resolution, and willing to help her cause. At first, she was sure it was because she had put him under the pain of death. But now, she felt, there was something else driving him. She couldn't express it.

"Yes, Granger, I do have a plan." A plan of desperation, she thought. Few other *yber* had achieved it.

"We shall go to the Father for help," she said.

"*The* Father?" asked Helman. "An *yber* father? He'll be able to help us? He's had experience with this type of thing before?"

Adrienne nodded. She felt tenseness inside in a different way from the way the humans felt it; the way she had felt it in her first life. But still she felt it now, crawling through her like a ravaging beast, digging into every part of her. *Yber* had control over their bodies. They didn't tremble: But in her mind, she shook.

"He is the oldest living *yber*."

The question hung silent and unspoken between them.

"More than nine hundred years," she said. "He has experience in everything."

Eight

The girl was dying. In minutes, the stress created by the shock of blood loss would strain her young heart beyond its capacity. On his bed, Lord Diego lay beside her, watching in fascination.

The girl was no more than twelve, her pale, naked body just beginning to show signs of maturity; a maturity that would never come. Diego had consumed her; drawing from her her childhood, her womanhood, and her blood. Now he watched as her life itself passed from her body.

Within Diego was the power to bring her back. By

sharing the Communion of his blood she could be born again into the world of *yber*. He was the taker and the giver of life, and, using that power, he toyed with her.

Delicately he ran his razor-sharp talon across the vein of his wrist. White liquid, the blood of the *yber* welled out from the separated flesh. He gathered it on his outstretched finger like sap. In the time it took for his finger to be coated, the wound had healed without trace.

Diego dangled his finger over the face of the dying child. Her eyes had rolled back and the unseeing whites stared uselessly from her half-closed lids. Her mouth was open, parched from labored breathing. Into it Diego dripped the blood of life. The girl's reaction was instantaneous.

Her eyes clenched shut as the first shock of the substance burned its way into her. Her mouth stretched open like a fish struggling out of water, desperate for more of what her body somehow knew was its only chance at survival. Groans rose from her. Her body arched as though in passion. Diego moved his hand away from her, slowly twisting it back and forth to keep the white fluid from dripping off. He waited until the reaction diminished, the child once again slipping close to oblivion. Then he held his finger above her mouth again. The blood of the *yber* entered her. Her body convulsed, desperate for life.

She is so strong, he thought. The children were always the ones who would last the longest. He marveled at it. Once he had kept a boy child on the brink of extinction and rebirth for an entire evening. Eventually, he had relented and decided such hunger for life should be rewarded. He had bared his neck to the boy, to let him share in Communion. But it had been too late. The child had died his first and only death. Since then, Diego had never relented, all his children had but one destination once he had taken them to his bed. He held his finger back from the girl, wiping it clean on the blood-stained sheets. She shuddered once, and was still. Her destination had been reached.

Diego pushed her useless body from the bed. It lay upon the floor like a broken doll. In the daytime, his familiars would remove it. The human who had provided her for the honored guest of the Eastern Meeting would demand more payment, no doubt. The girl would not be returned in usable condition. But the Conclave had more than enough wealth to reimburse him a billion times over, if they chose. Perhaps this close to the fruition of their Final Plan, they could simply dispose of him as well. Soon the order would be changed, and Diego could have whomever he wanted, whenever he chose. The feeling that thought gave him was good. Almost as good as the feeling of the child's blood in what now served as his belly.

He liked the feeling. He had spent his first two hundred years as an *yber* sleeping in rotting coffins and mausoleums. Each dawn he had passed into dreamless unconsciousness fearing the stake and the ax. Too many times he had returned to his sanctuary to find the accursed priests and the burning garlic blocking his way. But he had survived. Two hundred years of living like an animal, and he had survived.

The next two hundred years had been far better. He had met others. Not just others of his kind, but others like him. *Yber* who had not lost their sanity in nights of hunting and being hunted. *Yber* who had not totally turned themselves into the demons of Hell most believed they were. Some *yber* had maintained their intellect. With them he had formed the Conclave and struck back at the maddening Society of Jesus.

Soon there had been wealth and property. Dry, secure sanctuaries to spend the long days in safety. Travel and gatherings at night. And familiars. Always there were familiars. *Yber* no longer had had to hunt for survival. There were always enough humans who would give themselves willingly—for a chance at Communion and the immortality it promised. And if the nights were too easy, the humans always had wars. The homelands, Korea, Vietnam. Today Africa and South America both offered the opportunity of the hunt, the drinking of fear-charged blood. The savaged bodies, drained of blood, were never questioned. The *yber* roamed free. And soon they would be freer still. The Final

Plan was almost complete. Only Adrienne St. Clair had the power to alter its inevitable outcome. But she could not last long against him.

Diego stretched out on the bed like a cat. The girl's blood was being metabolized within him, restoring him. He felt at peace.

In a sense, he supposed he should be thankful to the woman. He had felt attracted to her when she had been presented to him for the first time in Geneva at the end of the last war in the homelands. At the time she had been with Jeffery, and Diego had kept his feelings to himself. He had lived for four hundred years and knew that nothing remained the same. Despite their love for each other, Diego could see that within a century at most, Jeffery and Adrienne would drive themselves apart. And then, Diego had thought, I will have her. Immortality tended to make the *yber* very patient.

To keep her near, he had vouched for her during the time of the slaying of the Unbidden. He had offered her and her mentor the use of his Spanish villa. He had supported their initial investigations into the nature of *yber*. Those investigations had made possible the Final Plan the Conclave was now embarked on. Those investigations had also threatened the Conclave's existence.

To himself only, Diego thought Adrienne was right. Whatever explanation there was for the existence of the *yber*, it lay in observable, understandable nature, not within the fire and brimstone of the Pit. But the Conclave ruled by fire and brimstone. The *yber* were content with their place within the supernatural realm the Conclave had created for them. The only disadvantage was dealing with the Jesuits, who also ruled themselves with knowledge of Hell. Some things of the human world Diego would miss when the order changed. But he would not miss the Jesuits. He would see to it that they were among the first to be consumed. He liked the feeling that thought gave him, too. He sprawled upon the bed for a long time, thinking thoughts about the coming destruction of the humans. The centuries of struggle would soon bear fruit. Beside him on the floor, the body of the girl was unmoving.

Eventually, Diego sensed the presence of another *yber* beyond the bedroom door. There was no knock. There didn't have to be.

"Come," he said aloud.

Mr. King entered, still in the make-up and clothing of his human disguise. His refined *yber* senses told him immediately that the child on the floor was dead; he completely ignored her. He did not feel jealous over this display of Diego's privileges. He preferred his prey older.

"We have received a message from Toronto," he said.

"She is dead?" Diego asked.

"It appears so, but Rice says the conditions are such that we cannot be sure."

Diego sat up on the bed. Dried blood had crusted on the corners of his mouth. "Explain," he said.

King told the story Helman had told Rice.

"So," he concluded, "either she was impaled by debris in the explosion and her body dissolved or, she simply left that pile of clothing as an attempt to deceive us."

"What is *your* conclusion, Mr. King?"

"In the confusion of the explosion, I don't believe she would have had time to create so elaborate a ruse, especially down to the detail of leaving a thick white fluid intermingled with the remains of her clothing. I believe she has been dissolved. The threat is ended. The human may be killed."

Diego ran his fingers around his mouth, removing the caked blood. "I agree with you, Mr. King. She wouldn't have enough time to prepare her clothes in that manner. But there is a third possibility."

"Which is?"

"She and the human may be working together."

"Impossible!"

"Don't be so quick, Mr. King. Do you know how the woman came by her Communion?"

"She was one of the Unbidden during the second major war in the homelands."

"Do you know what happened to her original mentor?"

"I have not heard the full story."

"He was dissolved by debris in an explosion exactly at the moment of transition from the first life to the second. Apparently the woman was literally drenched in the blood of life. It was enough for her to survive Communion."

King understood immediately. "Dissolved in the debris from an explosion," he repeated.

"Precisely, Mr. King. It's too convenient a story the second time around. She would not have had time to prepare her clothes, but she would have time to tell the human the story so he would tell us."

"But why would she work with the human who tried to kill her?"

"He is, it would seem, quite resourceful. She has no familiars, no contacts in North America. I think she has made a wise decision."

"If your conclusion is true, my Lord, what are we to do?"

"We are to win, Mr. King. We are to win."

King stayed silent. He knew better than to question a Lord of the Conclave.

"Of first importance," Diego continued, "is keeping the woman from contacting Washington—"

"You believe the claims of the Jesuit?"

"That the woman and Washington are somehow conspiring to enter into some form of alliance, yes. About Armageddon and all the other nonsense the Jesuits are fond of spouting, no. Our second goal, of course, is to kill her. Whom do we have in California?"

"Matheson, my Lord. But why California?"

"The woman is young, Mr. King. Still predictable. She has run out of options. She knows, despite her assassin human, that it is just a matter of time before the Conclave prevails. Her Final Death cannot be far away. In such a position, what would *you* do?"

King paused a moment. He could think of nothing.

"Pretend to repent," he offered, weakly. "Give myself to the Jesuits in return for forgiveness and sanctuary."

"Not even the Jesuits are so stupid, Mr. King. Where in the world is there a place safe from the influence of the Conclave?"

King had no reply.

"You have heard of the birthplace, have you not?"

"Nacimiento?"

Diego smiled, his fangs brilliantly white, devastatingly sharp. "Nacimiento," he agreed. "The fortress of the Father. Alone among all *yber*, he is free of the Conclave."

King was shaken. He had never thought of the Father as a possible refuge for the woman because it was unthinkable. The woman would not live a single night if she dared to intrude upon the Father's domain. Likewise, the Conclave could not survive the dissension if Diego advised the *yber* to move against him. He was the Father, Mentor to hundreds who still lived as *yber*. It was impossible.

"Surely, my Lord, you must—"

Diego spat at King. "Watch your tongue or you may be watching the next sunrise."

King checked his comment. He wouldn't risk it.

Diego resumed in a more natural, for *yber*, voice.

"Does Rice have watchers at all the points of exit for Toronto?"

"Yes, my Lord."

"You will tell him to remove them."

"Should we not maintain our watch on the human?"

"Why? If he returns to his sister, we shall have him. If he travels with the woman to Nacimiento, again we shall have him. He has only two destinations. We shall be at each, yes?"

"Yes, my Lord."

"You will contact Matheson in California. In the end the woman *will* arrive there. Rice must do nothing to prevent it. We dare not risk another failed operation. It will take her at least two nights of travel to arrive. We will be prepared for her this time. And this time, I will be there to deal with her myself.''

''Yes, my Lord.''

''When you have reached Matheson, put him through to me in the meeting room. Then you will travel to New Hampshire. West Heparton, I believe you called it.''

The human assassin was to be punished, King thought. ''The sister, my Lord?''

Diego nodded. ''And the children, Mr. King. After you have killed the sister, bring the children to me. I wish this human to see what happens to those who defy the Conclave.''

''Yes, my Lord.''

''And take this thing with you as you leave.'' Diego waved his claws at the crumpled form of the girl beside the bed.

King stooped to pick her up. Her body sprawled lightly in his arms. He would take her to the furnace like the others.

Diego watched him leave impassively. Already his mind had moved on to the nights ahead. How perfectly events were transpiring. The woman and her human would run straight to the only protection she believed still existed for her. And it would be Diego's trap. What's more, in that trap, the Father could finally be given the Final Death. Not out of revenge or maliciousness, but as a signal to the rest of the *yber* that the old times were coming to an end. The order would be reversed. And when it was, so would the Conclave change. In a world where humans were in the total control of the *yber*, a world after the Final Plan had taken hold, there would be much more to be gained by standing against the old ways of the Conclave. Diego planned to gain it all.

But first there would be the last battle at the birthplace. The woman would die, the last hope of the humans would die, and of course the human who had caused all of this trouble would die, after he had seen his beloved sister's children taken to the bed of Diego and consumed.

He left the bedroom and walked naked to the meeting room. He must arrange the conditions with Matheson. And he must send another message to the Jesuits. Not only could the *yber* rid themselves of many of the priests there, but the blame for the Father's death could be placed on them, too. Yes, it was all arranging itself perfectly he thought. This victory will be sweet.

As sweet as the blood of the children.

PART THREE

THE CLOSING

One

To the others sitting in the departure lounge of Toronto's Pearson International Airport, Helman was nondescript and appeared somehow removed from his immediate physical surroundings. Daydreaming perhaps, even though it was near midnight; maybe just one of those people who was apprehensive of flying. But within himself, Helman raged.

The redeye flight to Vancouver was due to receive its passengers within minutes. There was still no sign of Adrienne.

They had split up outside a small church in Toronto's east end where one of Adrienne's sanctuaries had been. It was the one in which she had cached two flight bags and a small hard-sided suitcase. She said they contained her notes and the results of some of the work Dr. Leung had begun. Helman had checked the suitcase through to Vancouver on the all-night flight in his own name. He carried both of the flight bags. It was important that she not have any luggage, but she would not tell him why. She *had* told him, that, as a matter of course, whether or not Mr. Rice had believed Helman's story about finding her impaled clothes, he would have an *yber* standing by any port of exit from the city. So Helman had gone ahead of her, purchased the tickets—hers left behind to be picked up at the customer service desk—and taken care of the luggage. She had said that she would come aboard at the last minute. The less time she stayed in one place in the airport, the less chance that another *yber* would sense her and be able to stop her. Apparently she was not concerned if they sensed her and discovered which flight she was on. She was only worried that they might do something to try to stop her from boarding.

A flight attendant began calling out row numbers to begin the boarding procedure. People began milling about the exit of the departure lounge leading to the embarking tunnel. Still no sign of Adrienne.

Helman's section was called. He stayed seated, trying to control the anxiety he felt. If they got Adrienne, his sister would be next. And the children. He wondered if Weston had gotten his agents to them in time. He wondered if they would do any good even if they arrived in time. Adrienne *had* to make it.

The last of the passengers were leaving the lounge. A flight attendant walked up to him.

"Excuse me, sir, are you—"

There was the sound of running in the corridor. Helman wheeled around in his chair. It was Adrienne, moving rapidly. He looked past her. His hand moved uselessly to where his shoulder holster would normally be. He had not had any way to bring his weapons past the metal detectors and the x-ray machine of the security checkpoints. Adrienne was running and he was defenseless.

She stopped in front of the check-in desk, holding her ticket before her. Helman watched the people beyond her in the corridor carefully. No one appeared to be following her.

"Excuse me, sir," the flight attendant began again. "If you're going to Vancouver, all passengers must board now." She saw Helman was watching the running woman check in. "Oh, I'm sorry," she said. "Were you waiting for her?"

Helman shook his head. "No. Don't know her. Must have been falling asleep I guess." He yawned convincingly, got up and went through the lounge exit. He could hear

Adrienne walking behind him. He slowed his pace to allow her to catch up in the tunnel. For a few moments they were alone in it; the flight attendants were checking paperwork back in the lounge.

"Did they pick you up?" he asked her in an urgent whisper.

"No," she said. After all the running, she was not out of breath. But she looked worried. "I didn't pick *them* up, either. It was as if they didn't have anyone watching the airport."

"If my story were believed, couldn't the watchers have been called off?"

They rounded the corner of the tunnel. Two flight attendants waited by the plane's hatchway.

"I don't think that's likely," she said in a pleasant, conversational tone.

"Why not?" he asked, equally jovial.

She gave him a quick glance, and smiled at the flight attendants as she showed her boarding pass to them.

They walked down one of the narrow aisles of the plane. Helman's seat was behind hers by several rows. She had said it was very important they not be connected to one another in anyone's eyes. Again she had refused to say why. Helman stopped behind another passenger who had opened the compartment above a seat and was filling it with flight bags and coats.

Adrienne moved closely behind Helman. He heard her whisper.

"The only reason they wouldn't be looking for me, for us, at the airport, is because they already know where we're going to be."

"Is that possible?" he whispered back.

"There aren't many options," she said.

The other passenger had sat down. Other people waited behind Helman. He moved on to his seat, confused and apprehensive.

What would be waiting for them in Vancouver?

Two

The children were sleeping.

Miriam sat up in her bedroom. A half-read book lay open on the night table. Granger's Remington lay beside her on the bed. For the past two days she had seen watchers in the woods behind her farmhouse and across the road. She had not let Steven and Campbell go to school. But Granger would be home soon and everything would be back to normal.

At least, she thought, the farmhouse is so rickety, no one could move through it without making the floorboards and the stairs creak up a storm.

The house was silent.

She watched in horror as her bedroom door swung open without a squeak of protest. It has to be a dream, she thought. And then they were on her so quickly she didn't even have a chance to scream.

The children did not sleep for long.

Three

Helman saw the whole, impossible thing, but denied it when the RCMP officers questioned the passengers on the plane. The officers were simply the security force for Vancouver International Airport. They had no knowledge of what had recently happened to their more highly placed colleagues in Toronto. They had no reason not to believe Helman's story. He was free to go with the other passengers an hour after the plane had landed. From the corridor windows he watched as the searchlights played across the tarmac, looking for the body. No one had believed the one passenger who had seen the woman run away. Helman had a hard time believing it himself. But he knew it had to be true.

The plane had been descending. Seatbelts were fastened and all the passengers, frightened or not, had been holding the seat arms just a little more tightly than usual as they waited for the first impact of the tires on the runway. All the passengers except one.

Adrienne St. Clair had gotten up from her seat moments before landing. She had held on to both her head and her stomach, as if sick and confused, and staggered down the aisle. Helman had heard the attendants shouting to her to return to her seat. Adrienne had continued.

Helman had slipped off his seatbelt and raised himself off his seat enough to turn his head and see what was going on. The senior flight attendant had unbuckled herself and gone after Adrienne. By this time, Adrienne was right where she wanted to be. The plane hit the runway with a jolt. Adrienne lashed out her arm and caught the unbalanced attendant across her midsection. The attendant went flying backward into the galley. Adrienne spun around to the emergency escape door and pulled and twisted on the large yellow handle. More attendants shouted.

Then the door popped open and Adrienne jumped out and hit the runway at one hundred and forty miles an hour.

She was safe.

Helman was impressed. Whatever was waiting for them in Vancouver had just been avoided by Adrienne. There did not appear to be anyone interested in him. Perhaps the *yber* watchers, if there had been any, had heard about the crazy woman on the Toronto flight who had committed suicide, realized what had happened, and were now scouring the areas beyond the runways.

Helman had not known what was going to happen. He continued on the way that they had planned. She had found him before in his Toronto hotel room. He had no doubt she would find him again.

The Ford LTD he had reserved from Toronto was waiting for him and he drove into the wet Vancouver night. Adrienne waved him down two miles from the airport. Before they drove on, she had him take the suitcase from the trunk of the car so she could put on new clothes. The ones she had worn in her jump from the plane were almost completely torn away by the force of the impact. Helman saw several dark ripples running along the pale skin that showed as she changed in the car. He asked her about them.

"That's the healing process," she explained. "Small wounds close up in seconds. If you can watch carefully, you may be able to see a thin dark line, almost as if a hair had been laid across the skin. More major wounds take a few minutes longer. Some can take hours, depending on the extent of the damage. The dark color is a type of antibody reaction we haven't been able to analyze yet."

Helman considered what Adrienne had said. Perhaps she would have an answer to his question.

"How can *yber* be so impervious to bullets and so fatally vulnerable to arrows or wooden stakes?"

Adrienne smiled. "Jeffery and I spent a considerable amount of time on that one, Granger. Essentially, despite the fact that there are so few outward manifestations of the changes from human to *yber*, inside the changes are extensive. What it comes down to is that *yber*, six months or so after Communion, experience a fusing of their internal organs. Instead of the dozens of specialized organs that humans have, each one prone to its own disorders, many capable of destroying the entire organism because of their own malfunction, *yber* possess a *generalized* organ. That's really about the only way I can think to describe it."

"*One* organ to do the work of all the others?"

"Essentially. It's like the brain. Certain areas of the brain, while they have no observable structural difference, serve as control centers for specialized functions. There's the speech center, sight center, tactile response, all of them with a more or less specific control point in the brain. But if one of those centers is damaged or destroyed, providing it's not one of the important ones that governs heartbeat or breathing, the organism is not destroyed. Almost every part of the brain has the capability of taking over control from any other part of the brain. Burn out the sight center of a chimpanzee. Leave the optical nerve structure intact so that the signals still can enter the brain, and within a few months you'll have a sighted chimpanzee back. It's the same way that stroke victims can recover. The brain tissue can't grow back, but as long as the signals can get to some area of the brain, there's a good chance that some form of recovery will take place as new areas take over."

"So if a bullet goes through the part of this generalized organ that is the center for, let's say the pancreas, some other part of the organ will begin the production of insulin?"

Adrienne nodded. "Other than the fact that *yber* don't produce and don't need insulin, that's the idea. And unlike the brain of a stroke victim, our generalized organ, which fills the chest and abdominal cavities, can regenerate itself.

Incredibly rapidly. Just like these.'' She held out one arm and rolled back the sleeve of her sweater. The dark ripples Helman had seen when she changed were little more than a light discoloration.

''So if that system makes you impervious to bullets, why doesn't it work on arrows and stakes?''

Adrienne rolled down her sleeve.

''Size is what it comes down to. *Yber* bodies are less dense than humans'. The tensile strength of the skin is less. Bullets, even the kind designed to mushroom on contact, don't meet much resistance when they pass through us. It's like throwing a stone through water. A stake or an arrow doesn't pass through the body as readily and instead of causing less than a cubic inch of internal displacement as a bullet does, it creates a permanent tunnel into the *yber* body that can't be instantly healed. The heart is one part of the *yber* body that is not absorbed into the generalized organ. There's only one. If a shaft of some sort impales it, stops its beating, our blood stops circulating, and our rapid metabolism almost instantly depletes our muscles of strength. We die. Same thing would happen if a powerful enough explosion hit us in the chest or if an enormous burst of bullets tore into our heart faster than the body could heal itself. Other than that, and barring massive destruction of the brain, *yber* are almost indestructible.''

''Makes it handy when you have to leave a plane in a hurry,'' he said.

They drove south on 99. With the change in time zones, there were still several hours of night remaining. They planned to be outside of Seattle by sunrise. At the very worst, if no sanctuary were available, Adrienne would be protected in the trunk of whatever car they stole to drive across the border. Helman could continue to drive through the day. If sanctuary were found, Helman could make arrangements for them to fly from Seattle to San Luis Obispo in California the next night. The Father's estate would be less than an hour's drive away.

Helman had many more questions, but for now he had to

concentrate on a plan for getting them into the United States without delay. He would not like to be sitting in a small, American customs interview room when the sun came up.

He drove toward the border.

The couple in White Rock, walking out of the restaurant into the parking lot, was perfect. They were middle-aged, obviously married, and moving as though they had had just a bit too much to drink. They were completely stunned when Adrienne stepped in front of them and told them that the man standing behind them had a gun. If they tried to run or scream, they were dead.

Helman closed in behind them. He held his hand menacingly in an empty coat pocket. He linked his arm with the woman's. Adrienne took the man's.

Helman smiled as he walked. "Just look straight ahead and keep walking to the blue LTD over there. Nothing bad is going to happen. We won't hurt you. Won't take any jewels or cash. Just need your car. Keep walking."

The man had rehearsed a hundred times what he would do if his wife and he were threatened in just this way, and all his plans evaporated. The shock of actually being in that situation made him incapable of doing anything except following the reasonable suggestions made by the reassuring voice of the man with the gun. Maybe it won't be so bad he kept telling himself.

Helman could tell what was going through the man's mind. He didn't tell the man how many people had gone quietly to their deaths thinking just those thoughts. He was just pleased that the man hadn't tried anything to cause a scene. It would have been unpleasant for everyone.

Helman got into the back seat of the LTD with the wife; Adrienne in the front with the husband. If the husband should try anything now, Adrienne could drop him instantly. Helman, however, was sure he would stay calm because of the threatening position his wife was apparently in. For people not used to it, violence was rarely necessary. The implied threat of violence, usually more vicious in their imagination than in reality, was generally all that was needed to keep those people in line. The type of people Helman hated dealing with were the type who thought they understood violence. By thinking they understood it, they somehow couldn't believe it could actually happen to them. That idea had given several people the incentive to attack Helman in similar situations. Helman was an expert. He had taught some painful lessons.

But this couple was cooperating. Both Helman and Adrienne were relieved.

Constantly reassured, the couple handed over their identification, car registration, insurance forms, keys, and even offered their cash. Helman turned it down. He still had more than $3000 left from the cash Rice had given him in Toronto. It could be easily exchanged for American cash in Seattle. And he still had the charge cards of his Osgood identity.

The LTD was angled away from the parking lot lights and not visible from any of the restaurant's windows. Helman slipped out of the back seat and opened the trunk of the car. He asked the man to follow him. Helman assisted him into the trunk. Then Adrienne brought the woman.

"Stay close because it's cold," Helman said. "And don't bother screaming because the lot is almost deserted and no one can hear you. When we get to Vancouver," he lied, "we'll call the police and they'll come and get you. We'll take good care of your car and leave it in a parking lot where they'll be sure to find it. All right?"

The man nodded. Fear was in his eyes and Helman knew what he must feel like being crammed in a trunk with his wife, completely out of control. Helman reached down to the edge of the trunk and ripped out the two wires leading to the trunk courtesy light switch. He twisted the bare ends together.

"The light will stay on when I shut the lid." He looked into the man's eyes. "Sir, I have a gun and I was ready to use it. You did exactly what you should have done. If you had done anything else, you both would be dead. There's nothing to be ashamed of. Do you understand?"

The man nodded.

Helman lowered the trunk lid.

"Stay close. The police will be here within an hour."

The trunk clicked shut. Adrienne and Helman walked quickly to the car the man had pointed out as being his; a white Buick Riviera from the days before downsizing. It started on the second try and they were at the border within twenty minutes. Within thirty minutes they were at an American service stop calling the White Rock police about a couple locked in the trunk of a car. Helman knew that by the time the police had gotten the story out of the couple and the Vancouver police had decided that the Riviera wasn't going to be found and perhaps the Washington State Police should be notified, two days of bureaucracy would have passed and the car would be long abandoned.

By the time the sun rose, they had checked into a small hotel north of Seattle and Adrienne was being protected from the light in a well-sealed, windowless bathroom.

As she stretched out on the mattress they had dragged into the bathroom for her, she looked up at him with a puzzled expression.

"I know it sounds odd, but you were very considerate with that couple in the parking lot," she said.

"None of this is their concern. They were in the wrong place, wrong time. Probably scared to death. The poor guy's going to feel worthless enough about not trying to fight for his wife. I didn't have to make it any worse for them."

"Not the sort of behavior I'd expect from a contract killer." She saw an incredibly sad expression flicker over Helman's face. "I'm sorry, Granger. I only meant—"

"It's okay," he shrugged. "You're not what I expect of a vampire. See you tonight." He shut the door. But despite what she had said, somehow he wanted to be in there with her.

From one of Adrienne's flight bags he took a large roll of black cloth tape and began to seal up the edges of the bathroom door. Adrienne had kept the other flight bag in with her. It contained what was left of the nutrient solution—the blood substitute—that she and Leung had developed. It wasn't yet adequate, she had told him, but it would support her for a few more nights at least. She had not wanted to discuss it further, as if the very topic of feeding were repugnant to her. Helman did not press her. But he felt both uneasy and, in a way, excited about what might happen when the artificial nutrient was used up.

After he had finished with the bathroom door, he taped the bedspread from the double bed in the room to the doorframe. He folded a blanket lengthwise and ran it across the top of the curtain track to keep light from reflecting up onto the ceiling. He followed the instructions she had given him precisely. It made him feel good to be her protector, but he didn't allow himself to dwell on the feeling. It made him think of his sister. And Weston and the Conclave and the Jesuits. And death.

When the sun had finally risen and the time of the *yber* had passed, Helman went to the lobby pay phone and dialed the first contact number Weston had given him. It had been a long night but he and Adrienne had survived it. He was afraid to learn if there were others who hadn't.

Four

Weston's chest was on fire with the pain of his coughing spasm. He was shocked by the ferocity of it. Time couldn't be running out this quickly for him. It couldn't. His mind flew back to the patterns of his childhood. It's just not fair, he thought. Not fair. He struggled to control the spasm. Fairness has nothing to do with it, he argued back at himself. The cancer is eating my lungs. It is neither right nor wrong, fair nor unfair. It is what cancer does.

"Now do what you're supposed to do," he said to himself, out loud. His voice was weak, but he didn't begin to cough again. A small victory on the way to total defeat.

A buzzer by his bed sounded. Weston reached out to touch the intercom bar. He and his men were staying in a safe house maintained by the American government in Toronto. It was made up of three apartments in an expensive condominium development on the shore of Lake Ontario to the west of the city. Most of the regular tenants of the complex spent half their time traveling so there were few familiar faces around to become concerned as a continual passage of intent-looking men arrived to debrief returning friendly agents or interrogate captured foreign ones, usually with extreme prejudice.

At this time, the place was quiet and Weston and his men were able to enjoy a few hours of rest while waiting for Helman's first call back. The voice on the intercom said that it had come.

"Where's he calling from?" Weston asked.

"Seattle. Holiday Inn north of the city. St. Clair is with him. No signs of surveillance," said the voice.

"Good," said Weston. "Get the details and tell him I'll arrive this evening."

"He wants to talk to you. Wants to know about his sister."

Weston's voice hardened. "Did you tell him?"

"Negative."

The tension relaxed again. For a moment, Weston had feared that he had lost Helman.

"Tell him everything is as we anticipated. I'll join him this evening."

"He's stubborn," the voice said.

"So am I." Weston took his hand off the intercom bar. Silence returned. He fought with the pain in his chest for another few minutes before he was able to instruct his aide to arrange for a charter jet to Seattle-Tacoma International.

He thought again about the description of the condition of Miriam Helman's body as it had been found by his agents in the early morning. He shuddered. Eventually he would have to tell Helman that they had been too late. There was still a chance he could lose it all. One way or another.

The coughing started again and he had to be sedated for his flight.

His agents didn't know whether to be embarrassed for him, or terrified for themselves.

For the most part, they were terrified.

Five

Outside, the snow-swollen clouds of the past few days had finally moved away and the sun shone brilliantly in the clear, winter blue sky. All the *yber* across the eastern seaboard were safely in their sanctuaries, except in the unassuming Scarsdale estate of the Eastern Meeting. Secure in the meeting room in the third basement where Helman had first been brought, and trained to resist the torpor of the day, Lord Diego beamed in satisfaction. His fangs were moist with the saliva of expectation as he contemplated the treat that at that moment awaited him from the hills of New Hampshire.

"Excellent, excellent," he said into the phone. "From Seattle to San Francisco. Transferring to a new flight arriving at San Luis Obispo at 11:27. I shall commend your industry to your mentor."

Across the continent, an eager young familiar trembled in the praise from a Lord of the Conclave. He worked for American Airlines and all he had done was monitor the reservation computers, as his mentor had instructed him, for the list of names and airports he had been given. Luckily, one combination had come up. And now Lord Diego himself was taking note of his work. The familiar did not think he could wait until sunset for his mentor to hear the praise being lavished upon him. He did not know that even as Diego talked to him, the Lord's own familiars were on their way to him to inflict upon him his First Death without benefit of Communion. Thus the information of the woman and her human assassin would be kept safely in Diego's hands. And in the hands of those he chose to share it with.

When the final confrontation at Nacimiento took place, Diego wanted no doubt to be raised that he and his emissaries and familiars took part only *after* the Jesuits had made their initial attack. The blame for the outrage must rest with the Jesuits until the Final Plan was well underway. And by that time, it wouldn't matter who knew the truth because the Conclave would rule the world of humans, and Diego would rule the Conclave.

Diego broke the connection with the doomed familiar on the west coast. He pressed a button on a console on the ornately carved table he worked at. A familiar appeared at the door to the meeting room.

"Yes, my Lord."

"Send the message to Father Clement. Prepare my familiars for the meeting. It shall be tonight."

"Yes, my Lord."

The familiar shut the door behind him. Diego took no notice. Already that familiar had joined the growing list of those who must be killed to keep their silence. Two hundred years ago, Diego would have thought of the murder of such well-trained familiars as regrettable. But the centuries had changed him. Now, he didn't think of it at all.

He thought only of his pleasure.

And he summoned it.

One of his own familiars appeared at the door to the meeting room. He was not alone.

Eyes clouded with the effects of the drugs which had kept them quiet on their journey, the two children stood motionless in the doorway.

Diego rose from behind the table and stood with his arms spread wide. His mouth spread wide.

"Suffer the little children to come unto me," he said.

With a gentle prod from the familiar, Campbell and Steven walked slowly towards the fangs and claws of Lord Diego.

The drugs, and the mind-numbing image of what they had seen done to their mother, kept them mercifully unaware of what happened next.

Diego felt a bit disappointed at having them drugged that way. It did spoil some of the pleasure.

But not, he was grateful, all of it.

Six

Helman was furious. He had spent the day in the Seattle hotel room unable to rest. The strain of the last days had reached a level where it interfered with the relaxation techniques he used to induce sleep. He had been roused three times by the persistent housekeeping staff who knocked on the door despite his Do Not Disturb sign. Each time he had thought it was the phone ringing. He had to have news from Weston, and now he was in the lobby of the Holiday Inn being told that Weston was out of touch.

"Why wouldn't he talk to me when I called in this morning?" Helman's voice was louder than was wise in the small lobby. The agent of the Nevada Project, quite unremarkable except for the heavy black leather gloves he wore, raised a cautionary hand to Helman.

Helman saw the puckered lines of stitching along the fingers of the palm of the glove. It was a Malther Hand. Helman quieted his voice immediately. The agent would be wearing a vest containing flat battery packs wired up into a step-up transformer. The leads terminated in the glove the agent was wearing. The black leather was actually an insulated rubber compound that would protect the agent when he gripped a victim with the Malther Hand and closed the circuit. The shiny suppleness of the glove was really a coating of a conductor cream to improve the current flow. The devices were manufactured in Germany, supposedly for police protection in crowd control situations only. The transformer could be set to deliver anything from a mild to fatal shock. The Malther Hands were in wide use in South America as an interrogation tool. Helman had no wish to see at what level the agent's transformer was set.

"Shall we go into the bar?" the agent suggested, lowering his hand.

Helman shook his head.

"Sunset's in less than half an hour. She'll be waking up soon. I can't risk being away. What's the news from Weston?"

"I told you. No news. His plane was forced down in Chicago by the weather. That's why he's not here. He wants to know if you have any idea where the woman is headed. He can move ahead and meet with you tomorrow." The agent's eyes constantly swept the lobby, looking for the one observer whose eyes stayed just a bit too long on Helman and him talking in the corner. So far, they were safe.

"What's the word about my sister and her children?"

"Everything is as we anticipated. That's all I know. Now where is the woman going?" With his hand which wore an ordinary glove, the agent handed Helman a packet of matches. "There's a number in there you can call to talk to Weston tomorrow. But for now, you talk to me."

The street lights were on outside. Adrienne would be waking. Helman needed the Nevada Project's protection. He had to cooperate. He slipped the match packet into a pocket.

"Nacimiento," he said. "A small town on the California coast. About halfway between San Francisco—"

"And Los Angeles," the agent said.

"You know about it?" Helman asked.

"A bit. When we first learned about the Jesuits, but before we knew that they *were* Jesuits, we thought they might be associated with an odd Christian cult that operates out of Nacimiento. Couldn't get closer to it. When we learned the truth about the Jesuits, we dropped the investigation. Is the woman involved with the cult?"

Apparently the Nevada Project didn't know everything.

"No," said Helman. "She's involved with the Father."

"The Father of what?"

"Tell Weston I've got some information for him whenever he decides to keep in touch." Helman was in control. He turned to the elevators.

"Tell *me*," the agent said and grabbed Helman by the arm. Helman was safe from the Malther Hand as long as it didn't make contact with his bare skin.

Helman turned slowly and whispered.

"Now look who's making a scene. Turn that thing on if you want to," he said, indicating the Hand, "but if I'm not up there when she wakes up, you've lost her. And from the way Weston's been going on, that's not a very good position to be in. Tell him I'll talk to him whenever he wants to talk to me."

The agent let go of Helman's arm. Helman went upstairs to unseal Adrienne. The agent went out to the car where Weston was waiting.

"You were right," the agent said as he got into the car and disconnected the wires leading to his glove. "She's going to the Father."

Weston signaled the driver to leave.

"That's what I'd do," he said. "How's Helman?"

"Looks strung out. Anxious about his sister. I told him a little about that cult we thought we had found in Nacimiento so he'd be a bit prepared for what he's going to find there. But I let him think we didn't know about the Father. I think it made him feel better to think that now you had a reason to get in touch with him. He accepted the Chicago story but he wasn't happy about it."

The driver took the cut-off from 5 to 405. At this time of day it was a faster trip to the airport than trying to drive through Seattle.

Weston stared out at the passing city for a long time before he spoke again.

''Have them close up Washington and meet us in Nacimiento.''

The agent was shocked. But at the same time oddly relieved. For the first time the battle lines were clearly drawn.

''It's finally come to this?'' the agent asked. ''You're sure?''

''Who else can we go to? Everyone will be necessary in Nacimiento. How long do you think our offices would stay secure if none of us come back? How long do you think our records would last? They'd be the hottest thing on the block in Washington since the unaltered autopsy report on William Casey. Too many explanations will be required and there'd be no one left to give them. By the time the first incubation period ends and the deaths begin, the government would already be paralyzed. Everything in the office has to be destroyed. Everything.''

''So it's all been for nothing, after all?''

''The Nevada Project by itself, yes.'' It hurt Weston to say it, but it was the truth. ''But we have a few other options. Starting next week, unless some of us are around to countermand the orders, there will be packets of information released to some selected writers outside the country. There will be enough conspiracy books on the market for people to realize that something is up. The government won't be able to suppress articles published outside the country.''

''Why not release it direct to the AMA? *The New York Times*?''

''They'll check anything this big through government sources. That's the last anyone will hear of it. It's got to be done outside Washington's influence. Remember, we weren't supposed to *suppress* the truth, we were to gather it. Fit it all together to spare the world from the half-truths and the panic of ignorance. Things just didn't work out. What a fitting epitaph that would make. Here lies the world. Things just didn't work out.''

The agent smiled without sharing Weston's humor. But

then, they all knew Weston was a dying man. He was allowed to say those things.

"Shall I cancel the coffee report for the *Lancet* article?" the agent asked.

Weston was instantly serious again.

"No. Let that be publicized. There's still a chance we'll get out of this one alive, you know. The *Lancet* article talks about airborne transmission because that's the only way so many could contract it at once. Except that with everyone in the United States drinking coffee everyday, there's enough room for an alternate explanation for the findings. The coffee report is a brilliant piece of forged research. I bet the *Lancet* won't even publish the airborne transmission work after they see a copy of it."

"At least we do some things well," the agent concluded.

"There's still Nacimiento," Weston said. "It means 'birthplace'."

"But of what?"

The car drove toward the airport.

Seven

Father Clement clutched at the crucifix beneath his coat, and prayed for strength. He was to meet one of *them* and his memories of Spain forty years ago made his stomach churn at the prospect. What if it happened again? The wind was cold and snowflakes made halos around the short lamp standards that burned along the pathway. Clement could feel them out there. Hiding like wraiths in the shadows of the trees and bushes. He wondered if more people than usual would meet their deaths in Central Park this night.

The noise of the city was a muffled background roar in each direction. Through the light, falling snow the twinkling windows of the apartments ringing the park flickered like exploding gaseous stars: a glimpse of Heaven in the midst of Hell.

Clement sat on a bench at the top of a small rise. A pathway ran down either side. A lamp standard shone behind him. Four scholastics, armed with hidden crossbows, stood well away, invisible in the shadows, guarding against the treachery of the undead. A figure approached along the pathway leading from within the park. Not even the muggers went deep within the park at night anymore. Clement clutched even tighter at his crucifix. The figure came nearer.

It was bent and appeared wrapped in a huge coat which dragged around his feet. As the figure drew closer to the shifting circle of light thrown by the wind-shaken lamp post, Clement saw that it was bent over and walking with a peculiar shuffle. The light caught something silvery hanging from the figure. It was another crucifix. The light captured more detail. The figure wore a monk's habit. A heavy cowl threw dark shadows across his face.

The monk stopped in front of Clement. Clement peered deep within the shadows of the cowl but could see nothing.

An old man's voice said, "Good evening, Father. It's rare to see such a one as you so late in this place."

"Who are you?" Clement said angrily, his breath steaming from his mouth. He did not notice that no breath steamed from without the cowl.

"A fellow traveler on the Lord's path," the figure said. He lifted his mittened hands to the cowl and pulled it back. An old man's face, softly framed by a thick beard of gray and black was revealed. "Might I sit with you awhile, Father?" the old monk asked, gesturing to the bench.

"No, no. Go away. You're interfering." Clement was nervous and confused. What was a *monk* doing in Central Park?

The old man shook his head. "That's hardly what I'd call Christian charity, Father Clement. Or perhaps you're waiting for an altar boy to come and do some special praying in your lap?"

Clement stood up in anger. "How dare you—" And then he realized the old man had called him by name. And then he realized . . .

The old man smiled broadly. His beard parted and his carnivore fangs glinted in the lamp light. Lord Diego had kept his appointment.

The moment was frozen as Clement stared at the fangs and the familiar eyes and recognized the face from forty years ago. The Pit was once again reaching out for him, calling him. He *must* resist. Clement ripped his crucifix from beneath his coat and held it menacingly in Diego's face. "Get back in the name of *God.*"

Diego smiled again and stared at the crucifix.

"What an elegant artifact, Father Clement," he said. "But not, I'm afraid, as elegant as mine." Diego lifted the crucifix hanging from his own neck and held it up in front of Clement's face.

"Observe the workmanship," Diego continued. "The artistry of the craftsman's skill. It was a gift to me when I was in the service of Father Lavalette, in Martinique, more than two hundred years ago. Surely you remember him, Father Clement? I was his financial advisor."

Father Lavalette was the Jesuit whose failed investments had brought ruin to the Society. Clement's mind reeled with Diego's revelation.

"*Sacrilege,*" Clement sputtered, his eyes riveted by the sight of the unholy monster before him holding an image of God. Yet the creature was unmarked! It was impossible. Clement himself had seen vampires burned horribly by the touch of a Holy article; scalded by the spray of Holy Water. Diego was playing a Devil's trick upon him.

"*Sacrilege!*" he shouted again and thrust his crucifix into the face of Diego.

Diego did not move. The crucifix smashed against his face, tearing away a portion of the false beard which hid his fangs. Diego brought his hand up and clenched it around

Clement's wrist. He squeezed. Bones painfully grated against each other in Clement's forearm.

"Are you sure you're holding it close enough, Priest? Why not closer?" Diego lifted Clement's hand away as though he were playing a child's game. He forced the priest to place the crucifix in the middle of Diego's forehead. Clement's arm moved in the vampire's grip as if it were a puppet's. Tears from the pain of the crushed bones streamed down his face, freezing in the chilling wind.

"What's this, Priest?" Diego said in mock surprise. "The flesh is unmarked by this most holy of artifacts?" He moved Clement's hand again. His forehead was unblemished. "How about here? Or here? Or here?"

Clement was jerked like a rag doll as Diego forced his arm from one position to another. He pressed the crucifix against each cheek, against his neck. Finally, with a savage twist that caused a snapping sound in Clement's shoulder, he forced the Priest to hold the crucifix against his groin. Clement could feel Diego's erection pushing against the image of Jesus. The Jesuit wrenched his hand and dropped the defiled crucifix onto the pathway. Diego laughed and released him.

"It appears that your God does not wish to harm me, Father Clement. What a strange turn of events. I think I would like to thank him."

Clement held his burning wrist to his chest. Why had God deserted him in this moment? How could that spawn of the Devil handle such a Holy object?

Diego reached down and retrieved the cross.

"In fact," he said, "I would like to kiss him."

Diego held the image of Jesus to his lips and sucked upon it. His tongue rolled around the edges of the tiny form.

"*Stop it!*" Clement screamed at the top of his lungs. "*Stop in God's name!*" The tears that flowed now were from outrage, not from the forgotten pain.

Diego, abruptly, stopped. He held out the crucifix to Clement. Saliva dripped obscenely from the small silver figure frozen in agony upon the cross.

"Would you like it back, Father Clement?"

Father Clement swung out his hand and smashed the crucifix from Diego's hand. It flew off into the dark, snow-sprinkled grass beside the bench.

"Ah," said Diego. "That is the first wise move you have made in years. Congratulations. You have rejected your silly superstition."

"You defiled it," Clement said.

"Think of all the times those things have defiled poor *yber* who didn't know any better. But I know better, Father Clement. I don't accept the superstitious beliefs of your church, and those superstitions become incapable of hurting me. I know that you don't believe in them either."

Clement's eyes burned deeply into Diego.

"Lies," he spat.

"Ah, *Clemencito*." Diego reached out a hand and brushed Clement's cheek. Clement pulled away as if burned. "You have aged terribly but the spirit I so admired is still there. I'm glad. I have missed you as a familiar."

Clement spun around to the dark shadows in the distance, where the scholastics hid.

"He is lying!" he screamed. "Kill him! Kill him now!"

Clement's voice was swallowed by the wind and the roar of New York.

"Your scholastics aren't there, *Clemencito*. If we end this meeting civilly, they will be released, unharmed. If no, they'll receive the same as your friend, Benedict."

"You said we would be allowed to bring others. You said there would be no interference." Clement was truly shaken at the breach of the truce Diego had called for the meeting.

"I am afraid I lied, Priest. But I'm not worried about going to hell. *You*, on the other hand, should worry about going to non-existence. I remember that you were worried about that a great deal when you first came to me, so many years ago. The meaninglessness of death disturbed you, incredibly so. But I offered you a way. I offered you *true* life eternal. Yet on the night you were to have joined me, you left. You joined the army of the black pope in a quest for some imaginary afterlife. And now look at you. You're old.

You're bent. Even if I took you now, you would spend eternity as an old man. Father Tithonus. Do you know what you have given up?''

Clement looked up into the night. He had tried to forget those early, questioning days; the times when his soul ached with the unanswered questions all must sometime face. He was confused. He was rash. And he had heard the stories of the strange philosopher near the ruins of Madrid who, it was said, offered answers. Clement had been astounded by those answers. He had brought himself to the brink of accepting them himself. And in the end, Eduardo Diego y Rey *had* helped Clement find peace. For Diego had shown him that the Devil did exist. And where there was a Devil, there must also be a God. Clement had fled the night he was to be inducted as a familiar in Diego's domain. Ever since, he had battled against Diego's kind. He had never expected to meet with him again. The memories confused him. The night was cold and the God he trusted had seemed to lose His strength over evil.

Diego waited patiently. After four hundred years, he knew what men thought. He knew what Clement agonized over: what if he were *wrong*?

''The girl, Clement,'' Diego began. ''The girl does not believe either. That is why she wants to join with the Americans. She thinks science can conquer her condition. She is deranged. She threatens you.''

Clement was not that confused. ''She threatens you too, vampire.''

''So let us combine for the moment to destroy the common threat.''

''Why should the Society help its sworn enemy?''

''Because you can't do it by yourself. No matter what means you choose. Heathrow was a disaster, Priest. Civilians killed. Soldiers with crossbows. Incredible. The colonel who was in charge of the bloodbath was found in his office the next day. Killed himself. Sounded like the work of someone I might know.''

''No games, vampire. We both know why we fight.''

"The woman must be eliminated."

"Yes."

"Our people are at cross-purposes. At Heathrow your soldiers forced my emissaries to leave in defeat. In Toronto, our assassin helped her to escape. We must cooperate."

"How?"

"The Conclave know where she has gone to hide. We cannot get at her. You can."

"Where is she?"

"Will you destroy her?"

"We will destroy all of you. Where?"

"The spirit of youth," Diego smiled.

"Where?"

"Nacimiento."

"The demon father has given her sanctuary?" Clement was astounded. "And *you* would dare to go against what he decrees?"

"*Clemencito*, your god, my Conclave, it's all superstition. The Father is not a demon. That crucifix does not embody god. When you pray, you are the only being who listens. I know you thought that once. Use your mind again and be free of the trappings of the old beliefs."

Clement backed away.

"Yours is the voice of the Devil," he said, his voice hollow in the snow and the night. "And even if it isn't, you are still Hell-spawned because of what you did to Father Benedict. Bad enough that it was done on the service of Hell. But it is twice cursed if it was done in the name of nothing. Of meaninglessness. We shall destroy the woman. And since the Conclave cowers in the presence of the demon father, we shall destroy Nacimiento. And then, vampire, *I* personally will destroy you. You may defile as many crucifixes as you choose. It doesn't matter. I carry my God within me where you can't touch him. I will see you thrown into the Pit. Vampire! Monster! Demon!"

Clement spat on the ground before Diego and ran down the pathway leading out of the park.

Diego stood motionless, reflective.

After a minute he pulled at the false beard he wore and removed it. His fangs were shockingly visible against his lower lips. He took off his mitts and his claws flickered at the tips of his long, bony fingers. New York was the one city in the world where no one would dare question his appearance, if indeed they noticed it at all.

He chose the best-lit route to where the limousine waited for him. One late-night jogger almost stumbled when he saw Diego's face in the lamplight. Diego was tempted, but let the jogger live. The meeting had gone exactly as planned. He had shocked Clement at the outset in the worst possible way that Clement could be shocked. In that condition, befuddled with confusing memories about the past, the Jesuit had leapt at the proposal Diego had offered him. He had accepted it uncritically. Diego could be sure that Clement would follow through with his threats to destroy with a fanatic's zeal, and a fanatic's lack of thought.

It was all so predictable. Just as Diego had known that young Clement, so long ago, would balk at joining the *yber* and run instead to the Church. Adrienne's assassin was the only human in decades upon decades who had offered Diego any challenge. It was unfortunate that he had seemed to throw in his lot with the girl. She was predictable too. Diego would have enjoyed facing Helman on his own.

He had certainly enjoyed facing Helman's nephews on their own. So much so that he had even made an exception to his own long-standing rule about Communion for children. He was glad that there were still a few things left for him to look forward to. He wondered if he might have a chance to actually talk with the Father. To see how he did it. How could one live nine hundred years without killing oneself? Diego had been *yber* for just over four hundred years, and already the boredom sometimes threatened to make him stay out to watch the sun come up. He desperately hoped that things would be different when the Final Plan was completed.

As he approached the limousine, he decided to arrange to have the four captive scholastics eviscerated and shipped back to the Jesuits in boxes. He would have them eviscerated alive because he knew the Jesuits' doctors could determine such things from an autopsy.

It would keep Clement in the proper state of mind.

Eight

When "the people" had moved into Nacimiento in the late sixties, the townspeople had been considerably upset. The formless fear that had grown with the hearts and minds of the conservative and middle-aged as they had watched the counterculture creep through America like dry rot, had finally been given a focus. Murders had taken place in Los Angeles. Words like "cult" and "Manson" were being thrust about like I-told-you-so's for five years of free love and marijuana. "The people" who had bought the Rand estate were peculiar enough to be called "hippies" by the locals. They expected the worst. But as the years passed, nothing much happened. "The people" went their way, wearing their white robes, but paying their taxes; the town went its way. Neither had anything to fear from the other. In fact, the only thing the Father feared as he stood looking out at the moonlit hills from the observation tower of the main building, was that all the required forces would not be properly assembled in time.

He had had more dreams.

The Rand Estate had been built in the late thirties by Charles Foster Rand. He had been one of the chief advisors and curators to the immense collections of William Randolph Hearst. A great many of the results of Rand's expertise in art history and shrewd business dealings had ended up in

Hearst's monumental paean to obsession: San Simeon, just a few miles up the coast.

Rand had spent many years involved in the ongoing and never-completed construction of the Hearst castle. Walls, ceilings and floors from ancient European structures were painstakingly disassembled and shipped to the California coast. There Rand and a host of architects would construct a concrete-walled, earthquake-proof box to hold the reconstructed rooms. The castle had grown like a cancer, continually branching out into unsuspected areas. Tenth-century rooms held a confused collection of 16th-century antiques, modern reproductions and clay vessels from before the time of Rome. After six years of working under such frustrating conditions, Rand had, in desperation, begun the construction of his own estate in Nacimiento. It was his answer to the Hearst Castle. He hadn't had Hearst's money to build it with, but he had something else that Hearst didn't: taste.

Originally, the estate had sat upon more than a thousand acres of rolling hills overlooking the Pacific. Through subsequent sales by subsequent owners, the holdings were now reduced to fewer than fifty acres. But the elegant main building remained.

Rand had modeled the basic layout after the spacious villas unearthed from early Grecian times. The main building was U-shaped, cupped to the west so that three sides overlooked the magnificent pool and fountain in the main courtyard and the stunning Pacific sunsets. At the bottom of the U, the main building rose in classic proportion to a height of four stories. On the eastern side, a hung-glass wall, an impressive achievement in its time, looked out over the formal gardens and sweep of land beyond. Everything was constructed in the most modern designs imaginable for the thirties. The estate was a perfect shrine to the style known as deco in its pure, cleanly spaced lines, and solidly defined spaces.

Photographs of the estate, originally taken in the fifties, appeared in almost every book that dealt with the history of western architecture. There had been no photographs taken inside the Rand Estate for more than twelve years. Ever since "the people" moved in: the familiars and emissaries of the Father.

Rand had died in 1959. He had been hopelessly in love with a boy under contract to a motion picture studio known for its children's films. The boy had returned Rand's affections with youthful passion. The studio had found out. The boy's contract was broken. He was sent away from California by his parents, back to their original home in Idaho.

The scandal had been vicious. Rand had thrown himself from the observation tower of the main building onto the marble courtyard.

A subsequent owner had attempted to cash in on the publicity surrounding the Hearst castle at San Simeon by trying to stage tours of the Rand estate. It wasn't garish enough. That owner had sold within a year. Nacimiento returned to being little more than a service community to Highway One. The only time its two motels were full was when the San Simeon and Cambria motels were all overbooked.

It was a perfect town for someone who was over nine hundred years old and wished to be left alone by humans and *yber* both. But it was not ready for the awesome forces that were converging upon it.

Far down the road to the south, the solid black, unblinking eyes of the Father saw the first of them arriving. Twin headlights would soon sweep along the coastal highway. They would take the small cut-off to his home. He descended from the observation tower to prepare himself.

That which he had dreamed of had begun many days ago.

Very soon now, it would end.

Nine

The rented Mustang hummed and more miles passed by them. They ran for their lives; the lives of those Helman loved, and in some obscure way, for the lives of all the people in the world. Helman thought that if he could tell Adrienne about his contact with Weston and the Nevada Project, if she could be made to understand why he had done it, then the two of them could find some understanding in the web of confusion in which they were ensnared. But the risks were too great. If she were as opposed to government involvement as Weston said, then the Nevada Project would lose her. And Helman would lose her. He didn't want that. He didn't know exactly what it was he did want, but he knew he had to have more time with her. An attraction was there. He was sure she felt it too. But both of them needed peace and an end to the running to come to terms with it. And then, perhaps, thought Helman, they would have all the time they could ever want. Forever.

"The turn off's coming up in the next few miles," Adrienne said, breaking his silent considerations.

"What does it say: 'This way to the vampires'?"

Adrienne smiled. She had never felt as relaxed around a human. Helman had accepted her as what she had said she was, a person like any other, but with a disease. If the Father would give them sanctuary, then she and Helman would have the time she felt they needed. She would be *yber* no more. She would be human.

"It says Nacimiento Reservoir. The town doesn't even have a city limits sign."

Helman stared past the forward illumination of the car's highbeams. The coastal highway was empty of other traffic but he kept on the alert for darkened vehicles at the side of the road which might suddenly spring into pursuit.

"A lot might have changed since you were here last," he said.

"The last trip with Diego's entourage was only five years ago. These small towns don't change that quickly. When the Father's familiars told Diego that the Father had refused to see him again, Diego considered burning the whole town to the ground. But he said it would be ten years before anybody knew it was gone."

"Diego sounds charming."

Adrienne became deadly serious.

"You mustn't underestimate him, Granger. He was the one who arranged for the evidence of the Delvecchio—" she faltered for a moment, unsure. Then she used his word for it. "The evidence of the Delvecchio murder to be used against you. Both King and Rice would be in constant touch with him. He was responsible for Jeffery's horrible death and I'm certain that his position in the Conclave rests on his disposal of me as well. Remember, he was the one who encouraged my work in the beginning. If either of us ever meet him face to face, we will not survive."

The turn-off sign came up suddenly and Helman braked in the darkness.

"Since the Father has refused to have any dealings at all with any of the *yber* for the past two centuries, why do you think he'll grant us sanctuary?"

"When the Conclave was formed and the Ways set out as our sacred teachings, the Father refused to take part. Even then he was too powerful, and too revered, for the Conclave to destroy. He is mentor to hundreds of *yber* around the world. Since then he has had a reputation for taking in those *yber* who have fallen from the Ways. Most who approach him to serve as his emissaries are rejected. A very few are accepted. No one knows what the conditions of his acceptance are. But at least you and I will have a chance."

"Will you introduce me as your familiar?"

"You aren't my familiar, Granger. I won't lie to the Father. You will be introduced as my friend. Helping me in my work."

A memory came back to Helman as he drove slowly through the narrow twisted road leading through the coastal hills.

"Back in Toronto," he said. "When Rice was giving me information about you, I asked him if you and Chris Leung were lovers."

Adrienne was impassive. She thought she knew where the question might lead.

"What did Rice tell you?" she asked.

"He said it was impossible. He seemed disgusted."

"To Rice, any such relationship between *yber* and human, unless it were part of Communion, would be like coupling with animals. Humans are quite beneath the *yber* in the *yber* view of things."

"Then, it's not impossible?"

"No, Granger, not impossible."

He asked no more questions about the past. Except for Adrienne's instructions, they drove the rest of the way in silence, both lost within their thoughts. Thinking of time uninterrupted.

The Father's familiars had told them that they were expected. Adrienne and Helman sat waiting in an enormous lounge off the spectacular four-story high entrance hall. Helman was sure that the Father was expecting them because the Father was now somehow linked to the Conclave. He felt he and Adrienne were sitting waiting for the trap to be sprung.

Helman had asked the familiar how the Father had known to expect them. The familiar had said that the Father had had a dream. He had said it reverentially, as though it were a rare and strange occurrence. Adrienne told him that it was.

"*Yber* don't dream, Granger."

"Never?"

"None ever remembered a dream. Jeffery and I attached ourselves to electroencephalographs for months without ever finding a dream trace among all the brain wave readings made while we slept."

"Why would that be?"

"Efficiency, I think. Just as our bodies become incredibly efficient, so do our minds. Our memories are virtually unimpeded. Our senses magnified. We concluded that *yber* don't dream because there is no need to. Our minds process all the information that comes to us in the course of a night instantly. There is no backlog of shuffling and filing that has to go on while we are in an unconscious state. That's generally thought to be the reason humans dream."

"Then why would the Father suddenly start dreaming after nine hundred years?"

Adrienne shrugged. "The first changes from human to *yber* occur within twenty-four hours. The old incisors fall out and new fangs erupt. Within six months the organs fuse. Within a year *yber* are able to detect each other at great distances with a type of sense we were never able to identify, probably telepathic in nature. Our bodies continue to change for centuries as our strength and abilities increase. Diego's body is quite different from one who has been *yber* for only a few years. The Father must be even more altered. Perhaps after a millennia we regain the ability to dream. Perhaps we might even be able to see into the future."

Helman felt that this was going beyond the realm of science. "Or maybe even turn into bats or clouds of dust?" he asked sarcastically. He had accepted the *yber* as a natural phenomenon. There was no room left in him to accept things even more fantastic.

But Adrienne's expression stayed serious.

"Though I know of none personally, the legends of shape-changers still live within the Ways. Who knows what further powers there are still to experience?"

Helman took Adrienne's hand. "You seem very human to me," he said.

She squeezed back. "I feel very human with you."

The doors from the entranceway swung open. A familiar, an older woman of about fifty wearing a simple white smock, with a high, tightly fitting collar, smiled at them. Behind her stood two other familiars, similarly clothed. Behind them was a tall, white figure that Helman's eyes refused to focus on.

"The Father will see you now," the familiar said.

The Father must be even more altered, Adrienne had said. And she had been right. Both of them had been totally unprepared for the sight of him as he entered the room. Adrienne adjusted to him first. Helman took far longer.

The Father was grotesque. Not that he was misshapen or twisted in bizarre and unimaginable forms, rather, there were so many small deviations from the ordinary that the overall impression was that of a figure seen in the darkness of a still room. From the corners of the eyes, the figure was acceptable. But if you dared look for detail, horror began.

The Father was well over six feet tall. He wore a simple white kaftan, similar to the robes his familiars wore. The three of them in the room gazed upon the Father with adulation.

His feet and ankles were bare and visible beneath the hem of the kaftan, as were his hands and forearms in the loose sleeves. No musculature seemed to exist upon his body. Thin, dull, white skin clung to his bones like vacuum-wrapped plastic. Each joint and rigid tendon was clearly visible. In less than bright light, the Father might appear transparent, or melted.

His face was the same.

No muscles seemed to fill up the deep hollows where the skin sucked in closely to the skull. He had no lips. His teeth, *all* of them stark white serrated fangs, emerged abruptly from the slug-white gums visible directly below the one nostril. The Father's nose had long since been absorbed back into his body and a single gaping hole burrowed deep within his death's-head face. Something else that was also black flicked within his mouth.

His ears were little more than small bumps that partially

hid the network of tendons, veins, and nerves that were visible at the hinge of his jaw.

He was completely hairless. Completely shrunken. And his eyes made him completely inhuman.

They were flat black. No iris, no pupil, no moisture. Just black like dry, dead stones. They could look directly at Helman and Adrienne and all the others in the room without moving. They saw everything at once. They saw many things that no one else could see.

Helman was drawn hopelessly into them, totally revulsed at the incomplete monster before him.

The Father held his gaze as he walked effortlessly to a chair in the middle of the room across from his two visitors. Helman had the impression that gravity was not working on the nine-hundred-year-old creature. He might have walked through a pile of crisp autumn leaves and not crushed one of them.

The Father smiled at Helman by turning two tiny corners of flesh at the edges of his mouth upright. His tongue emerged from between his fangs, flicking like a lizard's. It was shriveled and tubular and ended in what looked to be a conical scab that resembled a bee's stinger.

"You are new to such as ourselves," the Father said.

It took a moment for Helman to realize he had spoken. No lips were there to move. The voice had sounded dry and whispery like soft winds through deserts. A voice that whispered your name in the night when you knew there was no one else there.

Helman could not reply.

The Father turned to Adrienne. In his movement, the front of his kaftan spread open. Helman stared in shock. The Father was wearing a string of rosary beads that ended in a silver crucifix.

"You seek sanctuary here," the Father whispered to Adrienne.

"From the Conclave," she said. "I would like a chance to explain why."

The Father shook his head once. Slowly and ponderously

as if some sudden movement might snap it free and it would float away.

"There is no need," the delicate, breathless whisper said. "Sanctuary is granted."

Adrienne could not keep the look of surprise from her face.

"I have known you were coming," he explained gently. "I was given a sign. From God."

"From God?" Adrienne repeated doubtfully. She had had her suspicions that Diego might not have entirely believed in the Devil worship of the Ways, but she had never heard of an *yber* turning to the religion of the Kingdom of Light.

The Father tilted his head upward. Helman saw that he had no eyelids. He never blinked.

"Our sweet Lord and Savior, Jesus Christ, has come to me in my dreams and shown me that the end of my punishment is at hand. Praise God."

"What punishment is that, Father?" Adrienne felt a tiny tremor of panic grow in her. Had the Jesuits contacted, *converted*, the Father?

"For seven centuries I swept the earth as an agent of death." The familiars closed their eyes and nodded, as though listening to a sermon they had heard countless times before. "Thousands of innocents were consumed by my bloodthirst. Millions suffered because of me. I served the demons of the Pit. But the Lord came to me and directed me and I turned away from the evil of those I had gathered to me. They formed their unholy Conclave. I undertook the life of a pilgrim, to repent, though I knew I would never meet my Lord."

The Jesuits could be in the hallways even now. Crossbows cocked. What unfathomable senility had struck at what was once the greatest of *yber*?

"Why is that, Father?" Adrienne asked. She calculated the movements she would have to make to drop the three familiars in the room with them. Mentally she measured the distance she would have to cover to get back to the car. Undoubtedly there would be pursuit. It would be faster if she carried Helman. She shifted her position, preparing herself for the flight.

"All of us," the Father whispered, sweeping his ivory chiseled hand and claws across the room. "All of us must serve God in whatever way we can. Then, when we die, we may be transfigured and ascend to Heaven. But our kind, Adrienne St. Clair, can never die. Were we to stand before the rising sun or refuse to partake of the living blood, we would be killing ourselves by our own hands and we would once again belong to the Pit. It is our punishment for our curse."

Adrienne leaned forward, one eye on the door to the entrance hall. Who knew how many scholastics were waiting there.

"Is that what the Jesuits told you?" she asked. His answer would determine her actions. She could see Helman bracing himself. He had put it together too.

"The Church is in the grip of Satan Himself," said the Father. "Please sit back. You are safe here. I am content to let each of you come to the Lord in your own time. What is of first importance is that you have rejected the Ways. You search for better methods for our kind."

"Your dreams told you that?" Adrienne settled back into the chair. Perhaps they would be safe after all.

"No, Adrienne St. Clair. You have come to this place before in the presence of a Lord of the Conclave. Familiars will talk. I will listen. I know many things without having to have learned them in dreams. But now you must teach me of your work. And your human companion will have to leave."

Adrienne reacted immediately. "He can't go. He's in as great a danger as I. He must have sanctuary too."

The father rose, ending the discussion.

"He is not *yber*. He is not familiar. He does not belong here. It is necessary that he go."

"But he's risked so much to get me here."

"He has risked nothing. Since the first I have known he was coming. And now it is necessary for him to go. There is only risk when the outcome is uncertain. The outcome of what we face is already decided.'' The father turned to Helman. ''Leave us now, human. You know to whom you must go. There is no uncertainty. No risk.''

Helman stood. He didn't understand what the Father was talking about.

''I have no one to go to,'' he said.

''Then they shall go to you. You may return when night falls again if that is what you wish to hear. Now go.''

Two familiars, muscular beneath their Kaftans, gripped Helman by his arms and led him out of the room. He and Adrienne could only look apprehensively into each other's eyes for a moment before he was removed from her presence. The familiars kept their grip upon him until he had reached the car outside the gates.

Sunrise was less than an hour away. Helman drove toward the town center of Nacimiento to contact Weston through the number the agent had given him in the match packet. No matter. how or where that call would be forwarded, Weston had to be somewhere in the area. Helman would be safe with the Nevada Project team during the day. He would also find out about his sister. Weston's ambiguous message that all was as they had anticipated still angered him.

By now the Conclave would have realized that he had not returned to West Heparton. He would not be surprised if the Conclave could manage to trace him and Adrienne to Nacimiento in a matter of days. Or nights as they thought of it. He would have to force a definite commitment out of Weston about just what it was Nevada wanted from Adrienne.

A car pulled out from some bushes behind Helman. The sudden flash of the other vehicle's headlights in the rearview mirror startled him. Out over the hills to the east, the sky was beginning to lighten. The headlights blinked at him, signaling to him.

Helman pulled over to the side of the narrow road. Finally Weston had come to him.

The other car pulled up beside him. The power window hummed down. The figure inside was in shadows.

"It's about time," said Helman. "She's been given sanctuary, what do we—"

The figure turned out of the shadows.

It had fangs.

"You have betrayed us," the vampire spat.

Helman jumped back.

"So nervous, are you, human? I don't think your nephews would be very impressed if they saw the way you looked now. But then, I'm sure *you* would be quite impressed by the way *they* look now." The creature laughed hideously. Helman was frozen in helpless anger.

"Lord Diego will meet with you all tonight, human. For the last time."

The car squealed away in a spray of gravel. The chilling laughter still echoed in Helman's ears.

He realized that the Conclave must have always known where he and Adrienne would head. This last vampire had followed him only to make sure that Adrienne hadn't left the Father's sanctuary with him. They knew where she was. They knew where he was. And it seemed to be too late for his sister and her children.

The sun was coming. Its light was the only thing that had prevented them from killing him here on the road. It would protect him for only twelve hours more. Tears of frustration grew in his eyes.

He screamed out Weston's name to the empty hills.

Weston was going to tell him everything about what was going on or Weston wasn't going to be alive to see Helman's last sunset.

The twelve final hours would not be wasted.

Ten

The two men accompanying Weston had made two mistakes. First, when Helman's call had reached them from Nacimiento, they had told Helman where they were, and second, when Helman had arrived, they had treated him as an ally. When they had opened the door to the Santa Barbara motel room for Helman, one surprised agent had been kicked in the head while the other got a slashing elbow across the face. There was blood dripping out of that agent's nose as he lay spreadeagled across the bed. Neither had had a chance to draw their weapons. Now, it was Weston's turn to pay for his own mistakes.

Helman pressed his forearm against Weston's larynx and part of him hoped that the old man would say nothing, to give him the excuse he needed to crush Weston's throat and leave him there to suffocate. Part of him didn't care that he would never make it out of the motel room alive without Weston. He was facing certain death by sunset anyway. Why should the loss of a few hours of life interfere with what small revenge he could get?

But Weston had information. Weston had power. Helman wanted both. When Weston began choking and gasping for breath, another part of Helman won the battle. He eased the pressure of his forearm and slapped his free hand over Weston's mouth.

"The Conclave knows where she is. They know where I am. We haven't been dodging them at all. You and they all knew we'd end up at the Father's. I want the truth. I don't want any bullshit or stories about the end of the world. All I want is a way out of this alive. With St. Clair. And with Miriam and the kids. Nod once if you understand."

Weston nodded. His chest was heaving in a desperate attempt for air.

"When I take my hand away you can call out if you want to, but before they get that door half open I'll have crushed both temples and severed the spinal cord in your neck. Here goes."

Helman lifted his hand and forearm away from Weston. Weston slapped both his own hands to his mouth and wheezed gratingly. He pointed to a suitcase sitting by the door to the room. He gasped the word "Oxygen."

Helman looked suspiciously from Weston to the suitcase.

"Or I'll start to cough," Weston whispered hoarsely. He squeezed both his hands tightly over his mouth and nose. His body convulsed and sweat sprung out over his face.

Helman risked it. It was too good an act. He got the suitcase and removed the small oxygen tank and soft plastic mask connected to it. Weston held it to his face like a drowning man. He coughed into the mask once or twice, but he seemed to have whatever it was under control.

Helman watched impassively. "Hurry up and start talking," he said.

Weston gestured for Helman to help him up from the floor where he had been thrown when Helman had burst into a frenzy. Helman pushed Weston into a fake colonial chair by a writing desk. Weston seemed to be breathing easier. If he hadn't gotten the oxygen and a coughing spell had begun, the agents waiting outside would have rushed in and splattered Helman against all four walls. He couldn't let this end in a cheap Santa Barbara motel.

He took the mask from his face. Helman was tying up and gagging the two unconscious agents with their belts and ripped bed sheets.

"How do you know?" Weston asked.

"That the Conclave knows where we are?"

"Yes."

"After I left the Father's estate, a car started following me. I thought it was you. Or at least your men. It was one of the Conclave. A vampire. He said something about my nephews and then told me that Diego would meet with us all tonight."

"What exactly did he say about your nephews?"

Helman felt chilled. Weston's message to him *had* been a lie.

"He said I wouldn't like the way they looked. What's happened to them? Why didn't you send your men?"

Helman trembled with rage. The horrible fear he had fought against, despite everything he had done to prevent it, was coming true.

"I did send men. They were too late. I'm sorry."

"What's happened to them?"

"Your sister is dead. Your nephews are gone."

"Miriam," Helman choked. "How? They didn't drink..."

Weston shook his head. "No, Granger. None of that. It was quick. She was asleep from the looks of it. Didn't know anything. Feel anything." The lies were easy for Weston. He had seen the photographs of what had been done to Miriam Helman. He couldn't bring himself to use the words that would describe it to Helman. She had been trussed like an animal, gutted and bled. But there had been no blood splattered on the floor. The blood had been taken along with her children. But he had to spare Helman something.

Helman was quaking. The one thing he had cherished in his life had been taken from him. His family was gone. And he had tried so hard, undergone such hell, to save them.

"We're still searching for the boys, Granger. There was no evidence that they were harmed."

Helman bordered on the hysterical. "Of course they weren't *harmed*. They wouldn't be *harmed*. They're being given to Diego because their blood is so sweet..."

"I'm sorry." It was all Weston could say. It was useless. It was inane. But it was true.

Helman talked as if no one were there.

"I have nothing left now. I did everything for her. I

even killed for her. When we were kids. She looked after me."

Weston got up slowly and moved toward Helman.

"And then this bastard she worked for raped her. She told me about it. She didn't want to tell me but I made her. And then I went after him and I killed him."

"It's all right, Granger," Weston said. He put his arm out to take Helman's shoulder. "It's all right."

"I didn't mean to kill him. Just hurt him. But he was scared and he wouldn't stay quiet. And then I found out that he was being a bastard to everyone and that Mr. Dorsey wanted him dead. Mr. Dorsey looked after everyone on the streets. Numbers and protection and girls. And he found out I did it and he thanked me and paid me and said if I ever wanted to make more money I just had to tell him and he'd give me more work to do. And I did. For me then. And then when her husband died, for Miriam."

Weston put one hand on Helman's shoulder, still talking softly to him. He couldn't afford to lose him. Slowly he moved Helman around so his back was to the door. Weston was going to throw the oxygen cylinder against the door to attract the attention of his men sitting in the car in the parking lot in front of the motel room door. He swung his arm back slowly to lob it.

He felt Helman's fingers squeezing painfully in on the pressure points beneath his ears.

"Throw that and I'll break your neck," Helman whispered to him. His voice sounded distant and hollow. It was changed.

Weston lowered the cylinder gently to the floor.

"Can we get in there, get her, and get out before sunset?" Helman asked. his eyes were narrowed and cold. "I don't care about the Conclave releasing the evidence they have on all the murders I've committed. I can hide well enough from the government." He relaxed his grip on Weston's neck.

"You have nothing to be afraid of from the government, Granger."

"You put the fix in, did you?" Helman rubbed violently at his face, wiping away the tears and bringing back sensation.

"There's always been a fix in. You're Phoenix, remember?"

"I don't now anything about that." Helman's voice was flat. There was no anger in his denial.

"That was the idea, Granger. You don't have to worry about any evidence the Conclave has reaching the government. The government already has more information on you than any judge or jury would need to convict you. I've seen the files on you. On Phoenix. CIA. FBI. NSA. You're known to them all."

"What are you talking about?"

"You only went after criminals, Granger. The Justice Department couldn't get them. They looked upon you as doing them a favor. As long as you stayed away from politicians and businessmen, the government was going to look after you. It looks after dozens of people like you as long as your closings serve the need of the government. That's why your 'broker's' operation was wiped out by the FBI. They had an agent in place in Telford's operation. When they found out that Telford had been murdered by the Jesuits, they knew his insurance was going to hit the street. You'd be named in it and any investigation would show that the government was linked with you. Why do you think the FBI didn't have a pursuit vehicle ready the day you forced Roselynne Delvecchio out of her house to meet you in the parking lot? Word had gone out: 'No pursuit.' The government has always been there behind the scenes helping you do the things they couldn't. One of them told you that. *"Mr. Helman? Nothing to worry about on this end."*

Helman looked around the room without seeing.

"It's all been a lie? No skill? No intelligence? I've been watched over since day one?"

"Since the beginning," Weston agreed.

"So I had nothing to worry about when that package arrived at the farm? I could have told the thing on the phone to get lost and they would have sent the evidence to the authorities and the FBI or someone would have buried it?"

"You were protected."

"None of this had to happen at all?" The two shocks

Helman had been faced with were taking their toll. Weston could see signs of hysteria building in Helman.

"It *has* happened, Granger. And there's still a chance we can beat it. Beat them."

"Why should I help?"

"Because of Adrienne." Helman had just said he wanted to get her out of the Father's estate before the Conclave arrived. Weston sensed that something was building between them. He played on it. But Helman's mind was elsewhere.

"She's a vampire. Never met her. None of this happened."

"Think of your nephews. We might still be able to save them."

"Didn't happen. They're back in West Heparton."

"How about saving millions, maybe billions of other lives?"

"Bullshit."

"You wanted to know all about the Nevada Project the last time we talked. Still do?"

Helman smiled. It was a sneer.

"Sure, Major. None of it's ever going to happen. Why don't you tell me all about the end of the world."

And Major Weston did.

It began with cats.

In 1961 a new breed of cat was discovered in a farmyard in Scotland. Its ears were limp and flopped forward on its head. The single kitten was spotted by a man with an interest in cats who recognized its uniqueness. The cat bred true. The man obtained one of its kittens, and the breed known as Scottish Fold began.

In 1962, the breed showed up in a subdivision outside of Indianapolis. Research, conducted after the importance of this finding was realized, indicated that the Scottish Fold mutation responsible for the new breed had turned up in more than sixteen separate locations around the world. In only one instance were two of the locations close enough for there to be the possibility that the mutation was caused by the same tomcat fathering two litters. In the other fourteen cases it was apparent that the mutation had arisen spontaneously and in no way were the litters in question related to each other. Later researchers were certain that the mutation had turned up in even more locations. But with only a small percentage of the world's population of cats coming under the careful scrutiny of trained breeders and fanciers, they had gone unnoticed. Except for the one kitten in Scotland that had started a breed, and the one kitten in Indianapolis who had revealed to the world a horrifying future.

The kitten in Indianapolis had been noticed by a geneticist at Indiana University. In 1965 he read a report on the new Scottish Fold breed of cats from Scotland. He recalled his daughter's friend also having a kitten similar to the one described three years earlier. The little girl still had the cat. The geneticist began to work on the problem of two seemingly identical mutations arising simultaneously over great distances. At first he kept his work to himself. He felt he might be on the verge of making a significant contribution to the study of genetics. He didn't want another, better-equipped university to beat him in the rush to publish.

What he was looking for was the mechanism of evolution. He found it. The truth of it terrified him so much that he bypassed his university and went directly to the Department of Health, Education, and Welfare. It took him three months to arrange a brief meeting with an official he considered high enough in rank to deal with his findings. His research and conclusions were elegant. The official was skeptical but could not ignore them. It took nine months for the government to confirm the geneticist's findings. The Nevada Project was formed in the next five days.

Evolution was an accepted scientific fact. What was not accepted was an explanation for how it actually occurred. Many different theories had been constructed. Some described how small, individually unrecognizable changes would gradually build up over the generations until an apparent change slowly manifested itself. Others detailed how catastrophic mutations would dramatically result in a new species within one or two generations. No one theory seemed correct. And no one theory could explain how one change in one individual could so drastically affect the future of an entire species as the fossil records of the past showed.

That is what attracted the geneticist's interest when he learned of the two mutations in Scotland and Indianapolis. Was there a means whereby a mutation was transmitted outside an individual's body enabling it to arise within many members of a particular species in the course of only one generation? The answer was yes.

The geneticist had discovered a biological manifestation which he termed a mutation- or m-virus.

Mutations were constantly occurring in the sex cells of all creatures on earth. The vast majority of them were meaningless because the genetic message was so scrambled it was ignored. Of the mutations that did carry recognizable genetic messages, the majority of them were fatal. Only one in many millions of mutations would actually be beneficial to a species.

And the way in which this one beneficial change in the genetic message could arise in one individual and go on to affect an entire species was by becoming an m-virus.

The body responded to the creation of a recognizable mutation, either beneficial or harmful, and manufactured duplicates of the tiny strands of DNA that the mutation affected. Like viruses, the bits of DNA were encased in protective protein shells and expelled from the body.

The m-viruses would then be quickly contracted by the entire population of a species.

When a beneficial m-virus traveled to a proper site in the host body, it would be incorporated into the genetic code of that body's cells. The mutation would manifest itself in that individual and be passed on to the next generation. By allowing the identical mutation to be present in several individuals at once, the chances of its survival were appreciably increased.

The geneticist was excited with his findings. Similar theories had been proposed from time to time but there had never been a case of an observable mutation arising to confirm or deny the theories.

There was only one problem facing the geneticist before he could announce his discoveries: why wasn't the world's population of cats suddenly overrun with kittens of the Scottish Fold variety? When he had answered that question, he went immediately to the government.

When an m-virus was contracted by a host body of the proper species, it had to locate itself at the proper site within the body in order to be viable. If a genetic message attempted to transmit itself to improper receptor cells, the genetic material of the host cell was thrown into confusion. The resulting damage caused by the improper and accelerated reproduction of cells was almost inevitably fatal.

Thus the mechanism—the m-virus—which developed a beneficial mutation also ensured that the mutation would only be passed on by breeding with other individuals carrying the same altered genes, because it caused the extinction of all non-mutation carrying individuals who had contracted it.

The geneticist obtained biological samples from around the world to test for the presence of m-viruses. He even obtained fossil samples to test for the distinctive beta-tracings that would indicate that m-viruses had once existed within long-dead animals. He discovered that the m-virus mechanism of evolution was always occurring in some form or another in almost every species that existed, or had existed on earth. Sometimes it involved a random, simple mutation like the one which caused cats' ears to flop forward.

But at certain times in a species' history, the mechanism accelerated as though a built-in biological "clock" was forcing a build-up in evolutionary pressure. M-viruses were produced at a staggering rate by virtually every individual in a given population. Mutations abounded, as did the incidence of m-viruses confusing genetic messages.

At such a time, dinosaurs died out within a generation. But beneficial m-viruses allowed some dinosaur species to rapidly evolve into birds. Other species which experienced this acceleration without developing a viable beneficial m-virus were completely wiped out of existence.

The human species was now in that accelerated stage of mutation.

The scientists knew this as evolution.

The public knew it as cancer.

The bottom line was that cancer was contagious and, over the next generation, 100 percent fatal.

The only survivors of the coming cancer plague would be those individuals who contracted an m-virus which located itself at a proper site and passed on its beneficial mutation characteristics.

The Nevada Project was able to determine that that proper mutation had already occurred, slightly more than two thousand years ago, probably in Greece.

The individuals who carried that altered genetic material called themselves *yber*.

In twenty years, they would be the only human species left alive.

Except for a world of vampires, the rest of humanity would be extinct.

The room was silent.

Soft sunlight glowed through the heavy orange and brown curtains that shut off the view of the parking lot. The two bound and gagged agents who had been surprised by Helman still lay unmoving. The blood had stopped trickling from the nose of one of them. Either the injury had not been serious or he was dead.

Weston and Helman stared into each other's eyes in what seemed to be a duel of wills. Helman broke first.

"That's insane," he said and looked away from Weston. He got up and paced.

"Incredibly insane," he continued. "It makes no sense. Doesn't fit in with anything. Ridiculous." He ran out of words.

"I agree with you," said Weston. "It's all of those things. And it's also true."

"*Everything* causes cancer. Sunlight. Headache pills. Cars. Asbestos. You name it. It's all in black and white.

Has been for years. How can you say it's a contagious disease?''

''What you're saying means that the Nevada Project has been doing its job well. What you believe about the nature of the disease is what we've made you believe.''

''That can't be true.''

''It *is*, Granger. Almost twenty years ago this terrified little university researcher came cowering into the Department of Health. He told the same story. No one believed him but his research checked out. Cat mutations were springing up like weeds in the early sixties. Wire-hairs. No-hairs. Extra claws. No claws. And cats were dropping like flies from leukemia. Feline leukemia. Biggest killer of cats. And it's infectious. Any vet in the world will tell you. And if it's infectious in cats, why not humans? Incidence of it more than quadrupled when the mutations started. That's what the Nevada Project was all about. Downplay it. Keep gathering the information. Assemble a scientific team that would continue discreet research. But keep it quiet from the public until we had an explanation and a cure.

''Is there a cure?''

''*It's not a disease*. It's a biological incident that we have never faced before. That's one of the things that enabled us to obscure the issue. Research facilities that didn't know the truth just weren't looking in the right directions. There were enough environmental pollutants floating around causing cellular damage similar to cancer to keep doctors and scientists busy looking for a cure when they should have realized they were just dealing with incidents of poisoning. None of the studies with human subjects is worth anything because by now, everyone in the world has contracted the virus and it's incubating. Or like me, it's already started to transmit its message. But you've got it, Granger. All my agents have it. *Everyone has it*. The primary incubation period is coming to an end. The first wave will be on us within a year. Two at the most.''

''But they're always saying the statistics show that the incidence of cancer is decreasing.''

Weston raised his voice in anger. "For God's sake, man. Where do you think those statistics come from? Who do you think draws them up? *I do*. They all come out of the same government systems that told you we'd have peace with honor, and a balanced budget, and an end to inflation. I've never been able to figure out why so many people would believe those statistics when *everyone* knows someone with cancer. I figure the only way Nevada has managed to last so long is because the people *want* to believe. They don't dare consider the alternative."

"But surely other countries, other scientists . . ."

"The countries we trust are in on it with us. Others, like France and Canada, stay in the dark. If one of their scientists appears to have stumbled upon anything, we offer them well-paying positions at a facility where they can work on anything but cancer research. Or they have an accident."

"You *kill* people for this?"

"I faced that problem long ago, Granger. Believe me, better one or two people leave this earth a bit earlier than the others than have our entire economic and social structure collapse within a few days. Just think what we'd be like if the public knew. Business would collapse. Could you sit in an office next to people who might be breathing cancer viruses all over you? Even if you knew you had already got it, you would still hope there'd be a chance that you were the exception. Could you shop? Stay in the army? Do anything that required you to go outside your home? Farms would turn into armed camps within the two months it would take for the food supply chain to break down. There'd be anarchy. Civil conflicts. You'd risk that for the sake of one stubborn scientist?"

"Is there an answer, then? Has it been worth it?"

"There's only one place left to look, Granger. The *yber*."

"Do *they* know what's going on?"

"We're fairly certain that the Conclave know. St. Clair doesn't."

"Well, they'd have to cooperate. They feed on human

blood. What's going to happen to them when there are no more people left?''

''They aren't rational, Granger. As far as we know they could believe that Satan is going to set up restaurants for them to celebrate his victory over God on earth. We've tried dealing with them before. We've captured two of them in the past ten years. The first one died in a botched experiment when we tried to determine their sensitivity to sunlight. The second one escaped and tore up a town in Texas. A reporter caught on to the story. He wouldn't be bought off. His car exploded.''

''Why did you have to capture them? Why couldn't you negotiate with them?''

''Adrienne St. Clair is the first *yber* we've ever heard of who doesn't appear to be a devil-worshiper like the rest of them. All the *yber* we've had contact with are certifiably insane. What good would a vaccine prepared from their blood do us if, among the other changes it caused, it disrupted the normal function of the brain?''

''You think a vaccine against cancer is possible?''

Weston took a deep breath. He felt he was close to winning Helman over again. It had to happen soon if it was going to be of any value. The direction of the sun through the curtains was shifting. It was past noon. Less than half the day remained.

''The *yber* are not subject to the m-virus. The m-virus that operates in cats is communicable only through contact with bodily fluids: blood, saliva, excrement. The m-virus operating in humans is transmittable through air. That's what makes it so all-pervasive. But after the m-virus is properly accepted within the host body, some sort of biochemical shift takes place in the blood. It becomes incapable of accepting another m-virus through the lungs. But it *can* be passed on through the blood. That's why they have to almost drain the blood from their victims before making them drink *yber* blood. With so little blood left in the body, the m-viruses concentrated in the *yber* blood can't help but locate themselves in the proper receptor areas along the trachea and intestinal tract."

"I'm confused here," Helman said. He seemed to have totally forgotten that not more than an hour ago he was ready to kill Weston. A new challenge had, at least temporarily, taken hold. "You want to get Adrienne's help to use her blood to infect everyone in the world? If they're all vampires, they'll never get cancer?"

"No, Granger, you're oversimplifying. The *yber* mutation is very complex. It governs changes to the organs, brain, muscles, skin, digestive system, metabolism, almost every aspect of the human body. In most instances it improves them. Makes them more efficient. More resistant to disease and injury. In fact, since all our studies indicate that the *yber* are sterile and since evolution seems to be directed at only one thing, the survival of the genetic material, it would appear that a new evolutionary experiment is being tried. Instead of creating creatures that can pass the genetic material on from one generation to another for eternity, it looks as though a body has been created that, *by itself*, can carry the material throughout eternity. With the *yber*, immortality has been evolved. What we want to isolate in Adrienne's blood is the particular bits of DNA that govern the biological bloodshift that prevents the acceptance of the cancer-causing m-virus. Through gene-splicing, we can replicate that one section over and over, creating a vaccine to grant immunity to cancer. After that, we'll have time to isolate the other beneficial conditions. We won't all have to be vampires. But we should be able to share some of their abilities."

"Has anyone ever bothered to tell Adrienne any of this?"

"You don't really believe it. Why should she? Chris Leung was going to arrange it so she would arrive at some of the conclusions herself. It would have been a lot easier if she had come halfway to us by herself. But now time has run out. We'll have to risk taking her by force."

Helman sat in silence for long moments.

"That won't be necessary. I'll be able to bring her in. She'll believe me."

"You're sure?" Weston dared not look too expectant. If Helman had the least suspicion that he had been manipulated into his decision, he would, by nature, refuse to take part in anything to aid the Nevada Project.

"Will you guarantee protection for us?"

"Everything the government can provide."

"Will you give me all the assistance I need to hunt down Diego?"

"It will be next to impossible, Granger. I know from experience. But yes, anything we can provide to help you, you can have."

"It had better not be impossible, Major. One of you killed my sister and her children. If I can't get Diego, I'll get you."

"Understood. Now help me untie those two and get things in here back to normal. We've got a lot of preparation to do before we get Adrienne out of the Father's estate, and I'll have a lot of explaining to do about what's happened in here, and why we can trust you. If we can trust you."

Helman nodded once. "For tonight, Major Weston. And depending on how it does, we'll talk about it again."

In Washington the last of the Nevada files were going through the shredder. Except for four plain manilla envelopes sitting in a lawyer's office in London and a group of men and equipment waiting in Santa Barbara for the sun to set, nothing more remained of the project which had molded the world's perceptions for so long.

And whether anything at all would be left by sunrise tomorrow was something that none of them dared contemplate.

The final move was ready to be played and, for whatever it was worth, Helman was going into the endgame without knowing that he was still a pawn.

Eleven

The air force had never noticed the alterations which had been made to the hangar at the abandoned airfield. It had been constructed during the Vietnam conflict to handle the overflow traffic from Vandenberg. With the cessation of hostilities, it had become surplus. Occasionally, it was rented out to a movie crew to be transformed into a Hollywood version of an airfield of any world war, or of any country. But on that day, no one was on the field, and no one was within the totally light-tight main hangar. Except for the vampires.

They were the emissaries of the Western Meeting of the *yber*, assembled under Lord Diego. They were not like the business investors and financiers of the Eastern Meeting. They were feral and savage. Many had formed their bonding groups in Russia during the time of the pogroms. To the insane authorities of that time, one more dead Jew attracted no attention, even if the blood were completely drained and the throat horribly savaged. To the *yber* of the Western Meeting, humans were more than food, they were sport. And regrettably, in the modern world, the times for play were few.

Diego stood before the twenty-two of them. He was dressed as they were: form-fitting black jumpsuits that would not impede their preternatural reflexes. The suits included a black hood that held a cloth mouthpiece to hide the fangs of the *yber* who wore it. The Western Meeting had felt a thrill of bloodlust when Diego had told them it would not be necessary to wear the masks. Those that the *yber* faced that night must know who it was who would destroy them.

The *yber* sat and crouched like impatient animals on the crates that lined a wall of the hangar. Foam insulation had long ago been blown into every crack and wall separation that light threatened to sear through. Impatiently they waited for sunset and the massacre which would follow.

"We shall arrive forty minutes after the night begins," Diego said to them. "By that time the gates and the main entrances will have been breached by the Jesuits. The familiars of the Father are insipid and weak. His emissaries have renounced violence. They will offer no resistance. Those that survive the arrows of the Jesuits are yours to do with as you please."

The *yber* responded with unnatural snarls of anticipation.

"The Jesuits are to be reduced to manageable numbers. After the Father has been given the Final Death, *preferably* by the Jesuits, the Jesuits may be entirely taken. Also, not one of the *yber* associated with the Father must be allowed to continue. If one escapes to take word back to the Conclave, we are all doomed to see the sunrise."

In the darkness of the hangar, the breathing of the *yber* was like that of a cave full of unimaginable creatures.

"The woman is to be left to me. As is her human. He must be allowed to live long enough to see our surprise for him. So he knows what happens to those who dare betray us."

The *yber* snorted approval. The surprise for Helman slept in the back of one of the three vans parked at the main door of the hangar. They had undergone Communion much too recently to resist the powerful urge to rest when the sun blazed.

But when the sun set they would awaken from their dreamless sleep and once again be excited by Diego's promise that they could finally see their uncle.

Impatiently, saliva dripping from their expectant fangs, the *yber* of the Western Meeting waited.

Twelve

All except the scholastic who drove the U-Haul Adventure in Moving truck along the twisting road bowed their heads in prayer. It was a Holy War they were going to fight and Clement had instructed them to wear the symbols of their order. Unlike some of the more covert operations the older of the Jesuits had taken part in, this time their crossbows were not hidden.

Clement sat among the scholastics and novitiates in the back of the closed truck. His soldiers of the Church would be well protected by their crucifixes and vials of Holy Water. The stakes and hammers that most carried in the cases at their sides would be weapons enough if they were able to arrive before the sun set. But Clement was still shaken by the way Diego had been unaffected by the Holy artifacts. For Diego, Clement carried something more secular, and far more powerful against one who did not believe in the power of the Lord. He carried a hand grenade a lay brother had obtained for him. Clement would offer himself up to Diego. And when the unholy fangs sank within Clement's neck he would remove the pin, sending each of them to his fate. Clement, with the twisted logic that had always allowed desperate men to justify any means to an end, devoutly believed that both he and the Lord of the Conclave would have different fates awaiting them.

The truck slowed. The driver pounded his fist three times on the back of the cab. It was the signal. The estate was one bend in the road away.

The back doors swung open and the Jesuits filed out like trained soldiers. Two of them carried the equipment which would blow open the gates to the estate. Before them went the marksmen who would eliminate the familiars who served as guards.

The setting sun cast long shadows across the hills.

The Jesuits swept silently through the brush, approaching the gates of the estate. The marksmen prayed to God to guide them in their murder of the familiars.

But the familiars were not at the gates.

And the gates were open.

The Jesuits poured through the gates like a black tide.

All was as the Father had dreamt.

Thirteen

Helman searched the skies for the Nevada team. There was nothing but a few red-tinted clouds scattered through a purpling sky. The sun almost touched the ocean. He forced the screaming car faster.

Near the final turn to the estate gates, a large rental moving truck blocked the road. He took the car off the road in a squealing attempt to miss the truck and it became bogged down in the soft grass.

Helman jumped out of the car and ran the rest of the way. The gates were open. The courtyard was clear. But smoke billowed from the northern wing of the main building. Black figures scurried across the shattered windows on the ground floors.

He was too late. The Jesuits had already arrived.

Helman dodged over to the shelter of some ornamental

trees. The courtyard was filled with brilliant red light from the sun which was now half hidden at the horizon. Adrienne was inside that building. Just now awakening. Helpless before the weapons of the priests.

He charged toward the main entrance. The weapons harness he wore bounced jerkily against him, throwing him off balance. They were the weapons of the Nevada team, specially designed to be used against the creatures who could not die. The most awkward was the gyrojet, a handgun that served as a handheld rocket launcher for miniature, solid fuel rockets. They were far more devastating than any exploding bullet could be. They would detonate on impact even with the soft yielding flesh of the *yber*.

Helman drew the smooth metal-clad weapon and held it at the ready as he ran. It was just a matter of time before the Jesuits spotted him.

Then one was at the double doorway of the main entrance. Immediately he raised and fired his crossbow. Helman couldn't twist in time. The bolt struck him squarely in the chest and spun off the impenetrable Kevlar armor he wore beneath the harness. It scraped by his unprotected face as it ricocheted, tearing at the flesh and leaving a trail of blood in its wake.

Helman fired the gyrojet. There was a flash of the projectile's exhaust venting through the side baffles of the launching tube. Almost simultaneously there was an explosion at the marble staircase in front of the doors where the Jesuit stood. Helman had expected a recoil from the rocket gun but it had launched clean and his aim had been low. The Jesuit had been sprayed with hundreds of marble shards. He clawed at his blinded eyes and fell writhing to the pitted staircase.

There were no others behind him. Helman ran and scooped the body to the side of the entrance way. The Jesuit screamed. Helman lashed out with the solid butt of the gyrojet. The Jesuit stopped. Adrienne was inside. Nothing was going to stop him from getting to her.

He ripped at the Jesuit's black cloak and pulled it over his own head. The disguise might buy him a few moments of surprise.

The sun set. The red afterglow in the low-lying clouds near the horizon made the courtyard look as if it were being consumed by an enormous fire.

Helman prepared to enter the building. The air vibrated strangely. He looked up. Three helicopters grew in the crimson sky. The Nevada team had arrived. But Helman could no more wait for them now than he could wait for them that afternoon after Weston had equipped him. He would have to go in alone.

Screams filled the house of the Father. Helman nearly tripped over the bodies of two familiars, white kaftans stained red by the multiple arrows that pierced them.

Both their heads had been savagely hacked at. Both were attached by only thin flaps of flesh. The Jesuits fought the battle of Armageddon. The demons of Hell could be shown no mercy.

Most of the screams echoed up from a grand stairway at the side of the four-story entrance hall. Helman ran for it. Underground would be the best protected from the light of day.

A balcony ran along three sides of the entranceway at the second-story level. It stopped only at the four-story high glass wall covered with enormous theater-like curtains. The balcony could be reached only by one staircase at the southwest corner. Clement had wisely placed the marksmen there. They had seen Helman don the cloak of their brother. Their arrows stung down upon him. The fabric of his cloak held them after they had stopped against the Kevlar. Bristling with arrows he dived down the staircase which descended from the main level.

Into the basement, he thought. It was like a warning.

The helicopters touched down in a deafening throbbing roar in the middle of the courtyard. The last thirty men and women of the Nevada Project moved quickly. Two helicopters stayed down while crates of equipment were unloaded. The other was emptied of its human cargo and immediately soared up again. It would circle until the word came that St. Clair was ready to be taken away.

Weston deployed his agents as they had planned. The windows of the building had all long ago been covered over to protect the *yber* from the sunlight. Two squads of five people each began blasting the windows with gyrojet rockets. Some windows collapsed easily. Others, including the ones looking into the entrance hall, were armored and resisted the explosions.

The rest of the team assembled three giant banks of floodlights. Generators were started. The floodlights glowed an eerie violet color as the courtyard and the rooms behind the shattered windows were bathed in ultra-violet light.

The first *yber* was taken.

He appeared screaming in the ruin of a broken window, wearing the white robe of an emissary of the Father. He screamed piercingly as the light ate at him; blistering and blackening him as the humans in the courtyard watched, fascinated and chilled.

The creature fell from the second-story window. Only his white smock survived the fall to the ground. There was no body within it. All that remained was the white sludge of the blood of life.

Two of Weston's people immediately ran for the remains of the *yber*. They carried a metal case holding sterile sample jars. Quickly they scraped as much of the white fluid into the containers as they could. Weston called the helicopter down to retrieve the precious substance. He knew it would only last about an hour outside the body of an *yber*. But he hoped that one way or another, the operation would be over before that hour was up.

The lights formed an impassable barricade for the *yber*. Weston's team in the courtyard would be safe until the signal came that Adrienne was to be brought out. That last thirty seconds when the lights would be cut and Adrienne would be transported to the helicopter would be their most vulnerable.

The helicopter ascended again. Weston gathered the first assault team.

He led them in.

Diego knew that the Jesuits weren't clever enough to be responsible for the painful blue glow that washed across the Father's estate. The Americans had become involved.

But Diego had seldom been surprised in the past centuries. He was not surprised now.

He said the words "warrior suits" to the *yber* who waited for his command, and they knew what they were to do.

The *yber* of the Western Meeting placed protective enclosures of dark mirrored plastic over their heads. Thick hand coverings that ended in vicious spring-loaded steel hooks to replace their hidden claws were attached to the sleeves of their jumpsuits.

The *yber* were now impervious to the deadly radiation.

Adrienne St. Clair had begun a deep fascination for technology and science within Diego. He regretted that he would never be able to thank her adequately.

The carnage in the courtyard was awesome.

The *yber* were like cutting machines, whirling their metal claws too fast for the humans to see. The Nevada team remaining in the courtyard was sliced and gutted and scattered like hay before a scythe. Most never even saw the dark glittering shapes that burst from the shadows like eruptions of black lava. It was over in seconds.

Sparks flying from their blood-drenched steel claws, the *yber* ripped at the generator's cables. The hateful lights died. Far above the hovering helicopter tried to raise the ground crew on the radio. There was no response. Knowing the people on the ground would be at the mercy of the *yber* while the lights were off, the pilot did the only thing she could do. She went down to rescue her friends.

She realized her mistake only when the helicopter loading doors swung open after she landed and the *yber* swarmed in, engulfing her.

This time, without the killing lights, they needed no steel implements to replace their own.

With a final desperate push before the fangs and claws descended, the pilot jammed the rotor control forward.

The helicopter bucked wildly and flew sideways into the other parked copters. The fireball returned the red glow of the setting sun to the courtyard.

The concussion collapsed part of the south wing. More windows were blown out.

In the small town of Nacimiento, the explosion rolled through the streets like thunder. Some of the residents refused to go to their windows to watch. Many had known something like this would happen when "the people" had first moved in. Others tried to phone the State Police, the fire department, even the army. But the last command of Nevada was in place. None of the townspeople knew that there were codewords to be said before any arm of the government could move into Nacimiento.

The orders which had created those conditions were being traced hurriedly by nervous bureaucrats who were afraid to act against them. And undoubtedly there would be an inquiry into just what had happened that night.

But by then, it would be far too late.

The first basement level had been designed for entertaining. It was elaborately finished and opulently paneled. But now the sections of wooden paneling had been ripped from the walls by the frantic Jesuits. Behind some of the damaged wall sections there had been hidden alcoves because now, after the Jesuits, each alcove contained only a wooden stake driven through an empty kaftan stained with a thick mixture of white syrup and the dust of *yber*.

Helman ran frantically through the hallways. Stopping at each ruined sanctuary to see if Adrienne's clothes were lying amidst the horror of an *yber* death. Panic rose in him. *Where was she?*

Footsteps clattered behind him. He spun, crossbow hiding the reloaded gyrojet in his hand.

A scholastic shouted to him.

"They're all taken care of down there. We've got to find the Father. The sun has set!"

Helman nodded and ran with them. If they hadn't found the Father yet, perhaps Adrienne was with him. There might still be a chance.

They rounded a corner. Another Jesuit stared incredulously into Helman's face.

"It's him!"

Helman fired the rocket into the man's chest. His head and limbs flew off as his torso burst in the explosion.

One of the scholastics fired his crossbow. The arrow's impact knocked Helman back a foot. It hung limply in his robe.

The scholastic yelled "Aim for his face" to the other who raised his crossbow.

Helman swung up his arm and rolled into the Jesuit. The bolt tore through his upraised forearm. He bellowed in pain.

With his good arm, Helman smashed the Jesuit's head against the floor with a sickening wet pop. He unsheathed the special barbed bayonet tied to his leg and thrust up at the other Jesuit who was attacking.

Helman misjudged and his wounded arm slipped out from him on the blood that had sprayed from the Jesuit shot by the rocket gun. Helman rolled away. Trying to get himself out of reach of the Jesuit who now held a crossbow bolt in his hand like a stake.

The Jesuit charged.

Helman held the bayonet before him in a useless guarding action.

A black shape lunged out of nowhere and the Jesuit flew through the air. His neck crunched as he smashed against the hallway wall.

The shape solidified before Helman. It had fangs that dripped with blood.

A black clad leg snaked out invisibly fast and Helman's bayonet clattered down the hallway.

The *yber* grabbed at him.

"Diego has something special planned for you, human. We are all eager to watch," it snarled at him.

The mention of Diego enflamed Helman. As the vampire dragged him up from the floor, Helman reached down and grabbed the crucifix from the fallen Jesuit he had smashed to the ground.

Helman swung the crucifix up against the *yber's* face.

The result was instantaneous.

There was a sizzling sound of burning flesh. The *yber* screamed and twisted away, releasing his grip. His hands clutched at the cross-shaped burn that blazed across his face. One eye was closed by a ballooning blister.

"Diego said you didn't believe," the *yber* spat, warily cowering before the outstretched crucifix in Helman's hand.

"But you do, don't you?" said Helman as he rushed at the vampire, driving the long end of the crucifix up through the soft tissue under the jaw. There was little resistance. It sank rapidly into the brain.

The *yber* twisted and writhed on the floor. His arms shook like they were palsied as he desperately tried to control them enough to take the burning cross from his skull.

Helman retrieved his bayonet.

The *yber* pulled the crucifix from out of his flesh and threw it to the side. He snarled in pain and rage. The skin beneath his neck was blackened and his hands were swollen globes of red.

Helman leapt upon him, driving the bayonet through the creature's chest.

The scream as Helman lay upon the writhing thing nearly deafened him. Then it ceased as if a loudspeaker had shut off. Helman felt himself sink to the floor.

The bayonet had found its mark. The *yber* had dissolved.

Helman stood up, shaking.

His Jesuit's robe was covered in the white ooze that ran from the empty black jumpsuit on the floor. He ripped the robe off and threw it away.

He picked up the gyrojet, reloaded, and ran off in the

direction that the Jesuits had been heading in to search for the Father.

He had to beat Diego to Adrienne.

Weston stared helplessly at the burning ruins of the helicopters in the courtyard. Even if St. Clair were located, he had no idea how they would get her away to safety. Unless his agents could somehow eliminate all the Jesuits and *yber* who swarmed through the Father's estate.

The Jesuits would be easy. As long as they persisted in aiming their crossbows at his people's midsections, the Kevlar would protect them. And the Jesuits, who somehow thought that God was protecting them, made very little effort to hide or protect themselves on their own.

The *yber* were a far more dangerous matter. The white-robed *yber* who served as emissaries of the Father were not a concern. They had been, it seemed, completely wiped out in the Jesuits' pre-sunset raid.

The black-clad *yber* were devastating. They fell in the ripping explosions of the gyrojets, but only two of the guns remained with the first assault squad. The rest had been lost when the *yber* who had armored themselves against the UV floodlights had swarmed through the courtyard.

At least a third of them had been scorched to the Final Death in the Helicopter explosions. Surrounded by flames, the *yber* could not resist the massive moisture loss for long. But others had entered the building from other entrances. Everyone was engaged in a frantic search for the woman. Weston had no choice but to join in. He gathered the eight of his people who survived and led them deeper into the Father's house.

Helman found a passage to the sub-basement. Two Jesuits lay dead at the foot of the staircase. Their throats had been ripped out. He walked through the darkness slowly. One hand carried the gyrojet. The other carried a cross.

The basement appeared to run the full width and depth of the building above him. It was dimly lit by dull orange emergency lights. The fire in the north wing seemed to have triggered an antiquated fire control system.

As he walked deeper into the hidden recesses of the concrete-floored expanse, he could sense the air becoming damper, thicker. He could hear water dripping. He tried to recall his run through the levels of the building to determine precisely where he was standing in it. He was under the courtyard. The pumping equipment that was intended to run the pool and fountain was to his left. It was the source of the water. And the steady dripping noise that masked the other sounds of movement behind him.

A strong sense of *déja vu* overtook him. He could feel that he was no longer alone. That he had been in this basement a long time ago. Or, at least, another basement like it.

Something made a rhythmic splashing sound behind him. He spun, finger tightening on the launch button of the gun. The rhythmic sound sped up, came closer. It stopped.

A dry, sibilant voice whispered at him from the darkness.

"Looking for something, little boy?"

Helman remembered that long-ago basement. The door swinging shut. The throbbing of his wounded arm carrying the crucifix disappeared as he felt the hair on the back of his neck bristle in a response to fear far older than humans. He could actually feel his skin crawl as he stared deep within the darkness and saw the things he had feared so much as a child.

"Looking for your ball? Want to play with us?"

Helman looked down. The rhythmic splashing had been a ball bouncing. How could they know?

A deeper, harsher voice whispered out at him.

"We know what you dream, human. We can make them *all* come true. Dreams and nightmares."

Helman could feel the panic grow within him. They had touched something too deep within himself to resist. How?

He jerked his head backward and forward. He couldn't remember the way back to the staircase. More sounds of movement slithered out of the black. He was surrounded. A low groan of desperation came from within him without him knowing. *They were all around him.*

"Someone want to play with us?" two voices chanted out.

"Come find your ball, little boy. Come play in the basement."

Helman's chest tightened. His breath came in gasps. The sounds were wet and all around him. All around him.

And then four tiny hands reached out and gently took his arms and he stared down into those familiar, lovely faces with such small fangs newly growing from their mouths that he could almost believe that they were still the same.

"Uncle Granger," Steven and Campbell said together. "We've missed you."

Clement crawled slowly up the main staircase that led to the balcony running on three sides of the four-story high entrance hall. He had seen Diego. He would trust his young scholastics to find and destroy the woman, but Diego was his. And Diego was waiting in the room just off the end of the balcony closest to the thick, lightproof curtains of the hung-glass wall.

Clement slipped the hand grenade from his equipment pouch and tucked it into his robe and under his shirt. He left his shirt buttons undone so he could reach in for the detonator pin when the moment came.

Within the room where Diego waited, a black-clad *yber* sniffed at the air and motioned toward the open door.

Diego shook his head.

"Let him come. I've waited forty years for him to come to me. Let him come now."

Diego smiled. He could feel the thirst rise in him. The excitement of quenching it with the blood of Clement made his fangs wet with anticipation.

Father Clement appeared in the doorway.

"Come in *Clemencito*. I've been expecting you."

Sounds of fighting still rumbled through the half-destroyed building. Weston realized with a faint glimmer of hope that more of his people might have survived than the three who were now left with him. Some of the sounds he heard were the dull explosions of gyrojets. Others the bloodcurdling shrieks of the dying, human and *yber* alike.

The section of the mansion he was in seemed deserted now. The fighting sounded as if it had concentrated in the parts leading back to the entrance hall. He waved his three people to stay put and kicked open a door into a guestroom, gyrojet at the ready.

The room was empty. He checked the closet and under the bed. All the walls were solid. He went to the windows and pulled on the curtains. The track was heavily reinforced, perhaps as insurance that an earthquake wouldn't knock it out of the wall while visiting *yber* stayed within the room. But with a powerful enough yank the curtains collapsed and the room was exposed to the dark eastern sky.

The night had been long and in just over an hour the sun would rise again. Not that that will solve anything, he thought.

Then he heard the snarl behind him. The *yber* was in the doorway, the severed head of the last of the Nevada agents within his claws. The shattered bodies of the two others lay in the hallway behind him.

It charged at Weston.

The gyrojet flared.

The creature dissolved in the explosion like a blizzard of snow. Except the whiteness was liquid and it hung like a mist in the air.

Weston got up from where the concussion had blasted him. The tightness in his chest was building again and he knew it was time for another injection. The drug would ease the pain and make it possible for him to breathe. But he knew he had crossed the limit and the strain on his body was going to make either this injection, or the next, fatal.

He wondered if Helman were still alive. He cursed himself for not telling Helman about the pocket on the weapon harness that Weston had given him; the pocket with the slip of paper in it. Even if Helman were to get out of this alive, he would probably not find the paper, and even then he might now know what to do with it.

And when Weston cursed himself again for not reloading the gyrojet as another *yber* sprang at him from the shadows of the hallway and dug its claws into his neck, forcing him back against the wall.

His vision was sparkling with the black dots of lack of blood but he was able to see the face of the *yber* was a woman's. And it had no fangs.

Weston was looking into the snarling face of Adrienne St. Clair.

In the basement, they had fed from him. Depleted, drained, and forced to endure horrors worse than any childhood fancy, Granger Helman was led up out of the darkness to meet with Diego. His eyes wore the vacant expression of the damned. They did not wish to see further. His blood ringed the lips of the children who walked beside him and discolored the fangs of the women who remained in the basement. He bore many wounds that were not on the veins of his neck.

The children of his sister took him gently by the hands and brought him in to meet their new father, Lord Diego.

Faced with the presence of the monster who had destroyed his life, Helman felt empty. Everything around him which he had cherished, they had taken from him. Everything he held tightly within himself as his strength and identity, they had exposed and crushed. He had no more capacity to loathe Diego. There was nothing left to him that mattered. There was nothing.

But Diego was ecstatic. Clement and the betrayer assassin both in one night. Only the girl was required now, and from the sounds of the fighting, her capture appeared to be imminent.

"So, children," he beamed through his fangs. "You have finally brought your uncle to meet with me again. It seems like such a long time since I spoke with him in New York. Don't you think so, human?"

Helman stood silently. Nothing.

"My friend, Father Clement here, has finally come to his senses, human. He wants to be my familiar again as he did so many years ago. Would you like to be my familiar also, human? Stay with your charming nephews, forever?"

"Please, Granger. Please do it. What he says," the children said.

Helman looked down at them. Their faces so familiar, so monstrous. He said nothing.

"Watch how easy it is, human," Diego said and moved toward Father Clement.

The *yber* who had kept a grip on Clement since his arrival let go and moved away. Clement filled his mind with prayers. The hand grenade was cold against his belly.

"Father Clement here will make an excellent familiar. His mind is disciplined. Difficult to peer into." Diego stood in front of Clement, eyeing him like an insect about to be crushed.

"You, on the other hand, human, have a weak mind. There were too many things that you cared about. It made your mind open. Some *yber* are trained in such things. Like the woman in the basement. We know all *your* dreams, human. But for you, *Clemencito* . . . what is it that you dream of?"

Diego spread his arms like some hellish bat enwrapping its victim. Clement's hands moved up to his neck and worked at removing his cleric's collar and opening his robe and shirt.

Diego hugged the Jesuit closely to him and looked within his eyes. Helman watched impassively. The other *yber* in the room was entranced by the sight of a Jesuit giving himself freely to his Lord.

"What are your dreams?" said Diego. He brushed his lips against Clement's face and bent his head toward the exposed neck.

Father Clement's hands moved between them.

Diego stiffened.

Catlike, his clawed hand jerked in between them, clutching at something Helman could not see.

Clement clenched his eyes shut.

Diego's opened in surprise.

With one hand he lifted Clement into the air by his neck and with the other sent him shooting through the open doorway.

Father Clement's body was engulfed in midair.

The room shook with the force of the explosion.

Helman was blasted back against a wall and slumped against it. His nephews curled up on the floor. The *yber* guard stumbled backward but did not fall.

Clement's body had directed most of the explosion back into the room. The doorway had focused it on Diego. He turned slowly to face the others in the room. His face was a mass of dark welts and rivulets of thick, white liquid. His black jumpsuit was shredded. But he smiled. Delighted.

"How unexpected," he said.

His face and the flesh of his upper chest where the shrapnel of the grenade had torn through it was literally creeping before Helman's eyes as the accelerated metabolism repaired the damage.

Diego turned to Helman.

"And what tricks do you have ready for me before I rip out your throat?" he snarled.

Helman didn't raise his hands to protect himself.

He didn't even wonder what it would be like.

He just knew it couldn't be worse than what had happened in the basement, when the living needles of his nephews' fangs had slipped through his skin, deep into his veins and flesh and drawn so much more from him than just blood. After that, he could accept anything else. Anything.

Diego came closer.

Something moved in the doorway.

"Eduardo."

The voice from the doorway burst upon Helman's mind like a wave. He looked past Diego. Diego recognized it also and spun.

In the doorway stood Adrienne St. Clair. Behind her was Major Weston.

In her hands she held a Nevada gyrojet.

Diego opened his mouth as if to say something.

The gun erupted.

The explosion flowered from Diego's midsection. He flew backward through the air. Helman felt the intense heat of the explosion as the fiery body rushed past. Diego's legs, severed in the explosion, lay before Helman. They twitched once and then, like paper consumed by fire, fell in on themselves and were dissolved.

The *yber* guard was disintegrated by Weston's gun.

"Adrienne," Helman said. Something had come back to him.

She ran to him. Put her arms around him.

"It's all right," she said. "We're going to get out of here. There are too many *yber* here for the location sense to work clearly. They aren't able to detect me. Weston told me everything."

"You believe him?"

"If you believe him, that's all I care about. I saw them taking you here. I thought you were gone."

Helman felt life returning to him. He looked up at Weston.

Weston's face was frozen in horror.

"*Diego!*" he screamed.

A clawed thing dug into Helman's leg.

The maniacal face of Diego snarled up at him. One hand held Helman's ankle. The other clawed arm stretched up for his neck. It snared on the weapons harness and began digging in, ripping through even the Kevlar armor, tearing for Helman's heart.

Adrienne fell back. The explosion had not reached Diego's heart. He was little more than a torso with arms, but he lived. She grabbed at the bayonet sheathed on Weston's leg. Helman struggled frantically against the half-monster that crawled inexorably up his body.

Adrienne attacked. She jabbed the bayonet into Diego's back. He screamed and fell back from Helman. She did not release her grip on the blade and it slipped from him.

She went to slash at him again. Weston desperately tried

to reload the gyrojet with his trembling hands. Helman ran to help him. His nephews stared at the struggle in confusion.

Diego swung his arm savagely at Adrienne, catching her on the knees. She was down. He crawled on her.

Helman couldn't fire the reloaded gun without hitting her.

He kicked out and caught Diego on the temple.

Without his full weight to stabilize him, Diego rolled off.

Helman aimed.

Adrienne jumped up in front of Helman's line of fire and began hacking at the writhing torso of Diego. She screamed hysterically. All she could see was Jeffery writhing in the sunrise where Diego's emissaries had chained him.

She slashed again and again. Diego bled white blood like a burst infection.

"Go for his heart," Helman screamed at her. "*His heart.*"

Diego was almost out of the door onto the balcony. Helman reached out and grabbed Adrienne's shoulder to push her out of the way so he could fire at Diego.

She snarled at Helman. "He's mine. For Jeffery."

She turned back to Diego. He was gone.

She ran out on the balcony. He was crawling away. Helman ran out after her.

"*Face me, Eduardo,*" Adrienne screamed.

Diego twisted on the floor.

The bayonet arced down for his neck.

At the last instant he contorted his half-body.

The bayonet sliced cleanly through his right arm. It dissolved before it hit the ground.

Diego roared. He rolled and tried to push himself up with his left arm. Adrienne thrust the bayonet into the middle of Diego's back so violently he crashed through the balcony railing and whirled down onto the solid marble floor of the entrance hall. There was a solid thud as he hit. Then a final, hollow gasp of breath. Then silence.

In the near-darkness, there was nothing left. Helman went to her. "We've got to get back to cover. There are still more of them around."

She turned to him. In the dim light of the emergency fire lights he saw the animal look of hate fade from her features.

"He's gone," she said.

"He's gone," Helman agreed. "Now let's get back to Weston."

She turned once more to look over the railing into the darkness.

"Come on," Helman said.

She stiffened.

From the other side of the entrance hall, a shriek of triumph rang from the balcony opposite.

"Death to the daughter of Satan!"

Adrienne lurched back against Helman, her eyes open in shock. A crossbow bolt was imbedded at the edge of her shoulder. Her mouth opened to gasp for air and a slimy gout of white blood vomited out.

Adrienne clutched at her chest. Helman saw a Jesuit reloading his crossbow on the far balcony. He leveled the gyrojet and the Jesuit was consumed in the explosion.

He carried Adrienne back to the room where Weston waited. Campbell and Steven crouched in a corner, whimpering.

Helman tried to pull on the arrow. Adrienne stopped him.

"It's too close," she choked. "Touching the heart. Mustn't force it."

"What happened to your armor?" Helman asked uselessly.

"I'm wearing it, Granger." She tried to smile. "Slipped by on the shoulder."

"What can I do?"

"I need some quiet. Can't concentrate on healing like this. Got to work it out a bit at a time. Heal it slowly." She stopped with a gurgling series of coughs. More white blood trickled from her mouth.

"It's almost sunrise," Weston said. "It's got to stop then."

"Don't count on it, Major," Helman said. "She's told me about the offices they run in Zurich. As long as they're protected from the sun, they just keep going."

"I've got five charges left for the gyro. Maybe there aren't more than five of them left," Weston said and crouched in the doorway, keeping guard.

"Is there anything I can do?" Helman asked her.

"Just hold me," she said. "It helps me concentrate."

He held her.

In the corner, the two children, only two days from their Communion, sank into the dreamless sleep of day.

Outside, the sun was rising.

By two hours after sunrise the sounds of fighting were sporadic. Few screams were heard and the last two explosions had been Weston's. Two black-suited *yber*, wearing the dark mirrored helmets that had protected them from the banks of UV floodlights had dissolved.

One narrow shaft of sunlight shone brilliantly through a parting of the immense curtains that covered the hung-glass wall that faced the rising sun.

Weston had fired his gyrojet at them much earlier. The drapes were not substantial enough to cause the small rocket to detonate. It had torn through the fabric and shattered the glass behind it. Only a narrow beam of light showed where the explosion had taken place.

He had fired another at the center of the massive track that supported the curtains, but it too had been reinforced as a precaution against earthquakes.

Adrienne, Helman, and Weston stayed protected in the room off the balcony that Diego had made his headquarters. They had only one charge left for the gun. And in the dim scattering of sunlight, they could see that there were still Jesuits on the balcony and *yber* down below. From time to time they called out to the trapped humans above. The Jesuits would answer with a salvo of arrows which would clatter uselessly on the floor. The *yber* would howl with delight.

"How's she doing?" Weston asked.

"*She* is doing fine, Major," Adrienne said. "I've got about two inches of it out so far, but I'm feeling resistance.

I think it has a barbed tip. If I pull on it any more it will tear through the muscle of the heart. I'm going to have to leave it where it is."

"Is there nothing you can do?" Weston spoke with his back to them as he watched the developments in the entrance hall.

"If we don't have to hurry, I can walk. If I can get to a doctor all I need is to have my chest opened up above the arrow and have it lifted out from above. It will heal in a single night."

"Think we can walk out of here by tonight, Major?" Helman asked.

"I don't know. But take a look at this. Those Jesuits over there are up to something."

Helman crawled toward the doorway and lay down beside Weston. Weston's voice was weak and quavering. Helman had seen him give himself an injection. He had been rapidly looking worse ever since. Helman was familiar with the effects of many chemicals. Even if he and Adrienne were able to walk out of the mansion that evening, Helman doubted if Weston would be alive to join them.

"Those two over there," Weston said, pointing with the barrel of the gyrojet.

In the darkness, Helman could see three Jesuits crouched in a doorway off the balcony on the other side of the entrance hall, just as he and Weston were. They seemed to be preparing for something.

Suddenly one of them burst off along the balcony toward the glass wall. The other two jumped to the balcony railing and fired their crossbows into the darkness.

The third Jesuit leapt to the edge of the railing and dove off, straight into the curtains.

At least five arrows hit him while he was in the air. He crashed screaming into the curtains and fell the twenty feet to the floor. Black shapes scuttled out of the darkness and surrounded his body. The Jesuits by the railing were recocking their crossbows, screaming at the *yber* in the shadows. They fired their weapons down at the creatures dragging away the body of their brother. Then two figures swung up over the railing where they had been hanging like bats and took them.

The Jesuits' headless bodies were thrown off the balcony. The *yber* below shrieked in victory.

"It's just a matter of time before they get us," Weston said. "There're probably half-a dozen under our part of the balcony right now just waiting for the moment when they think our weapon is unloaded."

"And they're using the Jesuits' crossbows. They wouldn't even have to get close to us." Helman was thinking about what the Jesuits had tried to do.

"There's a way to do that properly," Weston said.

"Pull down the curtains?"

"The secret's not to get shot when you make the jump."

"How do you manage that?"

"When you start your run, I'll fire this straight in the middle of the floor down there. That will stop them just for the two seconds you need to rip those curtains off the track with the momentum of your body."

"My body?"

"I can't run, Granger. Where I'm laying now is where I'm going to die. I've taken so many stimulants and painkillers to get my lungs this far that this is as far as I go."

"What happens to Nevada?"

"You're Nevada. No one else is left. Some rumors will start soon when a few envelopes of our findings are distributed outside the States. But there's no one else to do our work. Just you. And Adrienne."

"How? I only know what you told me yesterday."

"In your harness. In the pocket there, by the clasp. All the information you need. Go do it. Get the sun in here before they decide to rush us."

Helman crawled back to Adrienne.

"I'm going to open the curtains out there. Bring in the sun." He pulled up on the rug on the floor and covered her with it. "I'll be back," he said.

"Granger—" she began.

He quietened her with his hand.

"It's all right," he said. "I'll be back."

He pulled the other half of the rug over the comatos
forms of Steve and Campbell, then joined Weston back a
the doorway.

"No way the enemy is going to come and get us out o
this one?" he asked.

"The codes are in," Weston said. "Nobody's going t
set foot here for days. The story's already going out to th
good people of Nacimiento that they're just filming anothe
movie up here. Somewhere in Washington the word is tha
there's a biological weapons spill up here. It's coded at suc
a high level that it will be days before any agency realize
that nobody's doing anything about it. We're on our own."

Helman clapped Weston on the shoulder.

"Get ready to fire then." He stood up against the door
frame. The path down the balcony seemed clear.

Weston forced himself to his knees. He was very un
steady and used both hands to steady the gyrojet.

"Now!" Helman snapped and tore off down the balcony

The *yber* below shrieked and hooted like animals.

Helman reached the end of the balcony. Weston lurche
forward and fired straight down. The explosion flared withi
the darkened hallway. Helman leapt.

Blinded by the flash, Weston heard more than saw th
dark shape that rushed toward him.

Helman made the jump easily. Not a single arrow cam
near.

He slid about five feet down the fabric as he swung int
it. The fold of cloth he clutched at burned like rope as i
ripped through his fingers. But he dug in and his grip held

His momentum swung him one way, then another. Th
track buckled just a small bit and when he swung back th
curtains parted for an instant and let in a killing shaft of sun

But then he swung back again. The shaft disappeared
And the track held firm.

Then they found him with their arrows.

Some hit the curtains where he hung. He felt others sto

against his Kevlar vest. He swung himself violently on the fabric. His injured arm gave out. He hung by one hand.

An arrow hit his leg. Another in his bad arm. The *yber* screamed at him. He felt dizzy. Another arrow in the back of his thigh. He fell feet first down the immovable curtains, smashing and rolling onto the floor.

He was stunned. Unable to move. But he saw that the entrance hall was still in darkness. And from that darkness, they came for him.

Fourteen

It was over.

The claws of the creatures dug into him.

He felt them drag him over the marble floor toward the dark room they gathered in.

They laughed down on him. They tore off their helmets to show him their fangs dripping with spittle and blood.

Their shrieking and howling washed over him until he heard it no more. The *yber* danced around him frantically, screaming for his blood. But Helman's mind protected him and he only had senses for the one narrow beam of light that shone through the small hole in the curtains.

The creatures dragged him farther into the darkness.

He saw dust motes dance lightly in the beam. Swirling gently. Then faster. Then madly.

He peered more intently. He realized he was seeing glowing motes where there was no light. They were caught in a luminescent tendril that snaked across the floor in front of the curtains. It was as if the one beam of light was spreading out and melting on the floor, forming impossible shapes.

It was glowing brighter now. Forming more densely. Swirling like thick smoke lit from within.

It rose from the floor. Contracting upwards. And then it was six-and-a-half feet tall and the swirling stopped. The glowing motes coalesced and the image of the Father stood before them in all his skeletal monstrosity.

And he lifted his arms and he said in a voice that shook the floor and wall, "Behold."

His hands, all joints and knuckles and tendons, stretched unnaturally far behind him and burrowed into the fabric of the curtains.

The jibbering of the *yber* had stopped. The hall was silent.

And the Father said: "I am the Resurrection and the *Light*!"

And he wrenched down and the curtains flew away like leaves in a gale.

The sun poured in like a tidal wave. The Father crumpled and swirled into dust in its impact.

The *yber* around Helman were smashed to the floor as if by an explosion.

The shrieking began again. And this time it was the haunting cry of mortal pain.

And through it all, Helman could hear Adrienne shouting out his name.

His legs were useless from the arrows and the fall. He crawled to her.

All around him black and red blistered things bubbled and writhed in the death grip of the sun. Frantically they tried to replace their protective helmets, but the shock of pure sunlight had stunned them. The *yber* in shadows were even more unlucky because the sun worked more slowly on them. Their skin puckered and flaked as if a flame thrower were being held against them. Finally the skin blackened and their cries turned to liquid gurgles. In the end, all that was left was a pile of empty clothes, and a rapidly drying, dust-thickened pool of the blood of life.

Helman crawled to the cries of Adrienne.

He pulled himself painfully, slowly up the stairs. *Yber* still dissolving around him.

He crawled along the balcony. He came to the door.

Weston lay there. Dead. A Jesuit's stake through his heart. A blackened, decomposing *yber* body lay across him. The curtains had opened just seconds too late.

Adrienne was half-uncovered by the rug. A brilliant shaft of light shone through the doorway. It had fallen against her exposed legs. Beneath her knees, her legs were blackened and charred stumps.

Helman dragged Weston's body inside the door and shut the door to the balcony. Light still spilled out around the door frame.

He went to Adrienne.

Her skin was red. Blisters had formed on the side of her face closer to the door.

"Weston saved me," she cried. "He got up and threw himself in front of the *yber* who was attacking. It jabbed the stake it had for me through him. And then the light came . . ." She cried in his arms and he comforted her.

He was tired and dizzy from loss of blood but he held on to her as if he were never letting her go.

"Whatever happened to our time?" he said to her.

"You can have it," she said through tears. "All our time. All you need. You can have it."

She whispered in his ear. Softly. Words meant just for him. Words he had dreamt of.

He held her close and whispered them back to her.

"Kiss me, Granger," she said. The blisters were blackening on her face. Her body shook. The arrow was too deep and the sun too devastating. Her hand moved at her neck. The blood of life flowed from her wound.

"Kiss me *now*," she said.

The taste was indescribable and made him ravenous.

Fifteen

The clouds that could be dimly seen at the horizon's edge were as red as the fire that consumed the Father's house.

Helman stood on a hilltop overlooking the Rand estate and watched the fire he had started eat away at the last resting place of the woman he had loved.

His nephews were safely hidden in the sub-basement by the pumping equipment. The fire would not reach them. If what Weston had said were true then they would be safe from human discovery for a week at least. The small game in the bush and forests would sustain them for the time being. Helman regretted that he couldn't take them with him, but he was confident that he would return for them soon.

The night would be short for all he had planned to do. He took one last look at the spreading fire and turned.

Something in the tall grass hissed his name.

Helman froze. His heightened senses detected subtle movement from a section of the grass to his right. Something was moving toward him.

The grass flattened before him.

Something unspeakable emerged.

It was a giant white slug thing, covered in thick raised weals of flesh. Two dark, human-seeming eyes peering out at him from a bulbous mass of scar tissue at one end. What he thought had been its tail swung around. It was an arm.

This thing was Eduardo Diego y Rey. Lord of the Conclave.

"Helman," it hissed at him again. Its mouth was swollen

shut from the dozens of deep slashes that Adrienne had inflicted on the balcony. Its words were slurred and indistinct.

"You are one of usss now, Helman. You must help me. Take me to sssanctuary with you. You must."

The thing pulsated slowly in the grass. It was forced to breathe deeply to force air down its multiple severed throat.

"I may be one like Adrienne. But I'll never be one like the Conclave. *Never*," Helman said to it. "Humanity will survive. I have the power, now."

It looked as if a smile was being forced through the lumps of scar tissue.

"Of course humanity will sssurvive," it gasped at him. "Where would the *yber* be without the living blood of humansss? Where would *you* be now, Helman? We are far ahead of your governmentsss and ssscientists. The girl showed us the way. It'sss all part of the Final Plan, Helman."

"What final plan? What did she show you?"

"That our gift isss not from the powersss of Hell. It'sss like a disease. Or a mutation."

"You know about that?"

"Far ahead, yesss. Far, far ahead. We have the cure, Helman. We have the cure. Interferon from the blood of life. All our familiars take it. Immunity from the cancer plague. Immunity for all the humansss we choose. The Final Plan is the final cure. Humanity survivesss as our food supply. Asss it should be. Yesss? You'll take me to sanctuary and I'll tell you more?"

Helman felt the primitive anger he had seen in Adrienne course through him.

"You disgust me," he snarled at Diego. "You don't even deserve to crawl."

Helman reached down and grabbed at Diego's one arm. New strength burned through his muscles. Diego's mangled arm was no match. Helman braced a foot against Diego's shoulder and pulled and twisted brutally.

The arm ripped out from its socket.

Diego's screams split the night air.

The arm dissolved in Helman's hands.

Diego's torso writhed and twisted in horror.

"I can't move," it screamed. "I'll never reach sssanctuary. The sssun will find me. *The sun will find me!*"

Helman walked around the gnashing white mound.

"Come back! The sun. The sun!"

When Helman had gone about a mile the screams were faint and hard to hear. After two miles, there was nothing.

Helman kept walking. The arrow wounds in his legs and arms were completely healed and he was surprised at the energy he felt. The only discomfort he felt was in his mouth. His incisors had fallen out while he slept during the day and the new ones were painful as they were erupting through his gums.

But he knew it would pass. And he knew he would need them soon. He could feel the thirst grow within him.

Highway 101 was still about five miles away. He could cover that easily in an hour. He could hitch up to Salinas by daybreak and find a quiet, safe church to sleep in.

Tomorrow night he would be in San Francisco and he would meet with the doctor whose name was written on the slip of paper that Weston had put into his weapon harness.

The doctor was an epidemiologist. He had made some surprising discoveries recently concerning the distribution of carcinomas in communities with little or no air pollution.

He had also turned down all of the Nevada Project's covert offers to accept much higher paying positions in Canada and France to conduct research on anything except carcinoma distribution. He had proved very stubborn to Weston. So much so that Weston had written the words "car accident" beside his name.

Helman took that to mean that the doctor was very close to the truth. Helman hoped so. It would mean that the explanations he would have to make would be simpler.

But then again, Helman thought as he checked out the new length of his rapidly growing fingernails and rubbed them experimentally across his neck, perhaps this first explanation would be even easier if he left all the talk for later and simply began by offering the doctor a drink.

He felt certain that the doctor would find it indescribable.

Acknowledgments

I owe a special debt of gratitude to the original publishers of *Bloodshift*: Ellen Aggar, Mr. Beatty, Susan Bermingham, Mark Biller, Mr. Church, Dean Cooke, Peter Doyle, Maureen Ford, Warren Knechtel, Robert Massoud, Thad McIlroy, Rob Mitchell, Gary Murphy, Steve Osborne, Susan Perry, Dawn Philips, Grace Philips, Keesha Lorraine Philips, Joel Sears, Peter Selk, Ruth Shamai, Tom Walmsley, Walter Warner, Robert Webster, Mel Wilson, Graham Yost, and our faithful bank messenger, Mr. Gorilla—aka Virgo Press, 1977–1981.

"*. . .for one brief shining moment. . .*"

—*GRS*